THE
LAST
GUEST
HOUSE

Also by Caroline Mitchell

Slayton Thrillers
The Midnight Man
The Night Whispers
The Bone House

Other works
Witness
Silent Victim
The Perfect Mother
The Village
The Islanders

The DI Amy Winter series
Truth and Lies
The Secret Child
Left for Dead
Flesh and Blood
In Cold Blood

The DC Jennifer Knight series
Don't Turn Around
Time to Die
The Silent Twin

The Ruby Preston series
Love You To Death
Sleep Tight

THE
LAST
GUEST
HOUSE

CAROLINE MITCHELL

embla
books

First published in Great Britain in 2024 by

Bonnier Books UK Limited
4th Floor, Victoria House, Bloomsbury Square, London, WC1B 4DA
Owned by Bonnier Books
Sveavägen 56, Stockholm, Sweden

A CIP catalogue record for this book is available from the British Library.

ISBN: 9781471416286

This book is typeset using Atomik ePublisher.

Embla Books is an imprint of Bonnier Books UK.
www.bonnierbooks.co.uk

In The Loch House, the past is not just remembered, it lives.

'Everyone is a moon, and has a dark side
which he never shows to anybody.'
Mark Twain

1

Elita

I inhaled my mother's ashes. It was an awful moment, filled with grief, panic and disgust. We should have chosen a better time for our little ceremony at the loch. But fine weather brings tourists, Granny said, and they couldn't afford for me to be seen. Only six years old, I was far too young to cope with her loss. The gust of wind came from nowhere, just as Granny helped me tip the ashes out. Most of it made the water, but some blew back onto me. I cried an apology to my mother, my whole body aching for her. Granny stroked my thinning hair and gave me a tissue. Grandad, who was devastated that Mum had chosen to be cremated in her will, took the urn from my small hands and began to mumble a steady stream of prayers in Latin. I remember gazing at the dark, cold water of the loch rippling in the wind. When the prayers were finally over, we went back home and Granny made me change my clothes. Ten years later, we've never spoken about that day since.

I was four when Mum first brought me to The Loch House. I was then what I am now, the same little girl. Maybe I'm a freak of nature, but for me, time really has stood still.

I've seen what regular girls look like and none of them are like me. It wasn't too bad when I was a kid, but now it's a new level of suckiness, not knowing where I fit in. On the bad days, when the cold creeps through the house, loneliness wraps itself around me. I've seen my childhood photos. I didn't have the cutesy face that makes people go 'aww'. At the age of two, my wrinkled forehead and bulging eyes made me look like I was plotting world domination. Mum wrote in her diaries that I was clingy, as if I knew I didn't belong to this world. She never had a second to herself. Each time Dad came near me, I let out this raspy sound to make him keep away. I don't know how the hell they lived with me. Back then, Mum was at my mercy, carrying me around like a tired warrior. She wrote in her journals that she was in awe of me one minute, and scared for me the next. I couldn't make sense of that . . . at least, not straight away. I remember staring at what she'd written, wondering what she was so scared about. I saw the blots on the pages, where her tears had mixed with pen ink. Knowing that she cried writing those words made me cry too.

In the early days we lived in a different building with loads of other people. Mum wrote about how those 'happy-clappy idiots' were always shouting, laughing and singing without a thought for the rest of us. I vaguely remember music of some kind or another filtering through the walls. It was only when Dad smuggled us away to Scotland that we found peace. I can still remember the journey if I concentrate hard: Mum telling me to be quiet as we hid in the boot of the car. The smell of her body – perfume and fresh sweat. I remember the wind whistling through the gap in the tail lights. Her voice was all shaky and I hated the dark. But she told me to close my eyes, and whispered stories of magical places and faraway lands. J.K. Rowling had nothing on her. The journey felt like forever, and only when we were far enough away, were we allowed to get out and sit in the back of the car. Then we were in Scotland, with its roaming wildlife, misty mountains and dewy fields. Mum's entries about the Isle of Skye back then were like poetry. She wrote that from the minute we got out of the car, we were hit with the 'earthy aroma of damp moss, soil and the lingering sweetness of heather and peat.' She could have been a poet, I guess, or a writer maybe. What a waste. That first night on Skye, I surprised her by finally sleeping through the night. She said it was like everything in me relaxed. Maybe it was the country air, or that we got away from the people who were always so loud. She said it was like the island had a magical hold over me.

I liked that. The Loch House was our happy place. Two short years. That's all we had in The Loch House before she was taken away from me. I was only six years old.

Now the centre of my world is dead, and I'm stuck in that single spot in time when she was ripped away from me, ten years ago. But hey, don't pity me. I might not have a life, but while you're staying at The Loch House, I'll busy myself by living yours. It's not often that we have guests. How spoilt it is, having so many warm bodies filling its rooms. Soon I will know the *real* you, the part you hide away. You lot are clueless though, aren't you? Worrying about dumb things like if your dinner is too cold, or how long you had to wait to get it. You're in the middle of nowhere, you know? Anything could happen. *Especially* here, in the wilderness, miles from hospitals. Miles from anywhere.

I always make sure I'm long gone by the time you get back to your room. You don't know that I've already been there, having a good snoop. Yeah, that's right. I've checked out your meds, sniffed your perfume and judged you on your choice of undies (couldn't resist). I've even poked around in your suitcases. I hope you're not too shocked about the underwear thing. I'm nosey but not in a pervy way. You can tell a lot about someone by what they wear under their clothes. I've come across some *very* strange things over the last few years. I don't feel bad about it, because my life is so dull. It's just a little fun, right? I mean, Harry Potter got up to all sorts of mischief when he was my age . . . I also know what it's like to be different to everyone else and live in a part of the house where nobody else goes. I used to dream that I'd get my invitation to Hogwarts, but I'm getting too old for all that childish stuff now. Nobody's coming to rescue me. I'm stuck here until I rot.

I love trying on shoes – but they're always way too big for me. Hats are my favourite, but people only wear the woolly ones and they're a total yawn fest. Granny makes my clothes, but they're different to what other people wear. I like my pretty dresses, but I'm fed up with looking like a child. She works so hard to stitch them that I can't find the words to tell her that I want to wear modern clothes. Not that I'd find anything to fit my body. At least when I'm looking through your things, I can forget what I am for a while. I've touched the wrinkled clothes hanging in your wardrobe and swiped that crumpled up receipt from your bin. You're too worried about the storm to notice the little things, and as snow hits your windowpane, you're grateful for the shelter of The Loch House. You sit in your room and chat about stuff you wouldn't say in front of anyone else. I've seen what people like you can be when they think nobody's watching. When it comes to The Loch House, guests aren't always kind. You've a lot more to worry about than the cobwebs in the corner of your room. I've seen it all, the messed up stuff that went on here. The ugly things I can't get out of my head. I still hear the screams. Smell the blood.

Just follow the rules, yeah? Then you'll be, like mostly fine.

Probably.

2

Nicola

I never wanted our Mercedes Coupé. It's too low to the ground for my liking, its mileage is crazy high and not practical for ferrying my six-year-old son around. It was Matt's decision, bless him, my kind, sensible Matt. Probably the only outlandish one he's ever made. He'd said that it was alright for me, because I got my thrills from racing around Lincoln at night on a blue light run. I wish he understood that my job in the police isn't some kind of game.

I stare out of the car window, my surroundings a blur as my mind wanders to work. It's gone 5 p.m. which means a shift changeover and fresh briefing to follow. Friday nights are always busy in Lincoln. Skinny Izzy will be out on the town tonight, in her lime-green skirt, furry jumper and fishnet tights. I imagine her picking fights as she staggers out of Walkabout on the high street, but I only have to steer her towards the kebab shop to calm her down. She gives a whole new level to the meaning of 'hangry' and the thought of her makes me smile.

Then there's Christina, our owlish new probationer, who I've taken under my wing. My shift partner Liam says that she's too soft and won't last. Maybe she won't, but she deserves a fair chance, which is more than I got during my probation period when I first joined. My tutor gave me six months. I don't know why, but she took an instant dislike to me. I'd walk into a room and hear her sniggering about a mistake I made, or gossiping about my 'dodgy friends', just because I grew up on a council estate. Life was tough back then and

I wanted to make something of myself. So I bowed and scraped to her highness during my training, did whatever it took to make it through. I wouldn't let her bully me out of the best job I'd ever had. I had more empathy for the people we dealt with in my little finger than she had in her whole body.

I've lived among domestic incidents, and people who have spiralled into crime from lack of money or dependence on drugs. Not everyone in prison is born a scoundrel. Sometimes, in fact plenty of times, good people do stupid things out of desperation. I don't have to agree with their life choices, but I do treat them with dignity when I can. This weekend, call takers will be swamped with domestic incidents and there aren't enough boots on the ground to cope with them all. I gaze mournfully out of the window, wishing I was back on shift where I could help.

The windscreen wipers automatically pick up speed to deal with the thickening snow. I glance back at George, amazed that he's still asleep. His wavy brown hair falls in front of his eyes as he rests his head on the pillow we've brought from home. He's short for his age, but a little chubby because his love of pizza knows no bounds. When he looks at me with those deep brown eyes, it's like I'm his entire world and when he smiles, his dimples melt my heart. Matt slows to negotiate a bend in the winding road. We should have checked in to The Royal Hotel two hours ago, but our trip has been hit with misfortune from the off. Now the car is playing up. What began as mild concern grows into something bigger as evening closes in.

'We should've stayed in Edinburgh,' I say, focusing on the winding road. Visibility is poor, and the absence of streetlights means we can only see a worryingly short distance ahead.

'The city's too busy.' Matt stares into the snowy abyss. 'We've a much better chance of seeing the Northern Lights from here.'

But I never asked to see them. Neither did George. Matt means well but he's trying to squeeze a square peg into a round hole. Perhaps the age gap is too much. We will never be the perfect family he wants us to be. I groan as we hit another pothole. 'I felt that in my bones. This car isn't cut out for country roads.'

Matt sighs and guilt blooms in my chest. He's a good man and treats me well. My female colleagues are always jealous when flowers arrive at work, or when he whisks me away for some time off. 'Sorry,' I quickly add. 'For being an ungrateful cow. I'm sure we'll love it.' His broad shoulders relax as I caress his forearm. After three years together, I interpret his body language so well that he doesn't need to say a word.

He glances at me briefly before returning his attention to the narrow road. 'It'll be worth all the hassle when we get to the hotel.'

I shift in my seat, inhaling a sharp breath as a dart of pain shoots up from my spine.

'How's your back?' Matt asks, a concerned look in his eye. 'Still playing up?'

'It's OK,' I lie. But I can't help but wince as I try to find a comfortable position. I don't want to start another row. The people I help are worth every bruise, every scratch, every dangerous situation that I put myself in. The only thing I don't like about my job is that it takes me away from spending time with my son.

I press an imaginary brake as the car suddenly skids in the snow. He should have let me drive, as I'm trained to negotiate treacherous roads. But mention of my police training is a big no right now. My occupation is the catalyst for all our problems.

It's ironic that without my job, we never would have met. It was a run of the mill criminal damage report. Teenagers had graffitied one of the classrooms the night before. Matt had begun his new role as headmaster and wanted to do things by the book. There were a couple of follow-up visits, but we didn't exchange numbers until I bumped into him at the farmer's market in Wragby one weekend. My shopping trip turned into an impromptu lunch date at the Adam and Eve pub, and that was it. After a previous bad relationship, dating Matt felt like a good idea. Given he was in his late thirties when we met, he seemed a lot more sensible than me. And he didn't mind that I had a three-year-old son. I needed someone steady, a good influence in my life.

Mum immediately adored him, and would love nothing better than for us to get hitched. But in the last two years, Matt has grown so intense while I'm doing my best to distance myself. I just can't commit. It's too big a step. Perhaps soon I'll find the courage to tell him how I feel.

Matt's eyes are focused on the road. Snow is coming down faster now, hypnotic as it hits our windscreen from all directions. He's right about the Isle of Skye, it's breathtakingly beautiful, especially in November, with its snow-capped mountains and twisting frosted roads. And there's something about Scottish people that feels comforting to me. Their food is warm and nurturing, their accents like a verbal warm hug. Had the weather been better, we could have planned visits to the Cuillin Hills and Eilean Donan castle. Or the main town of Portree with its pretty harbour and restaurants. But the place we're going to tonight is at the far end of the island, miles away from civilisation. Matt doesn't like socialising. He's always been big on having me all to himself.

I activate the heaters to clear the windscreen fog. 'Not far now,' Matt mumbles under his breath.

Don't jinx it, I think. The car engine light came on half an hour ago. I don't want to contemplate what will happen should we break down on these unforgiving roads.

3

Nicola

'Look!' Matt points out of the window at last. 'There it is.'

A sense of relief washes over me at the sight of the large, luxurious hotel in the distance. My earlier concerns dissipate at the thought of relaxing in our room. As we pull up into the busy car park, Matt turns off the ignition and reaches over to squeeze my hand.

'I know the past few months have been . . . well, things haven't been right. No more fighting, eh? This is a new start . . .' He glances back at George. 'For all of us.'

I feel shitty, but I fix a smile on my face. 'New starts.' He doesn't know that I've been scanning Rightmove's online rentals section for somewhere to live. Matt's dogged determination to keep our relationship afloat is what's kept us together over the last year. He's been a great father figure to George, looking after him while I work. The problem is, I don't love him anymore. I can't burst his bubble here. We'll have this one last holiday. It's scary imagining the consequences of our break-up. George has always been polite with Matt, but not particularly close. Memories of his biological father are never far away. He was young when we parted, but some traumas run deep. Matt tried everything to win George over, but my son has always clung to me. At least I have my mother to support me when I need it. I'm not scared of being a single mum . . . it's Matt I'm frightened of. What he might do after I'm gone. But I can't put this off anymore. I'll move out when he's at work and Mum can help with George until I get back on my feet.

My breath is visible in the biting winter air as I lift a sleepy George out of the car. Twilight colours the snowy landscape in a twinkling blue hue. The storm shows no signs of abating and already, clumps of snowflakes have settled on my hair and clothes. Matt wheels our suitcases through the deepening snow. I shake the snow out of my hair as we enter the lobby, while Matt rubs the flakes from his beard. The hotel lobby is bustling with people, and the sudden surge of heat prickles my skin. I'm encompassed by smells of wood and smoke, and the scent of pine rising from the huge Christmas tree in the corner of the room. The walls are adorned with a stag head, vintage guns, and paintings of the countryside during brighter days. A well-groomed middle-aged receptionist greets us at the front desk.

'Welcome to The Royal Hotel.' She speaks with a gentle Scottish accent, pushing her thick rimmed glasses up the bridge of her long nose. 'How may I help you?' Her name is Sheena Campbell, according to her name badge. I always scan my surroundings – names, descriptions, body language. You never know when someone might turn.

'We have a reservation.' Matt returns Sheena's smile before providing our details.

She types something on her computer and her smile falls away. 'Sorry, what name did you book under again?'

I don't like the sound of this.

'I booked the honeymoon suite for Matt Barber and Nicola McKenna, with a fold-up bed for George.' Matt glances my way as my mouth drops open. 'It was meant to be a surprise.'

'Consider me surprised,' I say with a hint of reluctance. It took Matt a year to persuade me to move into his house. He's always been so sensible, with his monthly and weekly check lists and the life plan he renews every five years. I know what he's planned for me and the last thing I want is him thinking that marriage is on the cards. The thought of walking up the aisle makes my stomach churn. It's not fair to lead him on. Matt is ready for marriage, but he deserves someone who loves him for who he is, not because their relationship is safe.

'It's a bigger room with a Jacuzzi and a view of the mountains,' Matt continues, taking in my crestfallen face. 'Plus, we'll get the best view of the aurora from there.'

But my feet feel rooted to the spot. Anyone else would be thrilled – but we're not together for the right reasons and he's become too serious too fast. I'll try to be the person he wants though, if only for this weekend. 'Thanks,' I reply, trying to inject some enthusiasm. 'George will love the Jacuzzi.' My arms ache and I gently place my son on the floor.

'Are we here?' George yawns, taking in his surroundings. He has the longest, darkest lashes, and for a moment I see his biological dad, Gav. A dart of pain shoots up from my lower lip as I bite it too hard. I remind myself that I'm safe now. There's nothing to be frightened of. Matt is nothing like the violent man who made my life hell.

I want to reassure my son that we're finally here, but Sheena is now looking at us with worrying sympathy. I turn to George. 'Why don't you sit down on that nice sofa over there while we get this sorted out?' He happily does as he is told. Because judging by Sheena's expression, I'm not sure we have a bed for the night.

4

Matt

I can't believe the day we've had and it's not ending here. This was meant to be a special time. A chance to help Nicola see things my way. She won't acknowledge her injuries, nor the effect her job is having on our relationship. She goes out to dangerous incidents, works all hours of the night dealing with drunks and violent offenders. George needs her. We both do. I wish she'd settle down. Perhaps it's old-fashioned but I want to provide for our little family and keep us safe from the outside world. But lately, everything I do backfires. Like this trip, which is already not going well.

'I've found your booking,' she says. 'But I'm afraid it's for this time next week.'

My heart sinks as I bring up the booking on my phone. 'No, you're wrong. It clearly says . . .' I peer closer. 'Oh.'

'God,' Nicola turns to the receptionist after seeing the booking date on my phone. 'Can't you change it for tonight?'

But Sheena is shaking her head. 'Sorry, but we don't have any rooms available. We're fully booked with the wedding party.' Only now do I notice the laughter and live music coming from another room.

I glance outside at the settling snow. 'But the car engine light has come on. Is there anywhere else around here that will have a room?'

The receptionist shakes her head, her expression conveying concern. 'I'm afraid not.' Her voice is filled with regret. 'Everywhere is booked up because of the Northern Lights.' Record numbers have been flooding the area in recent days to see what has been described in the news as a 'stunning display'.

Tiredness seeps through to my very bones. I just want to eat a hot meal with my family, followed by a few drinks before bed.

Nicola throws me a worried look. This is about more than missing out on a Jacuzzi. We are stranded with a six-year-old in tow. I cast a glance over at George, who is so short for his age, sitting on the sofa, swinging his legs. He's a sweet kid, quiet and well behaved. I'd like a little brother and sister for him one day. I tune back into Nicola's narrative as she challenges the receptionist.

'The problem is,' Nicola continues, 'we can't rely on our car, and the road is like an ice rink. If you can't find us a place to stay, I'm afraid the three of us will be sleeping in your lobby because we're not going out in *that.*'

I shake my head miserably as I stare at the Booking.com app on my phone. 'I can't believe I got the dates wrong.'

The receptionist pauses for a moment. 'Can you give me a minute? I'll see what I can do.' She walks to the far end of reception and makes a quick phone call. 'Good news,' she says upon her return. 'Mr and Mrs Hill, the proprietors of The Loch House guest house said they can fit you in. It's a twenty-minute drive away, and I've asked them to hold the room. I can issue you a refund if you like. Their rooms are a fraction of the price.'

'Thanks, we'll take it,' Nicola says with relief, as the blizzard swirls around outside. I bite my lip as I debate our next move.

'You said everywhere around here was booked.' I turn the receptionist's comment over like a coin. 'Why is The Loch House free?'

'Does it matter?' Nicola cuts in, as the receptionist is preparing to answer. 'Look at George. It's been such a long day.' She turns back to Sheena. 'You're a lifesaver.'

But as Nicola gets George, I catch the uncertainty in the receptionist's eyes. I wanted an answer to my question, and had Nicola not stepped in, I might have got one. What might she have told me? I have an uneasy feeling thinking about it, but brush it off. After confirming the room, the three of us head back out into the chilly night air. Our earlier footprints have already been camouflaged by the thickening snow.

My limbs are heavy with tiredness as we follow Sheena's directions to the guest house. I only hope that we can get there in time.

5

Nicola

'It was meant to be perfect.' Matt stares out of the window, slowly negotiating the treacherous road. 'This place must be a dive. Why else would it be the only available guest house on the island?'

'Because it's so far out,' I counter. 'C'mon, it'll be an adventure.' I don't want to be here either, but we may as well make the best of it.

'I suppose,' Matt replies with a sigh.

I check my mirror to see George sitting quietly in the back. 'We can go back to Edinburgh tomorrow if it doesn't work out here.' A sense of foreboding encompasses me as I stare out of the window at the winding snow-lined road.

Finally, after what feels like an eternity, the car headlights illuminate a crooked sign for The Loch House Hotel. It's hammered onto a piece of wood which juts out sideways from a ditch. But there's something else grasping for my attention. 'Slow down . . . is that?' I stare past the sign to see a snow-encrusted figure beneath the jutting branches of a tree. 'Stop the car!' I shout a little too loudly, as if instructing a probationer.

Matt says nothing as he slows the car to a halt. I barely wait for it to stop before jumping out, almost slipping on a hard patch of ice. While the snow crunches beneath my boots, I'm conscious that there's a hard sheet of ice beneath. George peeps through the windscreen as he watches me approach the mound. It's not the first time he's seen me go into police mode. I've had to pull my weight in the past when some teenage boys picked a fight during a train journey, and he's witnessed me give CPR to an elderly man during a supermarket shop. 'Jeez,' I exhale, my hand clasped to my chest. 'It's OK,' I smile, my face chilled by the icy wind. It seems the 'body' is a false alarm. Matt shakes his head from inside the car. I know what he's thinking – do I ever take time off from work?

I stare uneasily at the snow-encrusted scarecrow as snow seeps into the hems of my jeans. It is an amalgamation of twisted branches and tattered clothing, its stick arms outstretched. The 'face' is a macabre spectacle, crudely put together with sackcloth and black stitching which reveals a lopsided grin. Two black buttons resemble hollow eye sockets, and the body appears broken from its base, its legs jutting in unnatural angles. I poke it with my foot and detect the musty odour of wet mouldy straw. In the snowy landscape, the eerie scarecrow unnerves me. I get back into the car and press the internal lock. I've only been outside for a minute, but the tips of my fingers are almost numb.

'It's a tatty bogle,' Matt says, accelerating cautiously. 'A Scottish scarecrow. Someone must have rooted him from his post.' Matt is a walking encyclopaedia and has obviously prepared for our trip. He's the perfect team member when it comes to pub quizzes, but he'd never get on with my shift partner Liam, who would take the mickey out of him and call him a swot. Matt drives on, describing in detail the folklore surrounding tatty bogles, and how 'tatty' means potato and 'bogle' means family of spirits, evil demons or ghosts.

I am more concerned with how the thing got there. It should be in a field, not propped up next to a weather-beaten sign. It feels like a warning, but it's too late to turn back now.

Mystery on the Mic Podcast

The Watts Case Series: Episode 1

Alex: Hey, everyone, and welcome back to another episode of 'Mystery on the Mic'. I'm your host, Alex, and today we'll be discussing a true crime story that's been making headlines all over the world. Joining me is our resident true crime historian and expert, Sarah. How's it going, Sarah?

Sarah: Hey, Alex! It's great to be back. I'm looking forward to diving into this intriguing case with you.

Alex: Absolutely. Welcome back from your holiday. We've missed you.

Sarah: (Chuckles) It's typical, I go away for two weeks and all hell breaks loose. The case we're about to discuss today has to be the biggest of the year.

Alex: You're not allowed to go away in future. And I'd say it's the case of the decade, so, let's get right into it. We're talking about the shocking and tragic incident involving multi-millionaire music mogul Ronnie Watts and his young wife, Heather Watts. This has got all the elements of a gripping mystery: fame, fortune, family drama and a whole load of unanswered questions. It's such a tragic case.

I can't imagine what the families of the victims are going through.

Sarah: Indeed, and we pass on our sincere condolences to them. Ronnie Watts was a huge name in the music industry and best known for discovering and nurturing new talent, most recently 'London Lads', the Britpop boy band sensation that soared in the charts. And who could forget Eddy Blake and his brother Andy, who've had five consecutive number ones?

Alex: Ronnie Watts made Simon Cowell look like his apprentice. The music world has been left in a state of shock from recent events.

Sarah: I don't want to be disrespectful of the recently deceased, but Ronnie's recent marriage to a much younger Heather stirred up its own share of controversy too.

Alex: It sure did, Sarah. I can't help but feel sorry for the member of staff who discovered them dead in their Surrey mansion. It's reported to have been a gruesome scene, with blood up the bedroom walls. Apparently, the security cameras were out of action too.

Sarah: The circumstances are so mysterious, aren't they? Ronnie's car was still in the driveway, when he was meant to be away. The mansion was unlocked and was said to have been a mess – it's the kind of stuff you see in crime dramas.

Alex: And the mystery deepens, with rumours swirling about the possible involvement of drugs. Reports mention an unidentified white powdery substance found at the scene. It's not uncommon in the music industry but has raised some eyebrows in this case.

Sarah: That's because Heather was said to have been such a great influence on Ronnie. She was totally against substance abuse after losing her best friend to a drug overdose when she was just sixteen. It was the driving force behind her tireless charity work which took place behind the scenes.

Alex: That's right. What's also really heartbreaking about this case is the impact on their families. Ronnie Watts had some longstanding tensions with his sons, Caleb and Ronan, stemming from their mother's death. And now, with his tragic demise, those unresolved issues are even more complex.

Sarah: It's a difficult situation indeed. Ronnie's marriage to Heather had already caused tension with his sons, and now this tragedy has added a new layer of grief and unanswered questions. You can't help but wonder how they feel. I don't like to say it, but we're not known for holding back here on 'Mystery on the Mic' . . . they stand to make a big inheritance from this.

Alex: You're only saying what everyone is thinking. And speaking of grief, Heather's parents have shared their devastation over their daughter's sudden death. In a heartfelt statement to the press, they described her as a 'kind and beautiful soul'. It's clear she meant the world to them.

Sarah: It's so sad. Everything I've read about Heather portrays her as a sweet and caring young woman, who shied away from the limelight. Her family's request for privacy during this difficult time is completely understandable.

Alex: Absolutely, Sarah. And Ronnie Watts was a huge icon in the music industry. Tributes have been pouring in from all corners. It's a major loss. His impact on the music world cannot be overstated.

Sarah: I have a feeling that there's a lot more to come with this case.

Alex: Yes, we'll be awaiting the results of autopsies and toxicology
        reports which will hopefully shed light on the cause of their
        deaths. Police are being very tight-lipped about the actual
        cause of death, but I imagine it won't be long until we get a
        hold of the truth.

Sarah: You can say that again. In the world of true crime, sometimes
        it takes time for the pieces to come together, but the truth
        usually comes out in the end. In such a high profile case
        as this, police will be under a lot of pressure to get things
        resolved. We'll be keeping a close eye on this case as it
        unfolds.

Alex: Thanks, Sarah. And thanks to all of you for tuning in to
        this segment of 'Mystery on the Mic'. We may only be a
        small channel, but our subscribers are growing daily and we
        appreciate all you curious true crimers. We'll be back after
        this sponsored ad with more captivating cases!

6

Nicola

The guest house is hidden deeply, down a road so remote and unused that it jolts us in our seats. I stare in awe at the vast loch which glimmers beneath the light of the rising full moon. It stretches out before us, as beautiful as it is mystical. Matt drives on in silence, focused on the road ahead. Tall pines suffocate the feeble evening light, and as our car headlights strobe the entrance I glance up at the two-storey building that looms ahead. It exudes an air of faded grandeur as it overlooks the loch, which is a short walk away. The stone building isn't big enough to be a hotel and seems too big to be a home. It falls into the realms of guest house, and this one has only scraped a two-star AA rating. The guest reviews I skimmed on the way here before my iPhone battery died have not been kind. They warn of strange, eccentric hosts, dusty old-fashioned rooms and the constant feeling of being watched.

As Matt parks up, I turn to see George looking happy in the back seat, cake crumbs stuck to his cheek. The receptionist was so kind, sneaking him out some food from the wedding for our journey. George loved his car picnic, gobbling down the sandwich and chocolate cake, but as our car slipped and slid on the remote roads, I was too worried to eat.

I follow Matt for the second time tonight, dragging my overnight case along the snow laden path with one hand, while balancing George with my other arm. It's worth the back pain to hold him close. He has wrapped himself around me like a monkey and I take comfort from his warmth. Time with my son is so precious, and I push the feeling of foreboding away. In the distance, the high shriek of a creature in the wild fills the air and I hesitate. 'Here,' Matt reaches out. 'Let me take that.' He lifts my heavy case with a grunt. Matt has always been chivalrous. He's aged well and is good looking in a teacherly sort of way. I imagine his adolescent pupils, dreamy eyed in his presence.

The Loch House is a poor substitute after the obvious luxury of the previous hotel. It looks more like something out of a Stephen King novel than the Good Travel Guide, but I'm grateful to have a bed for the night. The imposing entrance door groans in protest as we push it open. I take in the unwelcoming foyer, telling myself that it's only for one night. It's barely six o'clock but it feels like night has closed in.

The gloomy atmosphere isn't helped by the mahogany wood panelled walls and paint flaked high ceilings. As I inhale a musty scent it feels like I'm stepping back in time. But it's not a good time. There's something dark and heavy lingering within these walls. I've felt it before, in the aftermath of violence. I wouldn't call it a psychic insight or anything daft like that, just a feeling I can't quite shake off. Matt wipes his shoes. 'Sorry, sweetie,' I murmur to George. 'I'm going to have to put you down.' I dread the day when he's too heavy for me to carry. I may work long hours, but I treasure every moment with my son. I shake the light dusting of snow off his hair and wipe my boots on the mat. My feet are freezing, and the dingy carpeted floors are uninviting, to say the least. 'Do we have to stay here?' I whisper to Matt. I've been in worse places in my capacity as a uniformed officer, but I'm actually paying for this.

'We've got no choice,' Matt whispers. 'This is the last hotel room left.'

'Quite right!' A thin voice rises from the corridor. The thick but worn carpet muffles the elderly woman's steps as she approaches. She's wearing black lace-up ankle boots and her bright colourful clothing appears wildly out of place. 'Hello, little man,' she bends at the waist to greet George, before turning her attention to us. 'You must be Nicola and Matt.' She extends her purple nail varnished hand in such a fashion as if expecting it to be kissed. It's impossible not to stare. She must be in her late seventies but looks like an ageing Bo Peep. White lace gloves grace her hands and a set of dentures flash between her thin pink lips. But her glowing white teeth are the least remarkable thing about her. The heavy blonde ringlets which frame her thin face must surely be a wig. She is heavily made up with blusher, eyeliner and bright blue eyeshadow. A thick diamanté-crusted necklace adorns her collarbone, with the matching set of earrings dragging down her ears. Her dress is impossibly tight at the waist, expanding outwards at the hips, making her look like a purple fuchsia. I elbow Matt in the ribs as he stares, lips parted in disbelief. But the woman titters beneath her breath.

'Don't worry, dear,' she flutters her eyelashes. 'I have that effect on men.' She winks at Matt. 'It's my teeny-tiny waist. I don't eat, you see. Maybe a piece of fruit every now and again. You don't need food when you can live on air.'

'Really?' I say, as our trip takes a bizarre turn.

'What age do you think I am?' She turns back to Matt.

'Um . . . I'm not very good with things like that.'

'Twenty-one,' she chuckles. 'That's what people take me for. Now, you can call me Dorothy.'

'Like out of *The Wizard of Oz*,' George says, his eyes twinkling. He loves old movies, and *The Wizard of Oz* is one of his favourites.

'There's no place like home!' Dorothy replies, clicking her heels together.

I feel like I've walked into a pantomime. 'Heeenrry!' Dorothy screeches, bringing me back to reality. 'They're here. You can lock the door now.' She pauses to check a silver plated pocket watch which hangs from a belt on her waist. 'And not a minute too soon.' She narrows her eyes as she peers down the dark corridor. 'My husband will be along any minute. Don't be alarmed.'

Don't be alarmed? I think. I think that ship has sailed. 'Can we get checked in please?' I ask, wearily. I'm used to meeting extraordinary people, but any hope of getting Dorothy back on track disappears as her husband towers over us. George clings to my side, his mouth open. I draw him towards me as a scarily tall man approaches, shadowed in the dim light. He must be almost seven feet. His eyes are dark with the deep, shadowed sockets of a man who's suffered from a trauma of some kind. His suit is too short for his frame, skimming his skinny ankles and upper wrists. It wouldn't be too bad if it was clean, but dirt stains are caked into the knees and lapels. Not normal stains, like food or toothpaste, but what appears to be cobwebs and dust. He looks like he's crawled out of a shallow grave. As he looms towards us, I notice the hole in his throat. I've seen it before and know exactly what it is. Matt, on the other hand, has grown visibly pale.

'You can lock the doors now,' Dorothy repeats, returning her attention to Matt. She looks down at George. 'Don't look so scared, dear. My husband is recovering from throat cancer. It's not catching.' She smiles at me. 'Not as long as you turn off your phones. Follow me!' She gestures towards the mahogany reception desk further down the hall as she complains about radiation in the air. 'It's everywhere. Gets in your clothes, your hair. Then it seeps into your skin and makes you ill . . .' Her thin voice echoes down the corridor. I'm holding George's hand, hoping he doesn't have nightmares. He's gazing up at the walls, which are lined with old portraits of the royal family.

'Where did she get those from?' Matt whispers just loud enough for me to hear.

'Dunno,' I respond in an equally low tone. 'But it feels like they're watching us.'

'Don't you just love our dear queen?' Dorothy heaves a dramatic sigh. 'I wore black for a month after she died.' The slam of the heavy front door is followed by a sense of finality as Henry pulls each bolt across.

'You're in room seven, upstairs. It has a beautiful view of the loch.' Dorothy gives Matt a strange, coquettish smile. 'But first, you have to agree to the rules.'

Rules? I groan. What fresh hell awaits us now?

7

Matt

At least I know why The Loch House was available. I feel bad for staring at Henry, but it's been a very demanding day. Now I'm faced with an eccentric woman who won't allow us to rest our heads until we sign up to a set of rules. As we stand at the reception desk I stare at a handwritten piece of paper with Nicola at my side, her lips moving silently.

Guest House Rules

1. *No smoking in the rooms.*
2. *No parties.*
3. *No loud music.*
4. *No pets.*
5. *No phones.*
6. *No leaving the building after 9 p.m.*

Rules one to four go without saying, but five and six are ridiculous.

'You are joking me, aren't you?' Nicola complains. 'I'm not handing over my phone.'

Dorothy gives her a hard stare.

'It's just one night,' I whisper. 'George is worn out. I'm not dragging him back to the car.' But Nicola isn't listening, she has that knot between her brows that she gets when she's annoyed. 'Why are we not allowed to leave after 9 p.m.?'

'It's for your own good.' The robotic voice that rises behind us is followed by a raspy gasp. Henry has placed a hand over the plastic device surrounding the hole in his throat, enabling him to speak. I know Nicola. She's too kind to argue with a man for whom speaking is such an effort. She sighs, and her shoulders slump in defeat. To be honest, I'm glad, because she would only be checking her phone all night for calls from work. She's either giggling like a schoolgirl over a text Liam has sent, or texting that young probationer who never leaves her alone. I don't know why she feels the need to get so involved. She has her family. What more does she want? I've tried to persuade Nicola to take an office job, such as CID. I resent the fact that this Liam fella gets to see more of her than I do. As for the violence . . . she's always the one who barrels headfirst into a tussle to break it up.

Dorothy shakes a small tin box in front of us. A crudely drawn label with the word 'phones' is stuck to the top. My eyes are sore from driving, and I could do with a rest. We turn off our phones before dropping them into the tin. George doesn't have electronic devices, just books and toys. I think there's an iPad in the case somewhere, but it's not linked to any Wi-Fi.

'What exactly are we being kept safe from?' I say, as Henry picks up our bags. Dorothy mentioned her fear of radiation in the air, but this feels like something more threatening than imaginary radon. But with both hands full, Henry is unable to speak.

'From the outside,' Dorothy utters a raspy whisper as she pokes me in the arm. 'But don't you worry your heads, you'll be quite safe as long as you obey the rules. Food is in half an hour. Cullen skink and slow cooked beef stew.'

My stomach rumbles as I explain to Nicola that Cullen skink is a traditional Scottish hearty fish soup. I'm not sure if George will like it, but he's already had a feast of sandwiches, chocolate cake, pop and sausage rolls. He holds Nicola's hand, more alert and curious as we follow Henry upstairs.

The air smells faintly of furniture polish, and the narrow wooden staircase is worn smooth, creaking beneath the weight of our steps. I glance around the upper floor as it reveals a series of guest rooms, each door numbered with a thick brass metal plate. We walk along the gallery landing, taking in the faded floral wallpaper peeling from the walls. Navy coloured paint lurks beneath, revealing glimpses of the past. Like downstairs, each space is dimly lit, as if the house doesn't want to draw attention to itself. Henry pushes open our room door and sets our cases aside. I wait for the key, but he turns to leave. 'Sorry,' I call after him. 'Our key?'

He presses his fingers against the hole in his throat, once again speaking in a sawing voice which sets my nerves on edge. 'Keyless rooms. Locks from the inside.' Then he's gone out into the hallway and I'm staring at Nicola in disbelief. I've heard about keyless rooms at wellness retreats, but not in guest houses. Nicola follows him out while I stay with George. She returns after a few minutes. 'I spoke to Dorothy.' She shakes her head. 'She said, "we're all friends here" and that she can safely store away any valuables.'

'Stranger and stranger,' I say, turning the inside lock, grateful that it works. The family room is outdated and spacious, with a four-poster double bed. We follow George through to an adjoining room. The bunk beds look out of place, but they are probably more comfortable than the fold-up bed in the luxury hotel I thought I'd booked. George's eyes are alight as he climbs the ladder. 'Look, Mummy, I'm going to sleep on top!' It's the most he's said all day. There's a dresser in the room and a shelf with a plethora of puzzles and games. The space is warm and comfortable, if a little dark, but George seems in his element as he explores his new space.

I exhale a low breath as Nicola and I return to our room. 'Talk about weird . . . this isn't exactly turning out as planned.'

'You can say that again,' Nicola laughs. 'Bless her, old Dorothy is living her best life, isn't she? I kinda admire her for that.'

'Yeah.' I can't help but smile. 'With her irresistible dress and teeny-tiny waist. What's the deal with her husband?'

'It's not his fault he can't talk.'

'I know, but did you see the dirt stains on his suit? And the way he looks at you . . . it's very Boris Karloff, isn't it?'

'Don't be mean. But yeah, they're both crazily eccentric. I mean, what's with all the rules? And more to the point, how will I manage without my phone?'

I shrug. 'At least we know why the place was available. I wonder who else is staying here.' I sit on the wooden four-poster bed and the mattress bounces beneath my weight. 'Seems comfy enough.' The ceiling is embellished with decorative dark timber framed covings which are mercifully cobweb-free.

'At least there's an en suite,' Nicola adds, her voice resounding from the tiled bathroom. 'It's tiny, but better than having to share.' She walks around the room and each cupboard creaks as she opens it. Wire hangers jangle in the wardrobe as she hangs up her damp coat. She checks her bedside table and slips out a bible. 'We might need this for the night ahead,' she chuckles before putting it back. But I know Nicola; she jokes when she's feeling uneasy. It stems from being in the police; it's her way of coping with the darker side of life.

I walk to the window to see that our car is already dusted in snow. Beyond it is the loch, which appears as a shimmering black mass between the tall trees. 'The storm has really picked up. We won't see the Northern Lights tonight.'

Nicola joins me and I rest my arm over her shoulders. She was in uniform when we first met, her dark hair coming loose from the bun in her hair. She'd smiled at me with such warmth that I'd almost melted on the spot. I've always had a thing for women in uniform, a guilty pleasure of sorts. It's the power, I'd suppose. My first crush was on Lynda Carter from the old *Wonder Woman* TV series. Perhaps I have a complex . . . I try not to overthink it. Or maybe it's because I work with young people all day. I'm not attracted to women who act like babies or are obsessed with selfies and social media.

Nicola sighs. 'As long as we can get away tomorrow.' Our eyes meet as she contemplates the alternative. 'You don't think we'll get snowed in, do you?'

'No. God, no. Even if we make it to another hotel we'll be fine.' But as Nicola turns away, I don't feel fine. The Hills' warning not to leave the building after nine is still ringing in my ears.

8

Nicola

My steps are heavy with tiredness as I follow Matt downstairs. As strange as The Loch House is, I'm relieved to be here. At least tonight we can get some sleep. But not before we meet the other house guests. I hear voices rising from another room and we follow the smell of food into the hall. The dining room is past the living room, which has the same dark mahogany panelling as the rest of the house. The floors, the walls, the décor . . . it's like everything is designed to be as depressing as possible. There's no joy in this place. The Tripadvisor reviewers were right. Perhaps my thoughts are coloured by their words but as I walk through the guest house, the hairs on the back of my neck prickle from a lingering feeling of being watched. I squeeze George's hand a little tighter and he looks up at me, eyes wide. He is feeling it too. I mask my discomfort with a smile.

I can't see a TV or radio in the living room, just a large brick inglenook fireplace, two worn Chesterfield sofas and lots of wide chairs. I try not to think of the glimpse I had of the gleaming furniture, deep rugs, tasteful armchairs draped with blankets, and roaring fires in the Royal's lounge. Having been so snotty about it I'd happily take the honeymoon suite tonight. As George tries out the ancient sofas I spot a huge bookshelf lining one wall. No point browsing the titles though as I plan on eating then heading straight to bed. My iPad is hidden under my pillow in any case.

I feel uneasy at the prospect of keyless rooms, but we can like it or lump it as far as Dorothy is concerned. It's only seven o'clock, so I shouldn't feel this tired. Perhaps Matt is right, and my gruelling shift pattern is catching up with me. My thoughts briefly turn to Liam, and I hope he's having a safe shift. He'll be working single-crewed tonight, as resources won't allow for a replacement while I'm away. I smile to myself as I imagine what he would have made of my encounter with the scarecrow earlier on – he'd never let me live it down.

The dining room is large, and rich with the smell of comfort food. Like the rest of the building, it has high ornate ceilings and panelled walls. It is an echo chamber, and every footstep reverberates across the hardwood floor. The sparsely furnished room holds a thick mahogany dining table and ten ornate wooden chairs. I cast my eyes around the table as Matt finds us a seat. There are four other people here. We gaze at each other expectantly, waiting for the first person to speak. Awkward silence fills the room. A shapely woman with bright red hair sits at the head of the table. She's dressed in layers and I'm guessing the sweet floral perfume I'm smelling comes from her. The woman to her left sits with her eyes cast downwards. Her red longline top pops against her smooth umber skin as she focuses on her plate. My gaze shifts to the young couple sitting on the other side of the table. There is trepidation on the woman's face. Her hand rests on her pregnancy bump and I seat George beside the man who I presume is her husband.

A tall man with deep set eyes and an authoritative presence strides into the room as if he's about to hold a board meeting. He's dressed in a shirt and tie, with navy trousers with a well ironed centre crease. Given the shine on his shoes, I wonder if he's ex-army. In my probationer days in the police, they would tell us to 'bull our boots' at home. You could always tell ex-army probationers just by the shine on their boots which took a crazy amount of time to do. As for me, I invested in shiny polish and dabbed it on in minutes before leaving it to dry. I rein in my thoughts. Even here, I'm still thinking of my job. It's such a big part of me that I'm unable to let it go. I watch as shiny shoes man sits at the other end of the table. I'm guessing he's approaching retirement age. At least there are bottles of wine on the table. I'll need a drink to get through the night.

'Hi, I'm Nicola,' I say, in an effort to break the ice. There's no sign of Dorothy or her husband, but I can hear clanging from the nearby kitchen. 'And this is my boyfriend, Matt.'

'Life partner,' he chuckles, shifting awkwardly in his seat. 'We're not sixteen.'

'Well, whatever the term is for it now. This is George. He's six, aren't you, my love?' He smiles shyly, his dimples on display.

'Hello, sweetie. I'm Bea. Bea Alderman,' the flame-haired woman at the top of the table says to my son. Her green eyes seem to twinkle with mischief as she takes us all in. I can't make out her accent, which seems to be a strange mishmash of Scottish and American. 'I'm a wanderer, with no fixed abode. Travelling is my passion. Who else came to see the Northern Lights?'

I raise my hand, as does the young couple beside me, but the woman in the red top remains quiet, a gentle smile on her face. 'I'm Steph,' the pregnant woman says. She has a warm and friendly face framed by long honey-blonde hair. 'This is Joey, my husband.' Joey is cleaning his glasses with his sweater, and he pauses to give me a friendly smile. I take in his man bun and tattoos and wonder if he's an artist or a creative of some kind. Then I see the musical notes etched on his skin.

'Let me guess, you're a musician?' I say.

'Is it that obvious?' He laughs, slipping his glasses back on. We are interrupted by Dorothy as she arrives, pushing an old-fashioned silver trolley laden with food. She flashes her unnaturally white teeth in a smile.

'This is nice, everybody getting along.'

I've no idea who has cooked the food, but it does smell good. 'Vegetable soup for you,' she says to the woman next to Bea. 'Although you're missing out!' Dorothy mutters something about vegetarianism being unhealthy. 'I have something nice for you, young man,' as she places a plate of chicken nuggets and chips in front of my son. 'Or you can have a grown-up meal if you prefer?' George thanks her for the chicken nuggets, and surprises me by tucking in.

Soon the rest of us are settled with our soup. 'This is good,' I say to Matt, as I butter a warm roll.

'Is it?' He watches me intently. I want to tell him not to worry, that we'll return to The Royal Hotel another time. But I can't stretch the lie that far. So instead, I smile, grateful for company. It's actually nice not to have our phones. Maybe we can salvage our break after all.

But there are two silent people at the table. The Asian lady in the red top who avoids eye contact and shiny shoes man, who stares at us each in turn. Dorothy returns to the kitchen and Bea breaks the silence, turning to the woman beside her.

'What's your name, dear?'

'Sunita,' the woman replies in a quiet voice. If Bea has noticed her discomfort, she's not making any allowances for it.

'Well, Sunita, you're a long way from home. What brings you here?'

I inwardly groan. Sunita surprises me as a gentle smile lands on her face. 'I'm here for the same reason as everyone else at this table. For shelter from the storm.' Her eyes suddenly rest on me, and I feel like she's seeing into my soul. Bea sniffs, moving on to the man at the end of the table who has already finished his soup.

'And you? What's your name?' She is unashamed in her curiosity as she awaits his reply.

'Bruce,' he booms. His voice is deep, his accent Scottish. 'Where are *you* from, Bea?' he says, turning the question back on her.

'I'm a nomad. I have no roots,' she says proudly with a wave of the hand.

Bruce's lips curl in a smile but his eyes are like flint. 'Yet you take one look at Sunita, and presume she's come all the way from India? Really? Are you that ignorant?'

I rest my soup spoon by the side of my plate. Bea turns a colourful shade of pink and the couple next to me shift in their chair. Sunita remains serene. 'I never said she was from India . . .' Bea falters, but then Dorothy comes in, bustling about as she offers more bread rolls. The moment is lost as Dorothy asks if we've enjoyed our soup. I'm not sure about Bruce. There's a coldness to him that makes me uneasy. I finish my soup, which is just what I needed after such a long day. We don't talk again until dinner is served, and Dorothy has returned to the kitchen.

'So, what about this phone ban?' I say, trying to lighten the mood. 'Anyone else going cold turkey?'

'God, yes!' Steph chuckles at the strangeness of it all. 'They were literally going to kick us out into the snow if we didn't hand over our phones.'

'They're an odd couple, aren't they?' Bea whispers conspiratorially. She's ignoring Bruce now, after checking with Sunita that she hadn't caused offence. I like Sunita. She's gracious and has a calming presence about her. But although Bruce appears well meaning, there's something about the way he acts that bothers me. It sometimes happens, given my profession; maybe I've seen him somewhere before. Although judging from his Scottish accent he's a bit far out for me to have dealt with him professionally.

'You all don't know about the history of this place, do you?' Bruce says, with a look that suggests he's in on a secret yet to be exposed. He has our full attention immediately.

'What history?' Matt says, slightly exasperated. He's tired and edgy and I don't blame him for wanting to get to the point. I feel like we're at one of those murder mystery weekends where everyone has a role to play. It's very surreal.

I notice a white line on Bruce's finger where a wedding band was once worn. I wonder if he's divorced, or a widow perhaps ... A sheen of sweat glazes his forehead as he taps a finger on the table. There may be a blizzard rattling the windowpanes, but this room is uncomfortably warm.

'You lot make me laugh. You complain about the rules, but you come here on the only weekend of the year that they're enforced. You can't blame our hosts for that.'

'The only weekend of the year? Why?' My curiosity is piqued now.

'This time ten years ago, every guest staying here was . . .' he glances at George and mimes a cut-throat motion with his finger when he's not looking '. . . including Dorothy's daughter, who was running The Loch House at the time.' He sits back in his chair, satisfied as he takes in our shocked expressions. 'So, you cannae blame our hosts for being jittery. I'm surprised they took in guests at all.'

'No.' Bea cups her hand over her mouth. 'You're lying.'

Dorothy appears behind her, and Bea jumps in surprise. 'It's true. Have some wine, dear. It will settle your nerves.' She fills our glasses.

'We moved here and took over the running of the guest house after that. The bills don't pay themselves.'

'Sorry for your loss.' Sunita places a hand over her glass as she declines alcohol.

'Thank you, dear,' Dorothy replies, and only now do I see the years of grief etched on her face. My mind is buzzing with questions, but I have to be careful how to word them, with George sitting beside me. 'Did they catch the people responsible?'

Dorothy shakes her head. 'They're still out there. Watching and waiting, which is why you can't leave after nine.' I want to know more, but Dorothy's breath catches, and she hurries back to the kitchen before I can ask.

'Bloody hell,' Joey mutters.

'I don't think I want to stay here anymore,' Steph says in a small, anxious voice. The atmosphere in the room has shifted and George picks up on it.

'What's wrong, Mummy?' He chews on his chicken nugget. He's a quiet child, often content to allow adult chatter to pass over him.

'Nothing to worry about,' I say. But then I glance over at Bruce and notice the hint of a smile resting on his face.

9

Elita

The truth is out. It didn't take you long, did it? I kinda wanted to watch you guys in your natural mode, you know? Now you're giving each other these weird looks, and everyone is acting all sneaky. You guys have such a mix of personalities, and even though you haven't had time to check us out, I've totally figured out a bunch of stuff about you. I know about the engagement ring, Matt. Seriously, you've gotta be more careful *A clumsy step leads to a painful fall.* My gran says it all the time. I mean, you should have known better. You're old. You must be . . . forty? Fifty? I dunno, I'm not very good with ages but you should have more sense than to leave it where anyone could take it. Lucky for you, I'm honest. I only take things that I know you won't want.

Maybe I should cut you some slack cos the last few hours have been pretty tough on you. I reckon you forgot that it was in your inside jacket pocket with all the fuss going on. I'm kinda curious about when you're gonna pop the special question to Nicola. The Loch House wasn't your first choice for a romantic getaway, was it? You can try to resist the vibes of this place, but trust me, it's hard to escape . . . I should know. My secret room is my own little hideout but can feel like a prison too. Once I step inside, everything changes. It has an odd kind of quietness, you know? But at least I have you to watch. There are no windows here, just the lights which cast long shadows on the walls. This house has an old-school feel, like something from a chapter of one of my books. Gran said it was built to protect the smugglers and pirates coming to the coast. That's why the secret places don't show up on any maps.

Can you even imagine *living* in this place? The smell of old wood and dust never goes away, and the walls that were once all vibrant and lively now look faded like an old photo. Some of the wallpaper is peeling, exposing the brickwork beneath. These walls were never painted, not like the rest of the house. But then, this place was only made for hiding. Grandad's done his best to cheer the place up, but the furniture is all so old. But it's not all bad. I like the deep, squishy armchair in the corner. It's perfect for curling up on. My bed is like a giant single, all decked out with clean, fresh white bedding and my desk is massive enough to fit, like, three computer screens on. It's one of those antique desks with these big drawers that I stuff full of knick-knacks from the guest rooms. The walls are decorated with portraits of various members of the royal family. Gran swears that they were presents to her. I've seen the photos too. She's not making it up. She was very pretty when she was young – not like me at this age. She's given me the best of the pictures. Each frame is carved all pretty and gilded with gold. It's funny that she settled for Henry, who was a butler for the royals back in the day. I know you think that she's batty, but there is *some* truth in her words. You've just got to figure out which parts are real.

I've been watching you, Matt. You don't listen properly when she speaks. Your attention is only ever on the person you're with. Nicola. You're very protective of her, aren't you? I've watched you pull out her chair, rest a hand on her back, lug around her suitcase. I'm not sure that she deserves all that trust that you're piling on her. Sure, she loves her little boy, but I dunno, her fondness for you seems forced. It's like she has to remember to return the favour. Her smiles aren't the real deal, but you don't seem to notice, and I can't help but feel bad for you. I'm worried that when you pop the question she'll say 'no'. What will happen to your family then?

Love, relationships . . . they're all a bit tangled, I'll never understand them. I've never been in love myself. Well, not unless you count fictional characters from books and stuff. I have a lot of time to read. George is lucky, having people who care about him so much. I try to imagine his life. Does he have heaps of friends in school? Does he go to birthday parties and munch on cake? Does his mum read him a story before tucking him into bed each night? Me, I don't have friends, not real ones anyway. Don't feel too sorry for me though. I'm different but I'm not stupid. I'm clever for my age. But being home-schooled means I've missed out on a lot. I'm not sure how to act around other people but I learn the best I can from books and DVDs. I wish I could reach out to George and tell him how lucky he is. To tell him to hide. Because Matt, you might not get as far as popping the question. You can't take anything for granted now.

Not everyone staying in The Loch House is being straight with us, that's for sure. Now the storm has closed in and it's hard to see where the ground ends and the sky begins. The world has gone all hushed, as if nature is holding its breath, waiting to see what will happen next. It's just like the storm we had ten years ago – the night my mother and the people who stayed here were killed.

I try not to dwell, it's not good for my mood. But those memories sneak up on me in my dreams when my guard is down. I haven't always understood what went down back then, so I've been leaning on Mum's diaries to make sense of it all. It's all I have left of her. A long chain of events set everything in motion. All the way back before I was born. Mum thought I was special, and she wasn't the only one. There was this guy named Caleb. Such a harmless sounding name. She put her trust in him. She was wrong. He's still out there, along with his crew. The people who took her away from me. I feel them getting closer and it feels like a dark omen as those snowdrifts pile up. The house's timbers are creaking under the weight of the snow. They're coming, and I'm defenceless. I just hope nobody else has to die.

10

Nicola

Everyone has moved to the living room, and given it's 9 p.m., George should be in bed. I don't want him listening to the conversation taking place downstairs, but neither will I leave him in our bedroom alone. He sits on the four-poster bed in quiet acceptance, not seeming to mind either way. He's not like other children, and readily accepts each situation with a tolerance beyond his years. He doesn't shout or scream or have tantrums. He does as he is told.

Sometimes, I almost wish he would misbehave. When he's quiet like this, I've no idea what's going on in his head. Is he happy? Sad? Does he even want to be here? I slip my iPad from its hiding place behind my pillow and watch his face light up as I give it to him. There are several games downloaded and some age-appropriate TV series too. He'd be just as happy sitting with a book, but the conversations downstairs have taken a dark turn. I think some of them have forgotten what it's like to be a child. They're all so worried about how they're feeling nobody has given him a second thought. All except for Dorothy, who genuinely seems to care about him.

After some initial misgivings, she even approved the device – as long as it's not connected to any sort of network, of course. She seems to like George and told me she's willing to bend the rules only for him. I sense there is good in this woman, but she has clearly suffered too. Pain shapes you as a person, lending a new lens of perspective to your world.

I feel uneasy in her husband's company though. It's nothing

to do with Henry's appearance. It's the air around him, a feeling of foreboding that I get each time he draws near. It's hardly any wonder I'm feeling on edge in this creepy old place. I stare out of the window as each flake of snow dances in the air, creating a mesmerising ballet of white. It's relentless as it piles up on the ground, and our car, which is barely visible under the weight of snow. The loch is somewhere beyond it, but I can't quite make it out. It feels like we're cut off from civilisation as nature tries to bury the outside world.

I fiddle with the sash window in an attempt to open it, but it feels glued down. A grunt escapes my lips from the effort, but the thing won't budge. The unease in my gut grows at the thought of being stranded here. When will the storm let up? With no access to TV, internet or radio, I've no way of knowing what the forecast is. *Why* did I let Matt drag us here? I should have told him it was over months ago, but his hold on me is so strong. I've been a victim once in my life already. Is it happening again? Unlike George's father, Matt has never been violent with me. But I've safeguarded enough victims of domestic abuse to know that it comes in many forms. Violence is the biggest red flag, but control and manipulation creep up on you. Have I allowed it to happen again?

'Can the little girl play with me, Mummy?' George clings to the iPad, his head tilted to one side. I turn away from the window and sit next to him on the bed, smoothing back his wavy hair, which is sticking up at the front. He hates getting his hair cut so much that I've resorted to trimming it myself.

'What little girl?' I've not heard mention of any other children in the guest house.

'The one looking out of the window. I saw her when we got here.'

I try to recall our arrival. I was so busy managing George and my bag that I hadn't thought to look up. 'Are you sure? It was snowy when we got here. Maybe your eyes were playing tricks on you.'

George's face scrunches in a frown. 'But she waved at me. She had yellow hair, like Emily.' Emily is his friend from school, a small, shy girl with wavy blonde hair. The pair of them are inseparable.

'George, to make this clear, you're telling me you saw a little girl waving from one of these upstairs windows? She was waving at you? Really? Are you sure?'

George nods. 'She was smiling. She was wearing a funny dress, like Dorothy's, but smaller.'

'Are you sure she was a child, not Dorothy, maybe? You know how things look smaller when they're far away.'

But George exhales a giant sigh. 'She was a girl, Mummy, smaller than me. She had a funny face ... it was like ...' He struggles to find the words. 'I dunno ... she was different. But OK.'

'Because she was smiling?' I ask him.

'Yeah. Can I play with her?'

'Not right now. Stick with me for tonight. If there is a little girl, she's probably tucked up in bed.' I make a mental note to ask Dorothy about the child later on. 'C'mon,' I gesture at George to get off the bed. 'Dorothy said she'll make you some hot chocolate if you want.' The thing is, George rarely lies, so I've no reason to doubt his account. I encompass his hand in mine and guide him out of the room. The house smells of smoke, it's a woody, earthy smell, rising up from the fire in the living room. The first floor landing is deathly silent, and a reticent quiet hangs in the air. If there are children in this building, they're not making themselves known. This place has such an oppressive quality, I cannot imagine children living here. Not happy children, anyway. A shiver of unease trails down my spine as George and I take the stairs. His steps are slow, his grip on my hand tight. He feels it too.

A heated discussion is taking place in the living room. Joey, Steph, Bea, Matt and Bruce are sitting around the fire. There's no sign of Sunita, and I'm guessing she's gone to her room. I settle George onto a comfortable chair, with my large noise cancelling headphones on his head. He looks so cute, and I feel guilty that he's not snuggled up in bed. Thank goodness he had a long sleep in the car. The group quietens as Dorothy briefly enters. She's wearing yellow marigold gloves and cautiously checks my iPad as if it's radioactive. 'Show me the Wi-Fi,' she asks George, but he responds with a shake of the head. 'There is none,' he says, bringing up the settings so she can check for herself. 'See?' She puts on her reading glasses which are kept on a jewelled loop around her neck. 'Alright, you can use it.' She turns to me with a smile as she pulls off her gloves and I know she's about to deliver one of her anecdotes.

'The royals play parlour games, you know. They don't trouble themselves with technology. At Christmas, they buy each other the most amusing gifts.' A small, tinkly laugh leaves her pink lipstick lips. 'It's all changing now, such a shame, but Charlie dear is a wonderful king.' I don't know how to respond so I simply smile and nod. Satisfied, she leaves to make George a hot chocolate. She seems to enjoy fussing over him, and I feel guilty for my initial assessment of her. She may be eccentric but there is kindness there too.

Matt is watching me, protective as always. I've taken some painkillers, so my back isn't playing up anymore. But how long will it be before I get the next injury? Liam's nickname for me is 'Scrappy', because I'm never afraid to jump into the middle of a street brawl. Nine out of ten times, it's me who breaks it up without needing to throw a punch. I don't get off on violence and, thankfully, people seem to listen to me.

Maybe Matt's right, and I should choose an easier life for myself. But having a job where every day is different makes me feel alive. I've no aspiration for promotions, I don't want to be a pen-pusher. How could sensible Matt understand when his Friday nights consist of marking his students' work? He doesn't like socialising, and rarely shows his face at any of my work events. Then again, I don't want him to, as the last time he met Liam, he was overly passive aggressive.

Matt is patting the space next to him on the worn leather couch. I join him, glancing at our guest room companions as the fire warms my legs. Logs are stacked on either side of the fireplace, which is throwing out a ferocious heat. If it weren't for the howl of the wind gusting down the chimney you could almost forget about the weather outside.

I cast an eye over clocks of every shape and size hanging on the wall above the fireplace. Only now do I notice that most of them have stopped. Have the batteries run down, or have they been deliberately stopped as a tribute to the loss of Dorothy and Henry's daughter?

It's unlikely they would have all run down at the same time – 11.11. It feels like this place is telling us life has no right to go on. I sink back into the leather sofa, which is worn and cushiony to the touch. I need to rein in my imagination. Call it a sixth sense, but I can't shake off the feeling that I'm being watched.

The Loch House is so eerily remote and the décor so uninviting that it feels like the last place left on earth. The world could have ended outside, and we wouldn't know about it. Given the tragedy that has forever shaped Dorothy's life, perhaps she prefers the isolation. Yet there are no pictures of her daughter on display. No family photos, nothing to bring a little warmth or personality to the place. Just the haunting aftermath of a tragic story which has yet to be resolved.

It might sound selfish but I hope it doesn't impact on our stay too negatively. George has witnessed enough violence in his short life.

11

Nicola

'I can't believe what I'm hearing.' Bea fidgets next to the fire, unable to stay still. 'You knew about the history of this place and came here anyway?' She is aiming her question at Bruce, whose expression is one of amusement. 'What sort of ghoul are you?' She shakes her head, not waiting for an answer before turning her attention to the rest of us. 'What if it happens again? What if history repeats itself?'

'Oh please, enough with the dramatics.' Bruce rolls his eyes. 'Nobody's coming after you.'

'Don't you look down your beaky nose at me.' Bea's voice is shrill. 'How do you know who they're coming after? Just what happened here and what has it got to do with *you*?'

'Hey, calm down, Bea. There's no need for things to get personal.' I stand, despite Matt trying to gently pull me back down. 'Even if what Bruce says is true, it happened a long time ago. In my experience, lightning doesn't strike twice in the same place.'

'And what experience would that be?' I feel the weight of Bruce's stare as he speaks.

'I'm a police officer.' I return his disdainful look.

Bea seems taken aback and regards me with new respect. 'Oh dear, not here in an official capacity, I trust?'

Matt stands now, resting a supportive arm around my shoulders. 'She's here to get away from her job, on a much needed break.'

'That explains the bruises, then,' Bruce replies. Nothing gets past him. I pull down the sleeve of my jumper. I hadn't realised they were on display.

'Exactly why I'd like her to give in her notice,' Matt says, with some affection. 'Nicola works for Lincolnshire police, so she has no jurisdiction here.'

That's not strictly true. I'm not officially a warranted officer here because the laws differ in Scotland, but I can make an arrest if I need to. I don't correct Matt because I don't want to show him up. The fire crackles and spits behind me as another gust of wind is driven down.

'Anyone can make a citizen's arrest,' Bruce stretches his long legs in front of him. 'Although the only officers officially warranted in England, Wales and Scotland are British Transport Police.'

'Are you in the job?' I say, but he shakes his head.

'My interests lie in true crime cold cases.'

'Is that why you're here? You're a true crime enthusiast?'

'Aye. I've been researching this case for some time.' He folds his arms and Matt and I sit back down. At least the sofas are comfortable, but the subject matter of our conversation is setting everyone on edge.

'Oh yes?' I ask, because now my interest is piqued. I knew from the moment that I entered this building that something dark went down here. 'It didn't get much coverage in the press,' I carry on, when Bruce doesn't continue. 'Have you got any theories?'

But despite Bruce being the one to bring it up, he now seems tight-lipped.

'I think Dorothy's the best person to answer your questions.'

'Maybe, but I'm asking you.' I cast an eye over my son, who is happily playing his game. Dorothy puts a stop to my questioning as she enters. This time, her rattling drinks trolley contains a teapot, cake and cups which are decorated with the faces of the royal family from years gone by. The cups rattle and the wheels squeak, adding to the feeling that we've stepped back in time. She's changed into a blue dress, with petticoats and lace. Her clothing doesn't come from any era but her own. With her bright white teeth and colourful clothes, she looks like a drag act. I stifle my smile.

'You look nice, Dorothy.' I figure that anyone who goes to that much trouble with their wardrobe is dying to be complimented.

'I do, don't I?' she agrees, swaying from side to side. 'The blue matches my eyes. I'm the most beautiful woman on the Isle of Skye.'

I don't know what sort of a mirror she's looking into, but I want one for my room. She hands George his hot chocolate, which is complete with mini marshmallows and cream on top. 'There's a pot of tea here for anyone who wants it, and whisky for those who don't. Help yourselves. We'll be in the kitchen if anyone needs us.' Her eyes dance around the room as she takes us in. She's a strange one. I like how she leaves us alone, although it's hardly surprising, given the topic of our conversation.

'Thanks.'

I follow her to the door. 'Dorothy,' I say, keeping my voice low. 'Are there any other children staying here? George mentioned that he saw a little girl standing at the window when we were arriving.'

She blinks her false eyelashes. A shadow crosses her face, a fleeting moment of concern. But she recovers quickly and fixes a rigid smile.

'No, dear. I can wholeheartedly say that your George is the only child under this roof.' She pauses, her gaze growing distant. 'I've always wanted lots of grandchildren, but it wasn't to be. Those evil monsters . . . they took everything.' She raises a hand to her mouth, pressing her fingers to her lips, as if trying to hold back her words. She excuses herself, and I watch her small frame scurry down the hall.

I've upset her for the second time tonight. Who are the monsters she's talking about? I approach Bruce, who has just snapped at Bea to shut up. I don't have time for their dramas as Bea inhales a shocked breath. It's time for answers.

'What happened here?' I say, before an angry-faced Bea can verbalise her disgust. 'You need to tell us.'

I'm surprised I haven't heard about the crimes that took place under this roof, but I've never watched much news, just immersed myself in work. Scottish crimes don't tend to get as much traction in the media as incidents in London, and I deal with so many incidents in my job that I'm sometimes blinkered to other high profile crimes. It's easy to feel overwhelmed. I made a vow to focus on my caseloads alone.

'Fine,' he says, regarding us all. 'I'll tell you. But don't shoot the messenger.' He gives Bea a meaningful look.

'Why don't you sit down?' I gesture towards the sofa. She's turned an unhealthy shade of pink and a sheen of sweat has broken out on her forehead. 'I was just about to,' she says reluctantly. 'The fire is getting too hot.'

I take my place beside Matt as Bruce throws another log into the flames. Is he purposely trying to wind Bea up? George is happily playing, snuggled on a comfy wide chair near the door, oblivious to our conversation. My mind is racing but I try to calm myself by picking at a thread on my jeans. The room falls into silence as we wait for Bruce to speak.

'Ten years ago, Dorothy's daughter Amelia was found dead in this room.' A beat passes as he takes a breath. 'She wasn't alone. Her guests had been poisoned. There were no survivors. Strangely enough, Amelia was shot in the head.'

A gasp leaves Bea's lips.

'Are you alright?' I ask, because all the colour has left her face. Her hands are clasped tightly on her lap, her knuckles white as she takes everything in. She delivers a nod and turns to Bruce, hungry for answers.

'Who . . . who would do such a thing?'

Bruce shrugs. 'There was nae sign of forced entry, and the killer was never found.'

'Killer or killers?' I interject. 'Because Dorothy called them monsters. Was she here?' But then I remember what he said about *everyone* here being killed.

'Not according to what I've read. There's a lot of speculation. Some say there was more than one killer. I mean, it would be hard for one person to control so many guests but not impossible.'

As a police officer I'm no stranger to violence but as the storm batters the windows, his words are giving me chills. Matt shifts beside me and I know he's feeling it too.

Bruce continues with his story. 'It could have been an inside job for all we know. Police found traces of poison in the food.'

'They poisoned the food?' Bea's hand falls over her chest. 'And you're telling us this now?'

Bruce actually smirks. 'Oh, I dare say if your food was poisoned, you'd know about it by now.' I watch in disbelief as he chuckles. This man is dark. The effect of his words on Steph are immediate as she clings to her husband for comfort.

'Motivation?' I ask, not giving him the satisfaction of looking as worried as I feel.

'If police knew that, then they would have found the killer, wouldn't they?'

'But you're a true crime enthusiast, aren't you? You must have your own theories.'

A thin-lipped smile spreads on Bruce's gaunt face. 'It wouldn't be very tactful to discuss it with her parents present, now would it?'

I look around the room. Neither Dorothy nor her husband Henry are in earshot. But Bruce gives me a look to suggest they are. In the police, you learn to read faces, to communicate without words. He glances up at the ceiling. The signal is brief, but enough for me to pick it up. In the corner of the coving, a small, shiny lens reflects the flickering fire. I drop my gaze before anyone else notices. My mind is racing. We are being watched.

Mystery on the Mic Podcast

The Watts Case Series: Episode 2

Alex: Welcome back to another episode of 'Mystery on the Mic,' folks! I'm your host, Alex, and thank you for joining us for this segment. Joining us for this segment of our podcast, is our resident true crime historian, Sarah. How's it going, Sarah?

Sarah: Hi, Alex! I'm doing well, but I must say this case is truly chilling. The Isle of Skye is known for its natural beauty and tranquillity, so a crime of this magnitude is virtually unheard of. It's early days, so the amount of information we have is limited. But it's definitely worth discussing as it comes in.

Alex: Absolutely, Sarah. We cover crimes from all over, but this is one of the most remote places I've encountered when it comes to true crime. So, let's get into it. Our story begins at The Loch House, a serene guest house on the Isle of Skye, where the owner, a young woman by the name of Amelia Evans, was found brutally murdered, along with her guests.

Sarah: That's right, Alex. Apparently, Amelia inherited the guest house from her grandmother, who ran it until she died. It's said that her grandmother Gertrude was a beloved figure in the community, known for her warm smile and generous spirit. Amelia was quiet by comparison, and apart from the guests she took in, she pretty much kept to herself.

Alex: According to locals, her parents made the journey from London to the island every couple of weeks. Unfortunately for them, they found her body, along with those of the other guests. Amelia had been tied to a chair and had a gunshot wound to her temple. To make matters even more baffling, the other guests were suspected victims of poisoning. Their bodies were laid out in front of Amelia and it's strongly suspected that she was forced to watch them die.

Sarah: Yes, Alex. It's utterly shocking and there doesn't appear to be any motive or suspects at this stage. Police officers haven't yet released the identities of the other guests. The fact that they may have been poisoned adds another layer of complexity to an already perplexing case.

Alex: I've covered a lot of true crime over the years, but this is even a lot for me, a hardened true crime podcaster, to take in. Sky News interviewed a very shocked local shop owner, Annie Campbell, who painted a picture of Amelia as a hardworking and kind person. It really makes you wonder, what could be the motive behind such a blood-chilling act?

Sarah: That's the million-dollar question, Alex. And it's one that has the entire island community on edge. The Isle of Skye has a reputation for being peaceful and safe, so this crime has shaken local people to their core. Up until now, it was the sort of place where you could go to bed with your key in the door – not anymore.

Alex: Absolutely. The whole island is feeling the impact, but on a positive note, it's heart-warming to see how the community has come together to support one another during this difficult time.

Sarah: It really is. In the face of such tragedy, their resilience shines through. Locals are hosting free coffee mornings in the local village hall, and there's a volunteer group visiting people who live in remote locations to offer comfort and advice. Police can only do so much. It's good that the locals have taken it upon themselves to look after their own.

Alex: Yes, and as police investigators work tirelessly to unravel this mystery, we're left wondering about the future of The Loch House. It was once a welcoming haven, but now it stands as a haunting crime scene. It makes you wonder if it will ever open its doors to the public again.

Sarah: That's right. The fate of The Loch House hangs in the balance, just like the search for justice for the victims and their grieving families. We've covered many unsolved mysteries over the years, but I really hope that we find closure here.

Alex: Indeed. Well, listeners, this is one case we'll be keeping a close eye on. Thank you, Sarah, for shedding light on this unsettling case. It's a wonder we can sleep at night.

Sarah: Thank *you*, Alex. It's always a pleasure to dive into these mysteries with you. And to be fair, crimes like these are so rare, it's not worth losing sleep over something that will never happen where you live.

Alex: (Chuckles) Let's hope so. And to our listeners, stay tuned for updates on this developing story. We'll be back with more 'Mystery on the Mic' after the break.

12

Matt

I pull the chain on the toilet. Even the bathrooms in this place are from another era. The cistern, positioned high on the wall, gurgles and splutters in protest. The wall mirror provides a distorted view as I wash my hands. Sunita had the right idea. We should have gone straight to our room after supper too. But now Nicola has gone into full police mode and there's no letting go. I tell myself that this is temporary, but it doesn't make me feel any better about the situation we've found ourselves in.

The feeble hand dryer gives off a dying wisp of air and I rub my damp hands on the back of my trousers. Why would anyone choose to stay here? As I walk down the hall, I try to imagine The Loch House back in the day. To me, it feels like the sort of place you'd come to if you were trying to hide. My footsteps echo as I walk a little quicker, checking over my shoulder. It's so dark, it feels like someone has snuck up behind me. But when I peer through the dim light, there's nobody there.

It's a relief to be in company and I take up a vacant spot on the leather sofa, more relaxed now that Nicola is back. I don't like her leaving my side in such a strange place. The others are talking among themselves. The air is warm in the sitting room, despite the freezing temperatures outside. The smell of burning wood offers a little comfort.

'I feel sick to my stomach,' Bea says, rubbing her generous waistline. 'We could have been poisoned for all we know.' I roll my eyes inwardly.

Her reaction is a mix of attention seeking, anxiety and hysterics. This is a woman who makes her presence known.

'It was years ago,' I say, in an effort to calm her down. 'Whoever poisoned the guests was hardly cooking for us tonight.' But Bea isn't listening as she complains about the food. It might have been nice to sit around the fire and chat, had everyone not been so fixated on the dark history of this place. I don't get people sometimes. Why can't they move on? But then I look at Nicola and remember that she's carrying baggage too. I don't mean George, he's a good kid. But his twisted father . . . I don't know what Nicola ever saw in him. I suppose it was his looks that turned her head. We couldn't be more different.

'It'll be fine. We're only here for one night,' Joey pipes up, and I appreciate another voice trying to calm things down. He and Steph sit entwined on the sofa, her hand resting on her neat bump. They seem like a nice couple. Musicians don't earn a lot of money, so I can see why they took their chances with a two-star hotel. They mentioned over dinner that this is their last holiday before their baby arrives. They have their whole lives in front of them, and if I'm honest, I envy them a bit. I may be financially secure, but I thought I'd be more settled by now. The couple are clearly devoted to each other, and I wonder why it's never worked out that way for me. It wasn't surprising that Steph is a beautician, with her perfectly arched eyebrows and flawless face. She told me she works from people's homes, doing their nails and advising on make-up and skin care, as well as in her local hairdressing salon a couple of times a week. They're saving for their new home, but now they've ended up in the middle of this.

'I'm sure the murdered guests thought they'd be fine too!' Bea is an out and out drama queen, and I'm not buying the whole California new age vibe. I haven't spoken to her as much as Joey and Steph, so I don't know her background. Although annoying, she seems nice enough at heart, and people sometimes overreact when they're scared. She managed to prise some information from Sunita before she wisely went to her room. It seems she's a yoga instructor who has come to Scotland with the intention of scouting some areas to hold retreats. I doubt The Loch House is what she's looking for. She seems like a private person, a little mistrustful perhaps?

'Do we know anything about them?' Nicola straightens up on the sofa. She's directed her question at Bruce but he sits back, his bony fingers steepled as he watches us all. 'Not enough to give us a motive,' he finally says. It's like we're pawns in his own private game. He has something against Bea, although they've not met before today as far as I'm aware. It's like he's enjoying drawing her out, fuelling her fear. He strikes me as a bully, taking pleasure in other people's discomfort. Like that challenge at the dinner table – he only did it to show Bea up. I've met people like him before and they don't impress me at all. It doesn't surprise me that he's a true crime fan. He wouldn't look out of place in one of those documentaries himself. How deep does his fascination with murder go?

George sits quietly, Nicola's soundproof headphones looking huge on him. He's a funny little boy. I thought he'd come out of himself as he got older, but if anything, he's withdrawn further from the world. As I say to my students, there's nothing wrong with being an introvert as long as you're happy. My fondness for George is another reason I want to marry Nicola. I'm not his biological father, but I want to remain a part of his life. The poor kid needs stability. I know about the injuries that his father, Gav, inflicted on Nicola. I guess it's why she keeps punishing herself. She needs counselling, not police work. I'm pretty sure that George witnessed his fair share of violence too. It took him a long time to accept me into his life.

Nicola is still asking questions. Her muscles tense beneath her jumper as I lay a hand on her back. She's in detective mode, trying to work out what happened here previously. I allow her chatter to wash over me as she questions Bruce about the past. She's a magnet for trouble. I feel guilty for thinking it, but I wonder if she's enjoying this. Why spend a night with me when she can sit among strangers, talking about her favourite subject – crime. Even on our journey here, she thought she saw a body on the roadside, when it was nothing but some creepy old scarecrow. It's exhausting sometimes. She's always getting involved. We can't pass a beggar on the street without her referring them to a homeless shelter. Then there's the kids in our neighbourhood that she's always keeping an eye on. I get that she's a compassionate person, I just wish she had a little more time for me.

At least it will do her good to have a break from her phone. I feel an edge of irritation as I think of the texts between her and her work colleagues. It's constant. Catching myself, I halt the thoughts which will only take me down a dark path. I love Nicola. She's kind and thoughtful and a wonderful mum. Because her heart is so big, she's so busy caring for everyone else that she sometimes forgets who's waiting for her at home. Life will be so much better when she leaves the police, and we have children of our own. We're both getting older. It's time to move things on.

Until then, I know she won't rest until she gets answers, and to be fair she has a point. Why have we been issued with rules telling us not to go outside? What is meant to be waiting for us out there? The wind has quietened outside, but snow continues to fall. I can't help but feel we're in the eye of the storm. We couldn't leave now if we tried.

Mystery on the Mic Podcast

The Watts Case Series: Episode 3

Alex: Welcome back to 'Mystery on the Mic', everyone. I'm your host, Alex. Today, we're back on the Isle of Skye, returning to the haunting case of The Loch House murders as we reach the ten year anniversary. As we've discussed before, this mysterious old guest house was the scene of a grim discovery when the owner and all the guests were found dead under chilling circumstances. To dig deeper into this section of our podcast, I'm joined by our fabulous true crime historian, Sarah. Hi, Sarah.

Sarah: Hello, Alex. This is such an intriguing case. Thanks for having me on board to discuss it.

Alex: We love having you on the show, and your detective skills are second to none. So, what can you tell us about The Loch House murders on the Isle of Skye? We've had a bunch of new subscribers who may not have heard of it before. How about we recap with the victims: who were they? What were their stories?

Sarah: I really had to dig deep to find out anything about this case. It almost feels as if the story has been suppressed on the internet and anything of relevance taken down.

Alex: Really? Is that possible? I mean, I've heard of internet suppression but I'm not sure how it works.

Sarah: It's difficult but not impossible – if you hire a team of people and have tons of money to pay for it. I can't say for sure that's what has happened here, only that information was unusually hard to find.

Alex: Which is why we're keen to share the story. This is such a tragic event. Five people lost their lives. We won't allow this to disappear. As listeners know, we keep cases alive for the families still searching for answers. They, more than anyone, deserve to know the truth. So, what *can* you tell us about the victims?

Sarah: They're a fascinating group of individuals, Alex. First, we have Linda, a sixty-three-year-old landscape painter. Recently divorced, she was reportedly staying at The Loch House to find inspiration for her art. Then there was the middle-aged couple, Brian and Alice, who were there to celebrate their wedding anniversary. It's said they met on the Isle of Skye when they were teenagers and returned every year. And lastly, we had Bertram Miller, a thirty-two-year-old environmentalist who was exploring the island and using The Loch House as his base. He had a particular interest in the loch.

Alex: That's so sad. They all sound like amazing people. What a waste of life. They were all found poisoned in the living room of The Loch House, correct?

Sarah: Yes, I'm afraid so. Police were tight-lipped but it came out in the inquest that they had been poisoned. Apparently, their bodies had been lined up on the floor in front of the guest house owner. A gruesome scene, I'm sure.

Alex: A chill has literally just run down my spine. I have so many unanswered questions. Now, let's talk about the owner of The Loch House, Amelia Evans. She ran the place all by herself, didn't she?

Sarah: Yes, she did. Amelia was a young woman who had been left to run The Loch House on her own after inheriting it from her grandmother. Amelia's husband, John Evans, left her not long after she moved in. We don't know why they split up. It must have been tough for Amelia, who managed everything from guest house bookings to catering for the guests. I've searched for details about John and read in a forum that he went to live abroad. He wasn't in the country when his wife died.

Alex: Yes, it can't have been easy, doing it all on her own. According to locals, her parents lived in London and visited to help out when they could. Makes you wonder why she stayed. She was also found dead at the scene, although she wasn't poisoned like the others. Isn't that right, Sarah?

Sarah: Correct. Amelia was found tied to a chair in the living room. It was as if she was forced to watch each of the guest's bodies being laid in front of her. A torture device, maybe, before she met her own violent end. For the life of me, I can't figure out the motive, though.

Alex: Yes, me neither. It's what makes this case so bizarre. The presence of a gun lends this case another strange twist.

Sarah: Yes, she was shot in the temple at close range. A shocking sight, undoubtedly, especially when contrasted with the peaceful surroundings of the Isle of Skye. I mean, it's not the Bronx. Anyone who's been there is immediately hit by its remote beauty. It's not the sort of place you'd expect someone to have firearms, apart from the people who use them to hunt.

Alex: This case is just filled with bizarre contradictions, isn't it? On one hand, we have this serene, picturesque location and on the other, such a gruesome, cold-blooded crime. But let's try and understand the motive here, Sarah. Why would someone poison the guests and then shoot the owner of the guest house?

Sarah: That's a good question, Alex. Theories have ranged from a disgruntled guest with mental health issues to a personal vendetta against Amelia. But nothing concrete has been established. As I said, it remains one of the most baffling aspects of this case.

Alex: Yes, and I just can't get my head around why someone as young as Amelia chose to live in such a remote place. After all, she could have sold the place after she inherited it. Was there anything in her past that could potentially point to a motive? Was she hiding from anyone?

Sarah: Amelia was quite reclusive, according to witness accounts. After her husband left, she cut herself off from most of her old life. Her parents, Dorothy and Henry Hill, were her only family, but they lived and worked in London most of the time. As far as we know, Amelia didn't have any enemies or debts. The people who came into contact with her said that she seemed really nice, if a little guarded. She was a bit of an enigma on the island.

Alex: It's interesting to see someone who's guarded also taking in guests. We've all got to make a living, I suppose. And what about her parents, Dorothy and Henry Hill? They run The Loch House now, right?

Sarah: Indeed, they do, which offers another strange twist. After Amelia's death, they took over The Loch House. It took quite a few months to get it back up and running and they don't operate it year-round like Amelia did. It's surprising, given what happened there. They were the ones who found the bodies. You can't easily shake off a traumatic event like that.

Alex: The Loch House has a bit of a reputation, doesn't it? There are some terrible reviews on Tripadvisor, from what I understand.

Sarah: You're not wrong there. Many guests reported feeling uncomfortable and it's said the place is a bit of a dump. Some mentioned a strange, oppressive atmosphere. Others complained about the remoteness of the location and lack of modern amenities, such as TV and Wi-Fi. After its heyday under Amelia, it's safe to say that The Loch House is no longer a popular destination.

Alex: All these elements make the case even more mysterious. Why do you think the police never got to the bottom of it, Sarah?

Sarah: There were many factors. The remote location, lack of physical evidence, and absence of eyewitnesses all made it difficult for the police to make any headway. It's also worth noting that the case did not receive much media attention, which meant less public pressure to solve it.

Alex: Yes, sad but true. I've said it a thousand times but it's such a baffling case. It's hard to comprehend it all – the poisonings, the shooting, the isolation of The Loch House, the odd reviews . . . I can't imagine just what went on there. Was Amelia running away from someone? Did they torture her before she died? But if so, for what? She didn't have any great wealth, and nothing was taken as far as I'm aware. Perhaps it was part of some bizarre satanic cult . . . These are just a few of the theories our listeners have mentioned online.

Sarah: It's a real head scratcher alright. The case of The Loch House remains one of the most enigmatic and unsettling cases I know of. It's a stark reminder of the mysteries that can lurk in the most unexpected places. Makes me all the more cautious when I book a holiday online.

Alex: You can say that again. Would you book a stay in The Loch House guest house, Sarah?

Sarah: (Chuckles) As interested as I am in the case, you couldn't pay me to do that!

Alex: I'm with you on that one! But on a more serious note, I do hope that one day we'll solve the mystery that continues to haunt the Isle of Skye. It would be good to find closure for everyone involved. As always, thanks for joining us today, Sarah. And to our listeners, thanks for tuning into this segment of 'Mystery on the Mic'. See the show notes for links to the original episodes on this case. Remember, truth can sometimes be stranger than any crime novel, so stay safe and keep your eyes open for the mysteries around you.

13

Nicola

George is still curled up on the armchair near the door, his head down as he stares at his iPad screen. He looks so cute in his *Fireman Sam* pyjamas. I'm dreading the day he'll leave all the childish stuff behind. He should be asleep, but I need to know what I'm dealing with first. How can I put him to bed, knowing that we're probably being watched?

Bruce was the first person to be aware of the camera and he's treating this like a game. What else does he know? Was he involved in the murders ten years ago? What if he's the type of killer who can't help but revisit the scene? The type who gets off on people's reactions, all the while reliving the violence on a loop in their twisted heads. The wind swirls restlessly down the chimney, mirroring my thoughts.

You can't judge people by their appearances, or so they say. I've been helped by a drug addict when a drunk was being violent, and once a sweet-looking young woman pulled a knife without warning during a domestic dispute. Granted it's unusual, and I pride myself on my intuition, but I'm not sure when it comes to Bruce. Not for the first time, I wish Liam was here with me instead of Matt. He'd know what to do.

I realise that I'm frowning and force myself to relax. Matt is watching me too closely. It's a good thing he can't read my thoughts. Not that I could tell my mate Liam about what's going on in my relationship . . . The very thought leaves me uneasy. Matt would never forgive me. I can tell he hates me analysing what went on here.

Every time I ask Bruce a question, I can hear Matt inwardly groan. He thinks that I'm overreacting, but I haven't told him about the camera yet. I'm not sure how he'll behave if I do.

The ice cubes clink in Bruce's crystal tumbler as he drinks the glass of whisky which he poured himself from the drinks trolley. Matt's displaying the same edgy quietness as when he doesn't get his own way. An only child, it's obvious he was spoilt by his parents. He doesn't just *hope* for things to go the way he wants – he *expects* it. I suppose it's why his students do so well. Heaven help anyone who doesn't make the grade.

Bea is up again, pacing the floor, her pastel coloured floaty clothes swishing as she moves. I wish she wouldn't stand so near the fire. I'm half expecting her to go up in a ball of flames. I need to get control of this situation. Feelings are running high, and I don't want George to get caught up in it. Thankfully he's still engrossed, and it's not been that long we've been down here really. He loves Tetris, or that game where you slice fruit in half . . . I can't wait to get him out of this place.

The guest house may be warm as the fire crackles in the hearth, but this room is heavy with a sense of desolation. I imagine the aftermath of violence ten years ago in this very room. Were the lights left on or off? Did the bodies lie in the darkness, blood seeping into the cracks of the timbers beneath my feet? They weren't found for two whole days. I imagine the old building standing witness to such horrors, the sounds of the many clocks on the walls ticking the seconds away. Then the creak of the front door as Dorothy and Henry arrived, their voices echoing in the hall. Did other guests arrive on the scene? Did they have children with them? What about the locals? How has life changed for them since the murders? Such brutality casts an eternal shadow. Do they think about it now?

It's easy for me to imagine the crime scene because I've been in such places before. The aftermath of murder leaves memories that are almost impossible to forget. The smell of dead bodies has a unique, dreadful aroma and you can't escape the distinct smell of spilled blood. It's not how people imagine. Crime scenes change by the second. What might be a river of bright red blood one minute soon changes into a thick congealed puddle of merlot – Liam's nickname for blood.

A hush descends as Henry enters the room, Dorothy behind him. Henry has discarded his suit jacket and the sleeves of his striped shirt are rolled up. His clothes look like something out of a seventies edition of *Kays* catalogue. He presses his hand against his throat, and I see Bea shudder from the corner of my eye.

'I'm locking up,' he says, his voice grating and cold. 'No one comes in or out until tomorrow morning.' I feel sorry for him having to live with his affliction, and I wish that Bea could at least try to disguise her obvious discomfort. Steph unwinds her limbs from her husband's and plants her bare feet on the ground. She must be tired, what with the pregnancy and travelling to get here. She has no recognisable accent, and I can't remember where they said they are from.

'Why all the glum faces?' Dorothy looks around. Her eyes are small and bird like as she curiously takes us all in.

'Dorothy, I think we'd all feel a little better if you could explain the reason behind the rules.' I turn to Bea, because I'll feel better if she calms down. 'Why don't you sit down? You must be tired, driving all this way on your own.' The truth is, I don't know where she's come from, but her pacing continues to irritate, and my gentle suggestion is enough to get her to sit.

Dorothy exchanges a glance with her husband before approaching Steph, who appears the most nervous of us all. 'The roads are impassable. All guest houses lock their doors at night.' She smiles, revealing pink lipstick-stained false teeth. 'It's not as if you're going out for a boogie-woogie, or whatever you young people call it these days.' She emits a giggle. 'I might look like I'm in my twenties but I'm not!'

I catch Matt rolling his eyes.

'Fine, but I want my phone.' Steph is obviously irritated. 'Why did you take them from us? There are people I need to keep in touch with.'

'I told you, the radiation,' Dorothy says, patting her hair. 'Do you like my ringlets? They're quite beautiful, aren't they? I bet nobody in your salon comes out looking like this.'

Bruce begins to cough as he almost chokes on his whisky. But Dorothy doesn't appear to notice as she delivers her signature coquettish laugh. I've encountered lots of people like Dorothy. Her behaviour could be down to any number of things. She could be an attention seeker, or delusional, or even suffering from dementia. Or this could just be her authentic self, who doesn't give a flying fig about how she's judged.

In the police, such people are part of the rich tapestry of my day-to-day working life. But here, in this isolated setting, it sends a chill down my spine. She's too far removed from reality for my liking. She's meant to be running this place. Who is cooking our food? What's in the tea that she's made? As for her concerns about 'radiation' – what other outlandish beliefs does she have? Her husband never challenges her. He just stands statue-like next to her, taking it all in. She virtually skips out of the room, with her husband sloping after her in her wake. She's ignored my request for clarity and I'm left, open mouthed.

'I want to leave,' Steph whispers to Joey. 'She's crazy. They both are.'

I inwardly cringe because I haven't told her about the camera yet. Bruce catches my eye and his eyes relay dark amusement. What is wrong with him? 'Steph,' I say, 'she's eccentric. I've met lots of people just like Dorothy in my job. Not one of them have caused an ounce of harm.'

But Steph is crying now, fat tears rolling down her face. 'I would never have booked here if I'd known.'

'Hun, if you want to go then we'll go. But . . .' Joey heaves a sigh. 'I'm not sure how far we'll get in this weather.'

Steph sniffles loudly. 'I'd rather take my chances in the snow than sleep here tonight. It's not that far to The Royal Hotel.'

'They're fully booked,' Matt chips in. 'We came from there.'

Joey turns to me for advice. 'What do you think we should do? I mean . . . as a police officer.'

An expression of annoyance crosses Matt's face as he answers on my behalf. 'We can either stay down here together and see the night through or go to bed and lock our doors.'

'But what about our food?' Bea chimes in. 'What if it's been poisoned?'

'Really, Bea?' I'm getting annoyed with her now, because she's not helping in calming things down. 'As Bruce said, if your food was poisoned, you'd know about it by now.' I turn back to Steph. 'Go to any hotel and you'll find history. Not as serious as this one, I grant you, but it doesn't mean anyone's out to get us.'

'But our phones . . .' Steph continues.

'A harmless rule.' My voice is low as I reply. 'It could be a psychological condition. I've seen it before.'

'And what about him?' She glances towards the doorway where Henry has just exited.

'Not the jolliest of men, granted,' I smile. 'But he's a cancer survivor, none of us would be a bag of laughs after that.' I pause for thought. 'Lots of people have stayed here since the murders. I've read the Tripadvisor reviews. Granted, they weren't great, but they all came out of it alive.' I can't help but chuckle as I try to put her at ease.

'I suppose . . .' she sniffs. 'You wouldn't stay here with your son if you didn't think it was safe.'

'That's right. The Loch House may be creepy, but it's better than the roads in their current state. Tomorrow will be a new day. We'll laugh about this in the morning, when we're on our way home.' I don't mention that there's no guarantees that the storm will be over by then.

'George?' Matt's voice breaks into my thoughts. I swivel towards my son, but he's not there.

'George?' I call out, seeing nothing but an empty cup on the table next to the chair. 'Where's George?' I glance around at my fellow guests, as if they'd somehow know. We're all on our feet, and I'm trying not to panic as I look for him. But he's not in the living room and I can't see him in the hall. My heart beats fast against my ribcage as I quickly take the stairs. This can't be happening. 'George! Where are you?'

'He can't have got far. I'll check the toilets!' Matt shouts as he thunders down the hall.

My palms are sweaty, and I grip the bannister as his name echoes throughout the house. I pause to listen but there's no response. He's in our bedroom, he has to be. I'm panicking over nothing. He probably needed the loo and was too shy to ask in front of everyone. Or maybe he's sleepy and has taken himself to bed.

Deep down, I know none of these things are true.

I'm finding it hard to breathe as I push my bedroom door open so hard that it hits the inside wall with force. He's not there. I almost trip over my feet as I stumble into the en suite, calling George's name. I catch my frightened expression in the mirror – eyes wide, face pallid. 'George?' I say, as I enter his adjoining bedroom. The silence is terrifying as I wait for a response. I drop to my knees and check under the bunk beds. There's nothing but dust bunnies gathered on the carpet, silent witnesses to my panic. Dread tightens my chest as I hear Matt calling his name downstairs. Where is he? Where is my little boy?

Mystery on the Mic Podcast

The Watts Case Series: Episode 4

Alex: Welcome, our curious listeners, to another intriguing episode of 'Mystery on the Mic'! I'm your host, Alex, and with me is our brilliant true crime historian, Sarah. How's it going, Sarah?

Sarah: Hey, Alex! I'm doing great, and I'm excited to share our latest case update with you today.

Alex: Fantastic! I'm in the mood for some true crime shenanigans too. Today, we're talking about an unexpected twist in the investigation into the tragic deaths of Ronnie and Heather Watts, the music industry power couple. Initially, it developed into a murder-suicide scenario, but hold onto your seats, folks, because things just got a whole lot more complicated.

Sarah: Absolutely, Alex. It's a case that had everyone speculating, and now it's leaving us all bewildered.

Alex: So, picture this: Ronnie and Heather Watts, found dead in their mansion with the presence of drugs in their room. Then, the plot thickened. Turns out, they'd been shot in the head, and Heather was holding the firearm in her lifeless hand.

Sarah: Right, and the mansion was in complete disarray. The lines of white powder added another layer of mystery as everyone in the industry knew that Heather Watts was very anti-drugs. And to add to the intrigue, it was cocaine, something she strongly campaigned against.

Alex: Yes, cocaine, of all things. Ronnie and Heather were said to be madly in love, despite the age gap. So what really went on that night?

Sarah: Well here's where it gets really interesting. Not long after the discovery of Ronnie and Heather's bodies, the focus shifted to Ronan and Caleb Watts, Ronnie's sons. Motive? Pretty clear, given the wealth they stood to inherit. But here's the kicker, there was no actual evidence tying them to the crime.

Alex: And don't forget the toxicology reports. High levels of drugs were found in both victims' blood. It's a rollercoaster of a case! There has been speculation that it was set up to look like a murder-suicide. The couple argue, take copious amounts of drugs, then Heather shoots Ronnie in bed before turning the gun on herself. But none of it rings true.

Sarah: You said it, Alex. The controversial brothers were released without charges. Talk about a shocker! The music industry is alight with gossip behind closed doors.

Alex: So many questions, Sarah. Was it really a murder-suicide, or is there a deeper, more sinister plot at play here? Plus, it's now come to light that there were bruises on Heather's body that no one can explain!

Sarah: I have my own theories on that one, but I don't want to be slapped with a lawsuit. Let's just say that certain people had a lot to gain from Ronnie and Heather's deaths. The nation is holding its breath for the truth to come to light.

Alex: That's right, Sarah. I'm definitely in your camp when it comes to this case. Strange how the CCTV happened to be out on the night in question, too. It's almost like someone on the inside planned it from the start.

Sarah: Hmm, say no more, Alex. There's a lot of powerful people involved in this case.

Alex: That's for sure. We'll be keeping a close eye on this one, folks. Stay tuned for more 'Mystery on the Mic' after this sponsored ad break. And remember, the truth is out there, and as long as we keep digging, we'll find it together!

Sarah: Yes, keep those detective hats on and stay curious.

14

Matt

The architecture of this building is like nothing I've seen before. It veers off from one room to another, each as dark as the one before. Dust rises from the carpet as I walk down some of the lesser used spaces, calling George's name. I breathe in the smell of varnished wood, taking time to stare out of the window of one of the vacant rooms. Snow swirls relentlessly outside and I press my hand against the pane before noticing that it's tightly nailed shut.

I stare in disbelief. This is totally against health and safety rules. As the headmaster of a school, I'm well aware that this sort of thing would get you shut down. The front door is tightly bolted. What if there was a fire? How would we get out? I run my finger over the crooked head of the nail which has been beaten into the woodwork with force. It's recent, and I catch my finger on a splinter, which produces a bead of blood. As I suck my finger, I contemplate the fact that George couldn't have made his exit this way. Not that he'd want to go outside on a night like this. But if someone was to try to take him . . . it wouldn't be easy for them to make their escape.

I remember Nicola telling me that when Gav got out of prison, the thought of him taking George kept her awake at night. It was Nicola's testimony that landed him in prison, after he assaulted her. What sort of man could beat a woman to a pulp, fracturing her jaw and breaking her ribs? Nicola always said that if Gav found and took George, it would be solely out of revenge.

I shake away the thought. George is *here*, somewhere. I'm usually so watchful. I can't believe that I didn't see him slip away. It's not the first time he's gone walkabout. He never purposely tries to upset us; he just doesn't think. I've told Nicola a thousand times, she needs to be more careful with what she says in front of him. It was bad enough when she jumped out of the car to check out the 'body' by the guest house sign. No wonder the poor little guy was spooked.

I exit the room, having checked the toilets already. I continue calling his name, keeping my tone light as if congratulating him on winning the game of hide and seek. 'C'mon out now, kiddo, if you're playing a game, you've won. And hey . . . if you're worried about anything, there's no need. I'm here to keep you safe.'

I pause as I absorb the silence. 'But your mummy . . . well, you know what she's like. She's having kittens, worrying about you!' I chuckle, hoping he'll suddenly appear. 'George? You don't want your mummy all worried, now do you? C'mon out, you're not in any trouble. Not one bit.' But all I can hear is the sound of my own breath and the creak of wooden floorboards beneath the thin carpet as I emerge into the hall.

Bea isn't helping as she marches towards me. As usual, she's making everything about her. 'I knew something bad was going to happen. I felt a low energy the minute I walked into this place!'

'Nothing bad is happening,' I snap. 'He's just a bored little boy who has taken himself off to explore.'

'He's not in our room.' Nicola meets us in the hall, breathless with panic. 'George!' she calls, staring into the empty spaces as if he'll suddenly appear. I know what's in her head. Her perspective is tainted with all the awful things she's seen. This isn't Nicola's first meltdown. She's been through worse than this. I need to keep her close – for her own safety. I shadow her as she returns to the living room, watching as she checks every corner. We're only there a few minutes when Dorothy walks in.

'What's all the shouting about?' Her lips are bright with a fresh application of pink lipstick despite the fact that it's now gone nine thirty, and her husband has locked us all up for the night.

'Have you seen George? Have you taken him somewhere?' Nicola is terse and edgy as she turns her attention to Dorothy. As I wait for

Dorothy's answer I notice that her hair is different, the long curly ringlets have been replaced by a short blonde bob. Her pencilled eyebrows rise.

'Of course I haven't taken him.' The thick lines of Dorothy's eyebrows knit into a frown. 'I've been upstairs. Maybe he got tired and went to bed.'

'He's not up there, I've checked.' Nicola runs her fingers through her tousled hair.

'Don't panic,' Bruce says as he approaches. 'We'll find him in no time if we spread out and search each part of the building.'

'He's not in the toilets,' Joey looks to each of us. I hadn't noticed him and Steph leave. I'm a bit irked by everyone taking over. I should be the one to take charge. I'm the nearest thing to a responsible father that boy has ever had.

'There's no need to go off searching,' Dorothy intervenes. 'This is my home and it's off limits to the guests.'

'I'm sorry, what?' I check that I'm hearing right.

She points a long finger in my direction. 'You have use of the living room, dining room and toilets. Your bedroom is your own space. But the rest of this guest house is mine and I won't have you all wandering around!' Dorothy's voice is growing louder with every word. Henry stands in the doorway, looking quizzically at his wife. How strange it must be, to be married but to share so few words. Better than too many, I suppose. Dorothy spins to face him. 'Little George has taken himself off somewhere. They want to search every nook and cranny of the house! I've told them there's no need.'

Henry's frown deepens, if that's possible. He presses his hand to his throat. 'He's not gone far. What are you . . .' He rakes in a breath. 'Worried about?'

'What am I worried about?' Nicola repeats, her nerves frayed. 'He's six years old. It's past his bedtime, he's in a strange place, and I don't know where he is. He could be hurt. Someone could have taken him. Who else sleeps under this roof? I want to speak to your staff.'

'You're speaking to them.' Dorothy is snippy in her response. 'And I don't like your tone.'

But Nicola doesn't seem to care. 'There are no chefs? No cleaners? Nobody else staying here?'

Dorothy's shiny blonde hair sways as she shakes her head from side to side. 'I cook your meals, and Henry helps with the cleaning. It's just us. How else could we afford to run this place?' I believe her, given how run down the guest house is.

'I think you're missing the point here,' Bea's cheeks redden as she waves her arms in the air. 'Had we known of the history of The Loch House, I doubt any of us would have stayed. As for those dreadful rules, and locking the doors . . . Where do you think you get off, keeping us all prisoner?'

'For your own . . . safety,' Henry stares down at her, sparing his words.

Bea pushes back her shoulders as she stands up to him. A flush is creeping up her neck. 'Yes, but why? What are you hiding? What really happened here? Because somebody knows who killed those people.' On and on, Bea argues, demanding the truth. I step away as I'm enveloped in a cloud of her sickly sweet perfume.

If I were George, I wouldn't want to return to this. I feel another jolt of annoyance. We should have brought him to bed and had an early night, instead of playing pretend detectives down here. I glance around the room. My heart falters a little as I notice that Nicola and Bruce are gone. Where is she off to now? She's not thinking straight. She needs to be by my side. Joey and Steph are in deep conversation, but judging by their whispers it's not for our ears. I don't blame them for being nervous, but right now, I just want George back. I leave Bea to her argument and resume the search. Because if we don't find George soon, I'm demanding my phone and calling the police.

15

Elita

I stretch my arms wide, blinking three times to make sense of the clock beside my bed. I've been asleep for a whole hour, dreaming of escaping this place. I'm too old to believe in princes, but a small part of me still falls for the fairy tales, wishing someone would come and rescue me from this odd existence. That's where you come in, dear guests. Each time one of you arrives, I wonder if you will be the person to whisk me away. The one who understands, instead of recoiling in disgust.

I guess I haven't properly introduced myself yet. My name's Elita. My grandad said it means 'chosen one' in Latin. He speaks the language and is into a lot of religious stuff. He treats me like I'm made of glass, and Granny Dorothy says that he's a bit in awe of me. Sometimes he comes in and brings me my vitamins then usually hands me a book. He likes to sit and watch me read. Other days, he'll read passages from his bible, and I try not to look too bored. I don't feel all that special. Instead, I feel like I'm stuck in a box and can't get out.

It's why I borrow other people's lives. Hidden away in my secret room, I quietly watch the outside world. But they don't look like me. They don't sound like me, and they sure don't dress like me. I tug at the frilly material of my clothes. Granny dresses me the way she likes, as if I'm her own special doll. I wonder about her and Grandad sometimes. I hate to even think it, but their point of view is, well, a bit twisted. It's taken me a while to come to terms with it, but deep down, I've always known that something isn't quite right with them.

My favourite bedtime story has always been *Rapunzel*. Go figure. But there's no point in being down. I open my mini fridge and take out the lunch that Granny has left for me. It's cut up into small chunks so I can chew it easily. She worries about me choking, but I'm used to eating soft things now. I take it to my computer desk and after a little effort, manage to sit on my swivel chair.

I chew slowly, barely able to tear my eyes away from my screens as I rewind the last couple of hours and watch. Your words are clear as they come through my headphones, and I try to figure out who's genuine and who's not. I enjoy piecing together stories as I observe you all. It's been that way for years. Your laughter, your conversations, those shared moments of happiness and sadness – they're my lifeline, filling the empty void. Gosh, I'm sounding all depressed, aren't I? I talk to myself sometimes, tell myself to snap out of it. I'm lucky to be alive. Tonight, everything feels different. Tonight, there are rules to follow, and I wonder how long it will be before one of you tries to leave. As if you could just walk away from here.

Your conversations are triggering some horrible memories for me. You all talk about The Loch House as if this place is some kind of hellhole, but you don't have a clue. Coming here was an escape from something far worse. But after Mum was killed, my life changed yet again as I was forced back into hiding, and now I struggle being alone. Some days it sucks big time. I'm stuck in this room for so many hours, but at least I have something to watch.

I've been in your rooms, touched your stuff, picked up the things you couldn't bear to leave at home. I've listened to your private chats, watched what you get up to when you think you're alone. It's all recorded, like some weird reality TV episode. (Oh yeah, I watch those too, but you're more interesting than what's on TV.) In my mind, I imagine your stories, and wonder what your lives are like at home. You're the nearest things I have to friends, even if you've no idea that I'm here.

I feel a tingly sense all over as I watch the young couple, Steph and Joey, interact. It's as close to romance as I'll ever get. I'll never become a woman, get married or have kids. I'll probably stay a child in this lonely room until the day I die. I tried once, you know. Tried to end it all because I hated being in my own miserable skin. That's when Granny gave me Mum's diaries. She wanted to show me just how much I was loved. She told me that I had to live, or Mum's death would have been for nothing because the monsters didn't come for her that night – they came for me. She said that I wasn't to blame myself, that those bad people would have killed everyone under this roof whether they found me or not. Gran kept going on about protecting me, and how important I am to the world. But if I'm so important, then why am I stuck here, away from everyone? What use am I here? Or am I something evil that the world needs protecting *from*?

I can feel my mood shifting for the worse and I take a few deep breaths. When I open my eyes, all the bad thoughts are gone. I've shoved them way down, and I turn my focus back to my most favourite couple of all.

I fast forward to Steph and Joey. They're so adorable. I imagine their future baby and know she will be beautiful. It's a girl, it's got to be, and she will melt hearts. As they chat about names in their room, their experiences become mine. They're getting ready for dinner now, and I tilt my head to the side, imagining what I would say in such social situations. I've never shared a meal with strangers. My gran says that people on the outside wouldn't understand why I've remained forever young. They wouldn't have real conversations; they'd only ask a thousand questions and then, when they've got what they wanted, they'd call the authorities. I'd be poked and prodded. Granny and Grandad might even be put in jail. But still, I long to be normal. I swipe away a tear as I wonder why I was born like this. I imagine Steph's new baby and wish that I was her, a beautiful soul coming into a new world with perfect parents and no monsters to fear.

The lights in my room dim, casting eerie shadows across the worn-out floors. Sometimes, when everything feels black inside, The Loch House comes alive. It reaches out and touches the guests. I see them shudder, or look over their shoulder as they feel it draw near.

The rooms are always gloomy, like the lights are too lazy to shine bright. I sit here, all by myself, as the darkness hangs heavy in the air. The Loch House, this old place, it has a way of making you feel things, even when you didn't want to. My grandparents tried to make it nice. I have a special low down shower because a real one is too hard to reach. I also have a sink and toilet that's made especially for me. There's a vent in the wall which sucks all the bad air away, and in the summer, they unblock the big vent which brings in fresh air through one outside wall. But it also brings in spiders and I don't like them at all. Granny says that everything seems bigger to me because I'm so small. I think she was joking. I told her that she's not what you'd call a giant herself.

The lights flicker again, making the shadows dance across the worn-out floorboards. It's as if The Loch House is stretching its old bones. Sometimes when I'm really lonely I'll talk to it, and it replies in its own way. I used to be frightened of this place, but there are worse things roaming around in the storm.

I take off my headphones and climb off the seat, my light steps echoing against the floor as I stretch my legs. Granny is late with my night-time snack, which is usually a hot chocolate and a Jaffa Cake. I don't sleep much, because it's hard for me to tell night from day. There's a special bell I can ring which goes through to the kitchen but when guests are here, it's only to be used in emergencies. Two walls separate me from everybody else. My place is pretty well soundproofed so nobody will hear me move. I take my smoothie from my desk and slowly sip it. My skin prickles from the cold as the temperature drops. There's an old mirror in the corner. It has seen better days and is covered in cracks and stains. I stare into it, half-expecting to see a ghostly face staring back at me. But all I see is my own sadness, the pain that has become a part of me.

'Mummy, are you here?' I whisper, my voice light on my breath.

Silence fills the room, but I can feel her nearby. It's like she lingers in the air, a comforting presence that whispers love. It feels like a hug from a memory.

Tears well in my eyes as I remember the sound of her laughter, the way she used to hold me when I was scared. I know she can't answer, but it feels good to pretend she is still around. Like she is watching over me in this creepy old house. I shake away my pity party for one, and turn back to the computer screen.

16

Nicola

As Bea unknowingly created a diversion, I took the opportunity to slip away. Dorothy and her husband were outnumbered, and they didn't notice me leave. Neither did Matt, or he would have been right behind me. Lately, he barely lets me out of his sight.

I wasn't long out of a bad relationship when I met Matt. With Gav, what you saw was what you got. Tattoos, leather jacket, a motorbike and a whole lot of attitude. He was outrageous, fearless, being with him was a buzz. It wasn't just his looks that drew me in, it was the element of danger. I should have known better. I wasn't supposed to mix with people like that. Yet, I was drawn in, attracted to one bad boy after another all my life.

Mum has always blamed herself. My father was not a good man. Our 'normal' wasn't the same as everyone else's. I thought that all mums were punished behind closed doors, until my primary school teacher took me aside. Mrs Logan was amazing. I was lucky to know her. She saw the bruises on Mum's wrists and guessed what was going on. Slowly, she prised it out of me, and told me that it wasn't OK. Then she approached my mum.

Dad was an alcoholic. He didn't attend the parent teacher evenings. That's when Mrs Logan managed to get Mum on her own. Mum surprised me with her strength. Perhaps she'd been looking for a way out. She spoke to the ladies at the refuge. Saved money. Hid a bag. After Gav, I did the same. I knew he'd eventually kill me if I didn't go. The biggest risk to victims of domestic abuse comes when they try to leave. It's one of the things regular people don't understand. 'Why didn't you just leave?' It was one of the first things Matt asked after I told him my story. How could he understand that it wasn't just as simple as walking away? Even when you manage to start a new life all over again, there are no guarantees that they won't track you down and make you pay. I should know.

I creep down the corridor, looking for forbidden rooms. This place is a lot bigger on the outside than it is within, like some kind of reverse Tardis. There must be secret spaces and false walls inside it. How else could George disappear? I don't see Bruce until he grabs my arm and pulls me to one side. I almost cry out, but I'm loath to draw attention to myself. We stand in the dark corridor, him blocking my path.

'What are you doing?' My limbs are trembling from the adrenaline rushing through my veins. Losing my son in this creepy old guest house has turned everything on its head.

'I need to speak to you on your own.' He's leaning down to talk to me, his breath smelling of whisky, his voice hushed. His demeanour is completely different. His expression is deathly serious, and all amusement has left his eyes. 'In here.' He gestures to the broom cupboard from which he appeared.

I hesitate. I don't want to be locked into an enclosed space with this man that I barely know. I don't trust him for a start, and there is no way of checking him out without my phone. If only I could call Liam and ask him to run his name through PNC . . . But the Police National Computer isn't easily accessed without good reason these days. On the other hand, Bruce carries a self-assurance that makes me wonder about his profession. I can't help but feel a kinship. As much as he's annoyed my fellow guests, there's something about his calm steadiness that resonates with me. He reminds me of my DI at work. Somewhat arrogant, takes no bullshit and unafraid to speak his mind.

'The cameras,' Bruce mouths, before placing a finger over his lips. He's right. They can probably pick up sound. I scratch my arm as my skin crawls with agitation. This whole scenario feels like a sick game. George needs me, and Bruce may be able to help. Taking a deep breath, I open the cupboard door and allow him to go in first.

The room is deceptively big, and judging by the number of hooks on the wall I'm guessing it was a cloak room once. Today it smells of cleaning fluid and stale mops. It easily houses the hoovers, cloths and detergents taking up shelf space. Bruce quickly checks the room. There's no ornate coving that could hide intrusive cameras, and the walls are bare and smooth. Bruce seems to be mentally preparing himself as he watches me with something akin to respect.

'I'm not the only copper here, am I?' The words have left my mouth before I've had time to think.

The corners of his mouth tug into a tiny smile and I know that I'm right.

'Ex-job.' His soft Scottish accent is spoken with new-found warmth. 'I retired as a DCI.'

I stand a little straighter. All this time I thought he was enjoying our situation, he was merely taking everything in. Granted, Bea provided enough entertainment to keep him amused. When you're in the police long enough, you become an amateur psychologist, monitoring people's behaviour and pre-empting their responses as the situation changes. He's met lots of people like Bea, and probably second-guessed her every move.

'Why didn't you say?' I'm a little happier in his company, now I know who he is. Strength in numbers, and all that.

'My dear, when you're in the job as long as I am, you'll keep it to yourself if you're after a quiet break.' He gives me an appraising eye. 'But something tells me you're not quite off duty yet.'

That's not how I do things, but I appreciate that he's right. 'Are any of us ever off duty? Why are you really here?' I fold my arms, unable to fully relax.

A beat passes between us as we hear rapid footsteps in the hall outside. I don't know who it is, but Matt wouldn't appreciate it if he found me hiding away in a cupboard with Bruce. He's jealous of anyone who spends time with me, apart from my son. I strain to listen as Bruce continues to speak in quiet tones.

'I wasn't lying when I said I was a true crime enthusiast. But what happened here is the *only* case that interests me. I was part of the investigation. It's given me plenty of sleepless nights, believe me.'

'But George . . .' I begin, my thoughts never leaving my son.

'He's probably with whoever's been watching us all this time. They have no reason to hurt him. He's not part of it.' Bruce speaks with such sincerity that I have no reason to doubt him.

'Part of what?' I appreciate his honesty, but I should be looking for my son. My intestines feel like they're twisting each moment I'm away from him. George is the one person in my life who loves me unconditionally, and I'm his mother. It's my job to look after him. 'Where is he?' I press, because I need Bruce to stop faffing about and get to the point. 'Can you help me find him or not?'

He nods. 'Of course I will. But you can't tell the others who I am. We don't want to spook them.'

'Them?' I ask as my frustration grows. 'Who is them? Because if you know something that I don't, then now is the time to tell me. I don't have time for games, Bruce.'

But Bruce exhales a tired breath. 'It's a long story that we don't have time for right now. I don't think Dorothy or Henry mean to do us harm. But they know a lot more than they're letting on.'

'Do you think they're capable of hurting my son?' I'm not sure I want the answer to this. Because if they cause him one iota of pain, I won't be responsible for my actions.

'No.' Bruce pauses to listen at the door. 'He mentioned seeing a little girl, didn't he? I heard you ask Dorothy about it.'

I nod. 'Why? What's that got to do with anything? She seemed pretty certain that there are no other children here.' By the way Bruce is looking at me, it feels like this mystery child is at the heart of it all.

'There *was* a child in the house on the night of the murders, but she'd be around sixteen, seventeen years old now. I need to speak to George to find out exactly what he saw.'

'How do you know that?' My impulse to search for my son is outweighed by the need to arm myself with details of the case. Only then will I know what I am dealing with.

'This was never released to the press . . .' He leans into me. 'But one of the victims didn't die straight away. They survived long enough to tell us that two men came looking for a child that night. That's what they were after. But Amelia – Dorothy's daughter – wouldn't tell them where she was.'

'Jesus,' I whisper. 'That's brutal. Amelia gave up her life to save her child? But how . . .' I frown, trying to work out the logistics. 'I mean, where was this mystery girl? Didn't the police find her when they searched the place?' I know how police treat crime scenes. They would have been thorough.

Bruce shakes his head. 'The victim who told them this died soon after he was discovered. His daughter said he had early onset dementia. Police put it down to that. That's why it never made it to the press.'

'And what about the two men?' I'm shocked by this information. 'Did you ever discover a motive for wanting this child?'

'We only got a vague description of the suspects, not enough to pin on anyone. Without finding the child, or even being sure she existed, we couldn't find any motive at the time. It seemed like such a wild theory. Plus, the poison could have had an effect, so there was no guarantee the information was reliable. It was safer to say it was a random killing than have people think there were mass murdering child snatchers running loose.'

I can see his point. The press would have gone wild, resulting in extra pressure on the police to come up with answers. When the press get hold of a story, people are less likely to forget. I tune back into Bruce's narrative.

'I thought if I booked a room, I'd be able to find the child and maybe she could lead me to the truth. A lot of people died that day, Nicola. They shouldn't get away with it.' He tilts his head. 'That's why I need to speak to George. He could lead us straight to her.'

I'm not sure what does it, but suddenly I wonder if the story that Bruce has just fed me is true. What if his authoritative demeanour is gained from criminality rather than being on the right side of the law? I press my hand on the door knob. I need to resume looking for my son. I don't want George getting caught up in any of this.

'We need to keep looking,' I say, thinking aloud. 'But I'm not promising anything. I'll ask him where he was but you're on your own after that.'

'Fine.' Bruce straightens himself up, a by-product of being tall. 'Just remember, we're being watched. If you need to talk, give me a signal and I'll meet you in here. The less said to anyone else the better. We don't want to spook them.'

'Is there backup? I mean, are the police in on this?' A small flare of hope lights inside me. Maybe they can get us out of here. But Bruce soon extinguishes it.

'It's a cold case as far as they are concerned.'

I consider asking Bruce more, but I'm not sure I can trust him. Isn't this what psychopaths do? Mirror the person they're trying to manipulate? My thoughts are spinning . . . all I know for certain is I want to escape his whisky breath and find my son. But he's not done talking yet.

'Did you notice when you came here, how much bigger the house is outside compared to inside? It's a real puzzle, this place. George could just be hiding. Or he may have curled up somewhere and fallen asleep.'

I had been too busy fussing over getting George inside to investigate the building. I feel like I'm off my game. 'Yeah, hopefully that's it. It's been a long day.' I force a smile. 'Let's keep looking, eh? There's no time to waste.'

I don't want George involved in whatever Dorothy and Henry are mixed up in. Are they protecting their granddaughter? Did they find her hiding in The Loch House after Amelia died? Are they aware of what went on, or were they somehow involved? As soon as I find my son, I'm going. I only hope I get to him before anyone else does.

Mystery on the Mic Podcast

The Watts Case Series: Episode 5

Alex: Ladies and gentlemen, welcome back to another episode of 'Mystery on the Mic'! I'm Alex, your host, and joining me as always is the brilliant true crime historian, Sarah. How's it going, Sarah? Great to see you back on the show.

Sarah: Hey, Alex! Yes, as much as I enjoyed my cruise around the Med, I couldn't wait to dive into this fascinating episode featuring none other than the Watts family. I don't want to sound insensitive, but they really are the gift that keeps on giving in the true crime world. You could have knocked me down with a feather when I read about Caleb Watts opening up about his life to the mainstream media.

Alex: Absolutely, Sarah. Just when everything goes quiet about this case, a new revelation is introduced into the mix. So for our new listeners, Caleb Watts, son of the late Ronnie Watts, music mogul extraordinaire, has shared his personal journey and countered allegations linking him to his father's and young stepmother's tragic deaths.

Sarah: It's a deep dive into a troubled upbringing, folks. Caleb candidly opened up to reporters about his childhood and what it was like growing up in the Watts mansion. In a heartfelt interview, he shared that after his biological mother's passing, he and his brother were left in the care of what he calls 'unsuitable' staff. Apparently the house was a revolving door of celebrities and drug-fuelled parties at the time. From what I've read about Ronnie Watts back then, it's most likely true.

Alex: I can't even imagine growing up in an environment like that. Caleb gets candid about how his father's grief led to his own struggles, especially during his teenage years when he felt lost and alone.

Sarah: Yeah, he turned to alcohol and drugs as coping mechanisms. It's a tale of how fame and wealth don't necessarily equate to happiness.

Alex: But then he starts talking about his journey to redemption, doesn't he? Things take a surprising turn as he shares how he's found solace in religion, particularly his deep connection to Christ.

Sarah: Yes indeedy, it's a surprising and powerful transformation. Caleb shares how music has become a tool for self-reflection and healing, turning dark days into something positive.

Alex: And it seems that he's not walking this path alone. Caleb's got a close-knit community of fellow believers who support him on his journey, although some would ask if they are followers or clingers on.

Sarah: When it comes to wealthy families, the two seem to go hand in hand. But he'll always be supported by his brother Ronan, who Caleb describes as his guardian and guiding light. Things certainly take a surreal turn as Caleb delves further into his spiritual journey, and to be honest, they raise a few red flags concerning his mental health.

Alex: When it comes to the Watts family, those flags aren't just raised, Sarah. They're flapping crazily in the wind! (Chuckles) I have serious concerns about Caleb's stability, especially considering the influence of his new-founded Fellowship on his already troubled past.

Sarah: That's a fair point well made, Alex. As the public grapples with Caleb Watts' latest revelations, he appears to be a soul in search of redemption. But from what? The legacy of Ronnie and Heather's deaths remains an enigma, leaving us all hungry for answers. There's no doubt now that the couple were murdered, but the trouble lies in pinning down the people responsible and I don't think we need to look very far.

Alex: That's right, Sarah. The truth is still out there, and concrete proof is just waiting to be unearthed. It's frustrating though, to be so near to yet so far from answers to this case. Thanks for joining us today, everyone, on this segment of 'Mystery on the Mic'. We've been recording episodes for many years now, but we won't give up our search for answers.

Sarah: Let's not count just how many years, Alex, you're making me feel old!

Alex: Never. Crime busting keeps you young. Just like our listeners at home! Stay tuned, folks, as we'll return to discuss a new case after this break.

Sarah: Yes, we appreciate all our listeners. Take care, and stay tuned. The opportunity to solve the mystery keeps us all coming back for more.

17

Nicola

I call out for George as I wander the corridors, but my voice disappears into the emptiness of the ageing building. My mind is filled with George, *my George*. It's like a part of me has been amputated, leaving me less than whole. I'm struggling to keep it together. What is it I say to parents whose children have disappeared? There was this one woman, whose four-year-old went AWOL in Asda. I told her that nine out of ten times, children returned home just fine. 'But what about that tenth child?' she'd cried, her face wet with tears. It was moments before my colleague discovered him hiding in the staff room. And now I'm thinking, what if my George is the tenth child? The thought leaves me cold. The Loch House offers little comfort against the storm, which shakes the very bones of this place. Its creaking timbers and rattling windows are enough to fill me with further dread. The walls feel like they're closing in on me, whispering secrets I'm too scared to comprehend. Beneath the surface of the faded wallpaper, something sinister lurks. I can't help but wonder if we're destined to join the ranks of the people who have died here before.

I return to my room and stare out into the distance, touching the pane of glass, which is patterned with frost. Why the hell did we come here? The guest house may be a refuge from the elements but are we any safer inside?

A thick blanket of white has covered the landscape and I can't make out the paths anymore. There is no sign of life as night unfolds in the quietness. I wish it was morning and the sun was thawing the roads. George couldn't be out there though, could he? Fear continues to course through my body as I imagine it, but he'd never leave. At least not on his own.

The thought of his biological father drives an involuntary shudder up my skin. I thought I was safe once before . . . the memory of what happened will haunt me until my dying day. It's this place. It's making me edgy. I thought I was strong until I met Gav. But little by little, he broke my confidence, dismantling each part of me until there was nothing original left.

It took time for the police to persuade me that Gav's sporadic violence wasn't my fault. It wasn't as if he beat me all the time. Once, I worked it out in a pie chart in my head. Seventy per cent of the time he was romantic, thoughtful and loving. Twenty per cent of the time he was violent. Sometimes it was without warning, but most of the time I could predict when he was in one of his moods. It could be that his team lost at the football, or someone took the piss out of him at work. It could be the fact that he had drank too much in the day. Then he'd come home to me, his handsome face hard with anger, driven by the need to take it out on someone. There were times when George cried in his cot, and he'd yell at me to 'sort him out' before *he* did. I could take a beating, but those threats against George frightened me the most.

The last ten per cent of his pie chart was reserved for remorse. It always felt genuine but came too late. He'd max out the credit card on surprise holidays. Then there were the dozens of red roses, chocolates, jewellery, anything he could afford would turn up at the door. He'd cry, plead and beg. He'd even get down on his knees. He was in genuine pain. He knew he was wired wrong. That's what made it so hard to walk away. He'd tell me he'd get therapy, that he'd do anything to put things right. Like a fool, I'd try to fix him. That was, until he nearly killed me, and I ended up in hospital with internal injuries and a broken jaw. When the police came to speak to me, I didn't send them away.

George was just a toddler when Gav was sent to prison for eighteen months. Eighteen lousy months for almost finishing me off. It was a plea deal for ABH, a lower offence. It was a turning point in my life, and the reason why, one year later, I joined the police. I may have been a victim once, but it will never happen again. If anyone tries to harm my son, I'll kill them if I have to – I won't hesitate.

I snap out of my dark thoughts. 'George?' I call, as I leave my room. My words echo around the landing as I try again. 'You're not in any trouble, sweetheart, but we need you to come out.' All I hear are the creaks and groans of the building as it is battered by the storm outside. I try Sunita's door. I heard Dorothy saying that she's in the room next to mine. It's locked. Her door rattles as I bang on it three times with my fists.

'Sunita, it's Nicola. Is George in there?' At last, I hear movement inside. But she's taking too long, and I feel like I'm suffocating. 'Sunita!' I bang again, because I'm not leaving until I get a response. There's a click from within as the door is unlocked.

Her eyes are large as she takes me in. She's wearing a blue silk dressing gown and blue pyjamas underneath. Her painted toenails peep out from the pyjama bottoms which are too long for her. 'What's wrong?' She touches my arm. 'Goodness, you're shaking.' She looks out into the landing before beckoning me inside. This small act of kindness breaks my defences, and I'm sobbing as I try to explain.

'George . . . he . . . he's missing. I can't . . . find him.' She locks the door behind her, and I sense wariness on her part. She guides me to the bed and encourages me to sit. 'Where did you see him last?'

'Downstairs.' I take a couple of deep breaths to steady myself. 'I changed him into his pyjamas then brought him down to sit with us until we went to bed. I . . .' Another strengthening breath. 'Dorothy let him play on my iPad. He was wearing my noise cancelling headphones so he couldn't hear us.'

'OK,' Sunita says. 'What were you talking about when he left?'

I notice that she says 'left' rather than 'disappeared' and it makes me feel a little better inside. Common sense dictates that the tatty bogle didn't come into the room and sweep him away. Neither did he silently disappear down a trapdoor. So why do I feel like he has? Despite Sunita's kindness, I don't want to be here. If George isn't in her room, then I need to move on. But I can hear Matt and the others searching and Sunita is only trying to help. I'm too close to

George to think sensibly, and as the most level-headed member of our group, Sunita may be able to suggest something.

'We were . . . um . . .' I try to compose my words. 'Bruce was talking about the history of this place. About the murders.'

'Right,' she nods. 'Enough to scare any little boy. What about the iPad and headphones. Are they gone too?'

I think for a second. 'Yes. Yes, they are. He'd drunk the hot chocolate that Dorothy made him. His cup was on a table next to his chair.' I bite my lip because a thought strikes. 'You don't think she drugged it, do you? Bruce said that the guests here were poisoned ten years ago . . .' I bite my lip as I realise how ridiculous I'm being. I'm beginning to sound like Bea.

'No, my dear,' Sunita's palm is warm as she touches me on the back. She moves her hand in circular movements, and it has an instant calming effect. 'Come, take some deep breaths. Motherly panic is making you feel this way. George probably heard what you were talking about and decided to play elsewhere. He strikes me as a sensitive little boy, and the subject matter was a little grim, wasn't it?'

I nod as I take a soothing breath. It was more than grim. It was terrifying.

'George wouldn't be gone this long without me though.'

'Are you sure? Didn't Matt say that you work twelve hour shifts? He must be used to you not being around for long periods of time.'

I exhale, hoping she's right. Sunita has been taking in more than I realised.

'And you know how addictive those games are,' she continues. 'He's either lost all sense of time or is curled up in a nook somewhere, asleep.'

'Then why doesn't he answer?'

Sunita taps the side of her head. 'Noise cancelling headphones, remember?'

Of course. She's right. 'This place is a labyrinth. Bruce said . . .' I stop myself.

'Be careful,' Sunita warned. 'You don't know who you're mixing with – or what their motives are.'

Her warning stalls me. 'I think that Bruce means well. Why are *you* here, Sunita?'

Sunita looks quietly affronted that I have turned the spotlight onto her. 'I already told you. I'm scouting the area for a wellness retreat.' She stares at me intently, reading my face. 'Just because I don't mix, it doesn't mean there's anything to worry about. But this place . . .' She looks around the room. 'It has a dark energy. I sense I'm being watched.' She's not the only one. I glance up at the dark ornate covings. There's a cobweb hanging from the corner, but I can't see any cameras. It doesn't mean they're not here. 'Will you join in with the search?' I ask, getting up off the bed. I don't want to detract from George's search by mentioning cameras now.

But Sunita shakes her head. 'Sorry. I'm not leaving my room tonight. As soon as the snow thaws, I'm going home. Don't worry. I'm sure George will show up soon. Just . . .' She takes me by the hand. 'Just come and tell me when he does.'

I understand her reluctance, and there are enough of us searching the house. I mask a yawn with the back of my hand as I head out of her room. Sunita closes the door behind me, and the lock clicks in the door. George is OK. He has to be, because I can't contemplate the alternative. I inhale a deep breath and begin to call his name.

18

Elita

I sit in my secret hiding place, my own private fort. My room is always twilight, apart from the flicker of my computer screens. That's OK. I've got used to the half dark. It's easier on my eyes. I've filled the place with shelves of books, computer screens and a whole load of surveillance equipment. A string of star-shaped fairy lights hangs over my bed, and at Christmas, Grandad comes in and puts up my very own tree. It's only small – I live behind the walls, right? But it's the thought that counts. I used to get so excited by the sight of it, but he doesn't seem to understand that despite what I look like, I'm too old for Santa now.

Christmas is a big deal to him. In the morning we lock the doors and I spend the day with him and Granny in the living room next to the fire. There are prayers of course, lots of them. But I don't mind, I'm just so happy to be out of my hiding place. In the afternoon we have this huge big feast, and then Granny tells me off for eating like a bird. After pudding, and if nobody's around, they sneak me outside and we go for a walk to the loch. That's when I whisper my own silent prayers to Mum. Grandad makes these funny little people-shaped figures out of reeds. Each year, he makes one for Mum and floats it onto the loch. Then, and only then, do we go back home for present time. They never give me what I want, but I'm grateful anyway. All I can give them is some crappy poem or picture that I drew myself. Still, I look forward to Christmas Day all year round.

I've caught up with what I've missed on screen, and it looks like your night has taken a crazy turn. Just when things were about to settle down, little George goes and disappears. Now you're all running around, searching deep into the guest house as you try to hunt him down. This place has been quiet for ages. It feels weird to hear shouting now. You won't find him. Nope, not where you're looking, but I know where he has gone.

So many of you are fake. Bea? Huh, not her real name. As for Bruce, he's keeping real quiet about what he *actually* does. But guess what? I know. I've already checked him out. He's a local on the island and has his own reasons for being here. They're not what he says. I think Bruce is onto me. He's acting all dramatic, like he's in some cheesy soap opera. I mean, this whole situation seems pretty surreal. I wish people were as worried about me . . . But how can you look for someone who doesn't exist?

As raised voices come through my headphones, it takes me back to that godawful day when those monsters came. Mum had braided my hair and I was rocking my favourite pink corduroy dungarees and my black patent shoes. The Loch House was a happy place back then, buzzing with upbeat music as delicious smells of Mum's freshly baked cookies wafted from the kitchen. Mum had always said we had to be careful and never let me mix with the guests. Her husband, the man I thought was my dad, took off a little while after we moved to The Loch House. He couldn't hack living out in the wilds. I don't think Mum missed him all that much, and I didn't either. Mum was always the centre of my universe.

She'd told me stories of our secret past, and what a special princess I was. Back then, I believed every word. But every fairy story has its baddies and she warned me about them too. She said they'd never stop looking for me. That made me scared. Then we had the rehearsals, and the special games of hide and seek. The Loch House was perfect because it was built for hiding people back in troubled times. The hidden rooms in this building aren't on any map, and their secrets were passed down from one family to another over the years. So when Mum inherited this place, it must have felt like an omen because she was trying to escape where she lived. Mum loved the island, and she often took me out to the most remote places for fresh air. I was in awe of the red deer that bounced through the heathers and wildflowers. Mum would speak in her lovely flowery language, talking about how the hills were painted in crimson, lavender and gold. She'd bring me out to see the seals, sunbathing on the rocky outcrops, and we'd laugh at the noisy screeching seabirds dive bombing into the sea. Some days we went coastal, others, she took me exploring in the hills and woods. I couldn't walk far, but when I got tired, Mum carried me on her back. It was magic. I sweep away a tear. She will always belong to this island and The Loch House.

So, when Mum swept me up in her arms and told me to be as quiet as a mouse as she hid me away, I did as I was asked. The bad man spent ages searching the guest house. I watched through an air vent in the wall, although I couldn't see a whole lot. I may have been only six, but I remember it like I was watching an important movie. After the guests had fallen asleep, Mum still wouldn't tell the bad people where I was. I was so scared that I wet my pants. Even when he held his gun to Mum's forehead, she kept saying that I'd died years before. I must have passed out after that as I don't remember anything else until I woke up on the dirty floor. I think by the end they believed it was true. But they shot her anyway, because that's what monsters do. I torture myself with the thought that maybe, just maybe, if I'd cried out I might have saved Mum's life.

I tried, you know. I opened my mouth wide, but nothing came out. Hiding in that dark cramped space, I blacked out. It happens when fear takes over. I read that somewhere.

I crawled out of my space when Granny and Grandad came. They'd been to The Loch House loads of times before, but they lived in London, so only visited every few weeks. By the time I came out of my hidey hole and fell into their arms, everyone else was dead. Everyone except the child the bad people came to kill.

My grandparents changed that day. Like me, they blamed themselves. The police closed the building and Granny snuck me back into my hideaway and stayed with me until they were done. Those days were the worst I've ever known. It wasn't like it is now. I didn't have my screens to see what was going on. It was a dark and cobwebbed hollowed out space, with no access to the outside world. All we had was running water, and enough food to keep us going.

But I was lost in grief for my mother and the life I once had. As the days dragged on, I walked the winding corridors, longing for some human connection. At least now, I come out when the guests go home. We're not that busy these days. Snooping in each of the guest rooms is my guilty pleasure. Granny would freak if she knew. Sometimes, when the weather is good, she brings me outside, but never to the coast or the woods. Lately, she's becoming more open to me having a life of my own. But just when I thought I could have a little more freedom, the anniversary of Mum's death closes in. The monsters have come before. And every year Granny and Grandad are convinced they will again.

Even after all this time, my grandparents haven't moved on. Maybe it's all in their heads. Maybe tonight will pass and everything will be OK. But I don't know . . . I feel all tied up in knots tonight. I jump as the door to my room opens. I stand stock still, unable to move. He's here. We stare at each other, waiting for the other one to speak.

19

Matt

Dorothy follows me like a lapdog, fretting at my side as I try each door in turn. I crane my neck as I look upwards. The corridor of the guest house is long and dark, which isn't helped by the gothic looking wall panelling and portraits either side. I've never seen anything quite so ornate as the ceilings, which are covered in the same mahogany coving. They're hand carved by the look of it. It adds to the moroseness of the place as I rely on light from the dusty lamps jutting out from the side of each wall. I've already searched the kitchen, which leads into the dining room. Bruce has thoroughly checked the living room and the closet and toilets further down. There's an event room at the end of the building which has chairs stacked up either side, and I walk the length of it as I check for hidden cupboards where George could hide.

'He'll come out when he's good and ready,' Dorothy frets, her heels clacking on the wooden floor. 'There's no need for this, no need at all.'

'Of course there's a need,' I snap, my patience wearing thin. Nicola is calling for George upstairs, so she's not had any luck finding him yet. It's not the first time George has gone missing. He's played hide and seek before, on the odd occasion when Nicola and I would have an argument. We only fight when she pushes back against my attempts to keep her safe. He's sensitive to disagreements, but that's hardly surprising. He may have been a toddler when his father was sent to prison, but such traumas run deep.

At least when George went hiding before, it was in the safety of our home. It will always be their home. Should anything happen to me, I've left it to them in my will. I've told Nicola that George should have therapy, but she wants them to move forward with their lives. It must have been a shock when his father was released from prison. Then when Gav turned up out of the blue like that . . . I wonder how much George knows. Nicola was drunk when she relayed the whole sorry story to me. I'll never forget that night, when she went into graphic detail about the violence Gav inflicted upon her. It made me feel physically sick. At least now, I can keep Nicola safe. I just need to find George. Satisfied the event room is empty, I walk across the hall.

'Stop!' Dorothy calls after me, taking two strides for one of mine. My hand rests on the handle of a door marked private.

'That's our private residence. You won't find him in there.'

'Unlock it. I need to check.'

But Dorothy raises a bony finger and wags it in my direction. 'You think that you can intimidate me, young man? I know your type . . .'

I'm hardly young and I don't like what she's suggesting. 'Woah.' I take a step back. 'I'm not bullying you, I'm just looking for George.'

'And I'm telling you he's not there. Not unless he can walk through walls.' She folds her arms, standing defiantly before the door.

'Then give me my phone. I'm calling the police.' I thrust my hand out like she's one of my students who have been caught with contraband. I don't know why I haven't thought to ask for it before now. I suppose I hoped that George would make an appearance, but it's gone 10 p.m. and Nicola sounds distraught. I half expect Dorothy to produce a key, but she continues to surprise me.

'Fine,' she says, striding sharply down the corridor. 'You can have your phone. In fact, call the police. Yes, by all means. Perhaps they will find you somewhere else to stay while you're at it, because I've had quite enough.' She mutters beneath her breath, stopping only when she gets to the reception desk. Our phones are locked away in a safe. I am happy to comply when she tells me to turn around, as she clicks the safe's dial this way and that. I turn back to face her, and she shoves an open tin box in my face.

I'm suddenly aware of someone behind me, and their flowery scent gives their identity away. It's Bea. 'Ooh I'll have mine too, thanks very much.' She grabs her pink phone from the box. We stare at our handsets in wonder as Dorothy locks the box away.

'Don't blame me if you get ill from radiation. I've tried to help, but would you listen? No. It's just like that time when I was inside number ten Downing Street. I said, Tony . . .'

I stop listening as she ventures off on another fairy tale. I'd charged my phone in the car on the journey over. Why isn't it coming on? 'It's not working.' I turn to Bea. She's frowning too.

'Neither is mine. Wait a minute . . . it's saying there's no SIM card.'

'So is mine,' I stare at my phone in disbelief. What on earth is going on?

'What in God's name?' Bea exclaims, 'Who's tampered with our phones?'

Dorothy cranes her neck from behind the counter. 'These phones haven't been touched. If the SIM is missing, then you've done it yourself.'

'Why would I remove my own SIM?' Bea insists. 'And how? When they're locked away. Have you got a landline?'

Dorothy seems deeply unhappy with this request.

'Why are you all standing around?' Nicola approaches us, arms open in a gesture of disbelief. 'Have you found something?'

I shake my head. 'Someone's taken the SIM cards out of our phones.'

'Well bloody well give them back!' Nicola insists, directing the command at Dorothy. 'A child has gone missing in your guest house. Don't you realise how serious this is?'

'Can you all stop shouting at me!' Dorothy looks behind us. 'Henry, please . . . I can't take any more. Make them stop!'

Henry looms over us, evidently furious at our small uprising. I don't know where he's been, but his sudden presence unsettles me. He presses a hand to his throat and each word seems tinged with rage. The skin on his neck is loose and wrinkled and seems to pulsate with each word he speaks. 'What . . . are you . . . doing?'

'George is missing,' Nicola speaks first, the heat leaving her words. 'We can't find him anywhere and now we can't use our phones.'

'Someone's removed the SIM cards.' I say, before he has a chance to respond. 'Why would anyone do that? And why are the exits and windows locked?' I tell him off and explain the fire hazards and health and safety laws.

'Just shut up, will you!' Nicola snaps at me. I round upon her, unable to help myself. I wrench her by the arm, fury tempering my movements as I pull her close.

'Who the hell do you think you're talking to?' I growl the words in her ear, my cheeks burning with the embarrassment of being shown up. Nicola visibly shrinks. She knows I'd never hurt her. I don't need to. I let go of her arm, and she apologises as she takes a step back. I hear footsteps behind me and compose myself. As Steph and Joey join us, I take a breath, regain my composure and smile.

20

Nicola

I feel physically sick as I step away from Matt. It's not the first time he's turned on me like that. I know I shouldn't have told him to shut up, but my nerves are frayed. As I rub my wrist, I think about how things have changed between us. Although his fingers didn't press hard enough to bruise, he's got me exactly where he wants me. This relationship may not be violent, but it's all about control. From now on, I need to be careful not to take my frustrations out on him.

Poor Dorothy, she looks shaken. I'm conscious that we're all ganging up on her, but I can't help but panic at how long George has been gone. It's ten past ten and we're no further on with finding him. My reaction is far removed from my training in the police. I need to calm the hell down. The feeling of helplessness is overriding my sensibilities and I'm glad when Bruce takes charge.

'Calm down, everybody. I'm sure Mr and Mrs Hill will be happy to cooperate.'

'Yes . . .' Dorothy clutches her thick necklace. 'We didn't ask for any of this.'

'And nobody here wishes either of you harm. I'm sure you won't mind if we use your landline, now will you?'

'Why I . . .' Dorothy looks at him dumbly. She seems lost in the moment, overwhelmed and a little afraid.

I take a step towards her and touch her arm for reassurance. 'Just a quick call. Please. It won't take long.'

She takes a breath to compose herself and straightens up her wig. 'Of course. One moment. No long distance calls mind. We're not made of money, you know.' She steps behind her desk and produces a retro handset from where it was hidden away.

I raise my hand to use the old rotary dial, but Matt takes the receiver. A flame of annoyance burns within. The call would be better coming from one of their own. But he's insistent as he gives me that patient smile I'm coming to hate. He frowns as he places the receiver to his ear. Then he dials, hangs up and dials again. 'There's no dial tone.'

'Let me see,' Dorothy says, taking the phone from his grip. But Matt is behind reception, checking the lead.

'It's all plugged in,' he says.

'It must be the storm. Sometimes the phone lines go down.'

'Oh God,' I whisper quietly. We really are trapped here. My hope of having the assistance of the police fades away. I bite my bottom lip, determined to be strong for my son. Bruce checks the phone for himself and hangs up the receiver.

'It's definitely out. Let's take this into the living room so we can work out a plan.' Dutifully, we follow Bruce, but I'm listening for every sound. 'We're missing one, aren't we?' Bruce casts his eye over our group as we gather around. 'Where's Sunita?'

I walk quickly to keep up with Bruce's long stride. It feels like I'm back in work during my days as a probationer. 'I've spoken to her. She said she hasn't seen George and she doesn't want to leave her room.'

'I see.' He pushes back his shirt sleeve and checks his watch. 'It is getting late, I suppose.' Bruce strides into the living room, and I feel like I'm in a team briefing as he runs through the situation so far. My old DI was Scottish, and the steady flow of Bruce's accent is triggering memories.

Bruce glances at each of us as if we're a band of unruly insubordinates. 'Henry, have you checked the perimeter? Have any of the windows or doors been compromised? Is there any chance George could have made his way outside?'

Henry wearily shakes his head. He appears calmer now as he

stands by Dorothy's side. They make an unusual couple: her with her flashy white dentures and colourful carnival clothes, and him with his dusty suit and sombre demeanour. I can imagine him as a butler in his younger days, but I'm not sure where Dorothy would have fitted in, in the royal household. 'Everything is locked,' he speaks in his grating tone. 'I have . . . the key.'

It's true. I've already checked the windows and couldn't open any of them. The place is sealed tight. Matt's rant on health and safety may have annoyed me at the time, but I dread to think what would happen if there was a fire here at night.

'Right,' Bruce continues. 'Have you checked the vehicles to ensure that none have been taken? It's not easy to get outside, so unless someone's driven off with him, it's more likely George is in the building somewhere.'

Dorothy interrupts. 'All the cars are still out there, covered in snow. We would have heard if anyone tried to leave. They'd need the key to open the front door, for a start.'

'Good, good.' Bruce thrusts his hands into his pockets, swaying slightly on the balls of his feet. If I didn't know any better, I'd say he was enjoying this. I watch as he shoves his hands deep into his trouser pockets. 'Who has searched where so far? No point in going over old ground.'

This is taking too long. I fight the urge to scream.

Matt discusses his search of the downstairs – he's checked everywhere except the locked room that Dorothy won't give him access to. He runs a hand over his hair, weary after the night's events. We exchange a glance, and I can tell he's sorry for grabbing me. I shouldn't have screamed at him in front of everyone like that. I turn my gaze to the floor. When I'm in my police uniform, I feel able to take on the world. But when it comes to our relationship, Matt is holding all the cards. I've become too dependent on him. I should never have moved in. I've got to get out of this cycle. I need to put George first. My chest becomes tight with panic.

Bruce is asking me a question about where I've searched. I tell him I've checked my bedroom and had a brief look in the other bedrooms and en suites that were unlocked. 'I didn't touch anything,' I say, as

Steph and Joey exchange a glance at the mention of me entering their room. 'Just a quick look under the beds, in the wardrobes and behind the shower curtain over the baths.'

Bea watches our interaction closely. 'I checked the kitchen. I must say, Dorothy, it's spotless. I don't know how you keep it so clean.'

A smile tugs at Dorothy's lips.

'Right.' As he clasps his hands together, Bruce doesn't even look at Bea, or acknowledge what she's said. 'Dorothy, would it be acceptable if just two of us, say, Nicola and I, escorted you into your private quarters and checked for young George?'

'But the door was locked.' Dorothy looks from me to Bruce. 'Unless he's able to walk through walls, he couldn't have got in.'

'Indeed,' Bruce continues. 'And you and I both know he's not inside. But it would really help to put a scared mum's mind at rest.' He looks at me benevolently and I give Dorothy a pleading look. God knows, I hate to be seen as weak, but I'll do anything to deepen the search. She sighs in defeat. 'Very well.'

But Bruce isn't finished yet. 'Henry, would you be so kind as to escort Matt and Joey into each of the bedrooms so they can conduct a more detailed search? Nothing too intrusive, just another check of any hiding places George may be curled up in.'

Henry exchanges a look with Dorothy before delivering a slow nod of acceptance.

Bruce turns to Steph, who appears distracted and on edge. 'Would you mind staying in the living room? It would be good to have a friendly face if George shows up.'

'I . . .' She appears reluctant to release her grip on her husband. 'I just want to go home.'

'I know,' he says, 'and you will. But right now, young George is our priority.'

'But the phones . . .' she begins. 'Someone took the SIM cards out.'

'A misunderstanding, I'm sure. We may not prescribe to the idea of radiation in the air, but we must respect our hosts' beliefs when we're staying under their roof. If we don't have any luck with this search, then we'll make headways into getting the phones up and running. And it goes without saying, if anyone comes across any SIM cards during their searches, bring them downstairs. OK?'

Nicely played, I think, with reluctant admiration.

'OK,' Steph says miserably, releasing her husband's arm and resting both hands on her bump. She may not get it now but one day she will understand. The fear of losing your child can eat you up inside. I should be taking charge, but my mind is filled with worry. I'm grateful for Bruce's presence as I follow him down the hall. A thin breeze whistles through the corridor, most likely emanating from one of the windows which have been nailed down. They may be shut tight, but the tall panes are old and weathered, the gaps big enough to create an unsettling draught.

Dorothy appears more reluctant with each step she takes down the hall. Her wig isn't quite straight, and she's walking as if she's in pain. What possessed her to open their doors tonight? Are they that desperate for money that they'd put themselves through this? She glances back at me briefly, as if she's picked up on my thoughts. She looks overwhelmed and I feel bad for the situation she's in. She should be taking it easy at her age, instead of cooking and cleaning for us. But even she must know that the strict set of rules was bound to cause concern. It gnaws at my thoughts, because surely nobody would enforce such strict rules unless they had a good reason for it. Do they really think their daughter's killers will return? I tug on the ends of my hair, nervous energy coursing through my veins as we approach the locked room. Dorothy mutters beneath her breath as she fiddles with a bunch of keys on the same chain as her watch.

'I want you in and out quick sharp,' she warns. 'Don't touch anything. There are a lot of valuables in here.'

I sigh. 'I'm a police officer, Dorothy. Your valuables are safe with me.' I deliver a gentle smile. I can't figure this woman out. Why is she living here in the very building that her daughter was murdered in? I can't imagine the awful memories that this place must hold. So why reopen the business and keep it going? As the door swings open, I half expect to see CCTV screens on the wall. I blink as she switches on the lamps. The room is filled with clutter. I see nothing of value here. There are dresses, belts, hats and shoes everywhere. One side of the four-poster bed is immaculate. A Dan Brown book rests on the mahogany bedside table next to a lamp and a glass of water. A pair of men's slippers are perfectly lined up under the bed, and as Bruce opens the wardrobe on that side, it reveals a few shirts and one spare suit. Some old leather shoes are resting in the bottom of the wardrobe and as Bruce pulls open the thick bottom drawer, it reveals ties, worn socks and underwear.

'Do you mind?' Dorothy is at his side, pushing the drawer shut. 'The child's hardly likely to be in there!'

Bruce stalls. 'Oh, I'm . . .' he stammers for the first time tonight. 'I do apologise.'

I know why he looked there. Force of habit. I couldn't begin to count the number of bedrooms I've searched during my time in the police. You search everywhere when you get the opportunity because you never know what will turn up.

I walk to Dorothy's side of the room. The air is thick with the smell of perfume, and I remind myself why we're here. 'George?' I call out, but silence is returned. Dorothy takes in my gaze as I look at the piles of magazines, clothes, old furniture and dusty ornaments. Everything is in complete disarray.

'We made a pact years ago,' she says, picking up a pair of tights off the floor. I take care of my side and he takes care of his. It prevents a lot of rows, once you make your peace with it.'

'No judgement here,' I say with a smile. 'Matt's the same, likes everything in its place. I'm the one digging my work shirts out of a pile on the ground.' I sigh, opening Dorothy's wardrobe. It's bursting to the seams with clothes and shoes but no sign of George. It looks like it belongs in the theatre, and the wardrobe is so old that it looks like a gateway into Narnia. This woman has a serious addiction for outlandish garments. I get a twinge in my back as I bend to check under the bed. 'Nothing but hat and shoe boxes under there, dear,' Dorothy says, and she's right. But where does this leave us now? I cast an eye over the many photos in frames on her dresser. There are politicians, members of the royal family and TV celebrities. 'They're my darlings,' Dorothy says. 'I know them all.' But something tells me it's her wish list of the people she'd love to know. 'I keep the naked ones hidden,' she chuckles. 'They were naughty scamps back then.' I see Bruce roll his eyes as he stands behind her. The images look like magazine cut outs, not one appears to be an original, so the possibility of her having nude photos of any of the people portrayed is slim.

'George, it's OK, you can come out now,' I call. 'You're not in any trouble. We just want to know that you're OK.' I sigh as nothing but the tick of a clock and the sound of the wind outside is returned.

I glance around the ornate coving, looking for a camera. There's nothing, because why would they be filming themselves? As Bruce follows my gaze, he seems to be thinking the same thing. 'Come along, that's enough snooping for now,' Dorothy says, ushering us both out. Bruce raises a hand, looking down at her. 'Not yet, we have one more question to ask.'

Dorothy emits a harsh sigh. 'Alright, but you must promise to leave once you've asked it.'

Bruce nods. 'Why are there CCTV cameras inside this building? You do know it's against the law to film your guests in certain areas without their consent.' I watch as Dorothy's mouth drops open. She wasn't expecting this. Given there's no response, he continues. 'How many cameras are there? Show us what you've recorded so we can follow George's steps.'

The room falls deathly quiet as Dorothy stares at us both. She is standing at the door, blinking rapidly as she buys some time to think. Shoulders back, she tilts her head defiantly as she stares up at Bruce. 'Those cameras were installed when the place was empty as a security measure. They're not in use anymore.' She sniffs as she gives me the side-eye. 'Don't you think that if I had any recordings, I would have checked them by now? It's not nice, being put under suspicion like this. Don't you know who you're talking to?' Her face flushes with annoyance. 'I'm related to royalty, I'll have you know.'

'How many cameras are there?' I refuse to be drawn into her dramas. I just want to find my son.

'I don't know.' Her wig becomes more unbalanced as she vehemently shakes her head. She pauses to fix her hair and checks her reflection in a cracked mirror as she tugs it on one side. 'After my daughter died, some undesirables tried to break in. There are a lot of ghouls out there and we had to take measures to keep the place secure.' She returns to the door and widens it for our exit. 'I don't know why you're standing here talking to me when you should be looking for your son.' She mutters to herself for a few moments before glancing up at us both. The expression on her face is one of hurt. 'We've been at your beck and call from the moment you arrived, and this is the thanks we get. Do you think any of this has been easy for me, coming up to the anniversary of my daughter's death?' She rests a hand over her mouth, gulping down air as her grief overwhelms her.

'I'm so sorry,' I say remorsefully, 'but I'm a mum too, and I have a right to look for my son. I'm sure we'll find him soon, and the minute it's safe to leave we'll be out of your hair.' I glance back at the room that she didn't have time to tidy. I soften my voice before reaching out and touching her arm. 'Maybe you should think about selling this place and giving yourselves an easier life. It must be very stressful for you both.'

'It has been,' Dorothy wipes away an errant tear. 'Especially with Henry's cancer. I think work is the one thing that helps keep his mind off it. But we do need to slow down.' She seems relieved as we both leave the room. I notice a tremble in her hands as she quickly locks the door behind us. I glance up at the loft hatch further down the hall. 'What's up there?'

Dorothy snorts. 'Unless your son is Spider-Man there's no way he could've reached that loft hatch. You're just being nosey now. I can see where he got it from. Curious George, causing all this upset.'

Dorothy's voice has taken on a hard tone and once more, her mood has changed in the blink of an eye. It's unsettling and I don't like it. I wonder if she has been playing me all along. But I don't have time to think about it, as Bea catches up with us. She waits until Bruce and Dorothy walk ahead before pulling me to one side. A sheen of sweat laces her brow as she keeps her voice low. 'Someone's been in my room.'

21

Nicola

Bea won't take no for an answer so I've no choice but to follow her to her room. My feet feel heavy as I drag myself up the creaking stairs. The feeling of helplessness is overwhelming. Her room is smaller than ours, and I wrinkle my nose at the cloying scent of her fruity vapes tinged with an unmistakeable smell of damp rising from the walls. Her four-poster bed is similar to ours, but the blankets are frayed, the pillows worn. Bea definitely got a raw deal with her room. The beginnings of tiny black spores blossom next to a rusted pipe jutting out from the radiator. There must have been a leak that was neglected for some time. The carpet is stained, a jaded shade of blue. The room is taken up with too much furniture that houses odds and ends – a cracked vase, a cheap heart-shaped ornament, a mirror too small to be of any use. An old clock radio flashes the wrong time in red, and there's no television. It's a gloomy space and my spirits plummet as I push aside the thick curtains and see the snow still falling thickly outside. It feels like we're stuck in a snow globe with no way out.

I turn back to Bea as she emerges from her en suite, drying her hands on the back of her clothes. 'Sorry, I was desperate. I hate using the toilet downstairs. I feel like someone's gonna jump out on me down there.'

I don't blame her. I've always felt like I was being watched in this creepy old place. At least now, I know why. I keep the presence of cameras to myself though. We're stuck here and Bea would only create a scene. Things are bad enough as it is. The radiator pipes rattle and Bea almost jumps out of her skin. I don't understand why she booked this place, given it frightens her half to death.

'I need to be getting back. George could be downstairs . . .'

But she cuts me off in a harsh whisper. 'That's what I'm talking about! I told you, someone's been in my room. What if it was him?'

'If he was here, he would have answered,' I reply, unconvinced. 'And I popped in to check earlier on . . . although I didn't touch anything.' I've put myself at risk, searching the rooms alone. If anything does go missing, I'll be the one getting the blame. But I've bigger things to worry about now.

'Well, there you go then.' Bea points at some ornaments on the sideboard. They're in line with Dorothy's tacky style so I'd presumed that she had put them there.

'Jerry was facing the window.' She picks up a ceramic ornament of a small grey rodent and moves it. 'When I came back here to freshen up, he was facing the door.'

'Jerry?'

She looks at me like I'm stupid. 'As in Tom and Jerry. It's an ornament of my dear departed pet mouse.'

For a second, I wonder if she's joking but her expression is deadpan. 'You brought an ornament of a mouse with you on holiday?'

'I couldn't very well leave him at home, now could I?' She looks at me quizzically. 'What if I was burgled? What if my house burnt down?'

Bea is going off track. I haven't got time for this. Although something is off, as I'm sure that earlier on she described herself as a traveller with no fixed abode.

'Has anything else been moved?'

Bea wanders around her room, checking the wardrobe for good measure. 'I can't say for sure, but it's a feeling, you know? Like someone's been here, snooping around my things. Earlier I saw Dorothy, taking a tray of food out of the kitchen. But when I turned the corridor to follow her, she was gone. Like she disappeared into thin air.'

'It's a big house, there's lots of side rooms.' But her comment intrigues me. Did George disappear into some kind of secret lair?

There's something about Bea that's unsettling me. She's looking at me like I'm going to solve her own personal mystery instead of putting my son first. Not for the first time, it feels like our stay here is part of one big game. My frown grows as I turn to face her.

'Why are you really here, Bea? Is there more to your visit than you're letting on?' I wasn't planning to challenge her, but I know she's holding back. 'Because earlier you said you're a traveller, with no fixed abode. But now you're telling me that you've taken your ornament from home. There's other stuff, too. Why are you really here? What's going on between you and Bruce?'

'Hey, don't start interrogating me. I'm an innocent victim in all of this.' She rummages in her bag and pulls out a vape. 'And as for Bruce, I've met people like him before. They can't handle outspoken women.' She looks me in the eye. 'Honey, don't let anyone steal your light.'

I feel a level of discomfort beneath the intensity of her gaze.

She touches my arm. 'I see how you are with Matt. Sure, on the surface, he seems like a nice man – thoughtful, kind and he loves George, there's no doubting that. But anyone can see that you're mismatched. Why are you with him? What kind of a hold does he have on you?'

I take a step back as my breath locks in my throat. I didn't realise that other people could see it too. 'My son is missing. Don't you think I've got enough on my plate?' I blurt. I feel exasperated, and I don't want to be under the spotlight when there's so much going on. 'I don't have time for your relationship advice or to investigate your . . . your ceramic mouse. George is my priority.'

Bea grips my arm as I turn to leave. 'Wait,' she says, desperation in her voice. 'I'm sorry if I've offended you. I'm an empath. I pick up on things, strong emotions filter through. But all I've done since I got here is rub people up the wrong way.'

I sigh. This isn't like me at all. 'I just want my little boy.'

'And you'll find him . . .' Bea's voice lowers as she quickly looks around the room. She dips her head and now she's back in my face as she quietly speaks. 'There's something you need to know.'

'The cameras?' I wipe a stray hair off my face. 'Yeah. I know about those.'

'There are cam . . . !' She realises she's shouting and lowers her voice to a whisper once more. 'There are *cameras*?'

I frown. 'There's one in the living room, hidden in the coving. I've seen one in the hall, too. There may be more . . .' I peer into the corners of the ceilings and notice a small, round glazed surface that could be glass. 'Don't look, but I think you have one too.'

'Christ on a bike,' she splutters, pulling her clothes together a little tighter. 'Why didn't you say so?'

'Because I didn't want to freak you out. Besides, Dorothy says they're not working, that they were installed to keep an eye on the place when it was empty.'

'Empty my backside. This place hasn't been empty a day since the murders. I should know.' A flush rises up her face.

Now she's got my attention. I rest my hands on my hips. 'What do you mean, *you should know*? What's really going on here, Bea? And where the hell is my son?'

22

Matt

This feels like the longest night of my life. Usually, I live with order. Everything is planned meticulously, my diet, my fitness regime, and most importantly, my job. Where I always seem to fall down is when it comes to relationships. My previous long term relationship ended when she travelled abroad to 'find herself'. I stand at the living room window, my anxiety rising as the memory of her departure returns. Carol was meant to be gone for a holiday, but as far as I know, she never came back. I must have sent her a hundred texts, left dozens of voicemails and poured my heart out in emails that took me hours to write. It took me weeks to realise that I was being 'ghosted', a term I learned from one of my students as we discussed social media in class.

This time, I was careful. It's not as if I was short of women wanting to date me. There were lots of single mums that I met through parent teacher meetings that seemed interested. But I took my time. Waited for the right person to come into my life. I really think that Nicola is the one. It's why I booked a romantic getaway. I had such great plans for this weekend.

We should be enjoying the honeymoon suite of a luxury hotel and seeing the Northern Lights. Nicola and I would have finished our romantic meal, and now we should be standing beneath Scottish skies glittering with the aurora borealis, with drinks in our hands. Then, just as she gasped in amazement at the beauty of the skies, that's when I'd produce the ring. God knows, the diamond is big enough to contend with anything the skies could produce.

I've played out the scene in my head a dozen times. Nicola wouldn't have been able to refuse. But nothing has gone to plan. It started when her mother backed out of babysitting George. She's always been flaky, with her depressive episodes. Nicola suggested calling the trip off, but I persuaded her that it would be fun to bring him along. I told myself we could make the most of it, and the hotel's babysitting service would give me time to propose. And I couldn't delay, not if we're to be married within the next six months. That's where I went wrong with Carol. We dated for years before she finally left. 'Strike while the iron is hot,' my father always said, along with little gems of wisdom like 'you've got to fight for what you want'.

I've already scouted locations and have the perfect place lined up – the very hotel where I was meant to propose. The only way of bridging the gap between us is to have children of our own. That would tie Nicola to me for good, and also serve to make her quit her job, with any luck. I just wish she'd let me show her how happy I can make her.

Now my plans are in tatters and George has disappeared. Joey and Steph are nice enough, but the rest of the guests are imbeciles. We've got Bruce, lording it over everyone like he's an ageing Detective Inspector Morse, and Bea, with her theatrics and annoying nasally voice, making everything about her. As for Dorothy and Henry – they're like an English Addams family.

I realise what I'm doing and take a deep, soothing breath. Breathe in positivity . . . breathe out stress. I have to do this three times before I feel any kind of calm. It's something my therapist taught me after my last relationship bit the dust. I need to halt my thoughts before they become too destructive. I unclench my fists and lower my shoulders an inch. But Nicola's absence makes me feel like I'm missing a limb. As unkind as my thoughts can become, I can't imagine a world without her or George in it.

I shouldn't have let her go off on her own. I call her name but there's no response. She can't have gone far. But then that's what we said about George . . .

I only make it as far as the hall when Joey grabs me by the arm.

Anxiety seems to have aged him in the short time we've been here. He's dressed in thick layers, with his long wavy hair poking out from beneath the beanie hat which is pulled over his ears. 'Steph and I have been talking. I'm going to get help. The roads look pretty impassable, so I'll hike to the nearest hotel and call the police.'

'Are you sure?' I say. 'It's treacherous. There's been no let up from the storm since we got here.' I check my watch. It's gone ten thirty. I don't want to feel responsible if something happens to him. 'George has gone missing before. I'm sure we'll find him soon. I wouldn't rush off just yet.' I'm trying to sound upbeat, but I'm honestly filled with dread. Too much time has passed. This old place, with its creaky floors and dark corners, carries a malignancy that turns my thoughts dark and fills me with unease.

'It's not just about George.' Joey punctuates the sentence with a sigh. 'Steph is scared, and it's not doing her or the baby any good.'

'We're all a bit freaked out . . .' I reply, but Joey interrupts me before I elaborate.

'Yeah, but Steph is worried what Dorothy and Henry will do next. First, they take our phones, then our SIM cards go missing.'

'The landline is down too,' I add, although it's not helping the situation. 'The storm has hit this place pretty hard.'

'I dunno . . .' Joey pauses to check his watch. He's edgy and can't stand still. 'I'm worried what will happen if we stay.'

It seems like he's made his mind up. 'And Steph? Is she going too? Because I'm not sure that's wise in her condition.'

But Joey shakes his head. 'She's going to stay here in case I run into problems. She wouldn't last five minutes out there.'

'And you would? On a night like this? It's below zero.' At least it is, according to the old-fashioned barometer in the hall.

Joey gives me a lopsided grin. 'I'm an experienced mountaineer. I've survived worse weather than this.'

'I don't know . . .' I'm not convinced that it's worth the risk. 'This island is so bloody remote. It's not as if you're going to bump into anyone else out there.'

But Joey's determination only seems to grow as he nails his point home. 'You've seen the storm. We could be here for *days*. What if history repeats itself? There was a bloodbath here. Everybody died and the killers are still out there. Or in here. What if it happens again?'

I can't disagree. The thought *has* crossed my mind, which makes me worry about George. I don't know why Joey is desperate for my approval but I give him a fatherly nod of the head.

'I suppose, and there might be people clearing the roads. Even if you spend the night with the police, it's safer than here. Do you want me to go with you?' I'm asking, not volunteering, because I don't want to leave Nicola and George.

'No need, man. I just wanted you on board. I feel better about leaving Steph knowing you and Nicola are here for her. Just keep an eye, yeah? I don't trust the others.' He shakes his head. 'I don't know why, but they don't feel genuine, especially Bruce. Keep a close eye on him too.'

'OK.' Again, I'm in agreement. And I don't like how that man has latched on to Nicola. I'm relieved that Joey's going it alone. 'But be careful. If the roads are impassable, or the conditions too bad, then head straight back here. You can always go in the light tomorrow.'

'Steph's already given me the full safety lecture,' he chuckles, as she joins his side. She rests one hand around his waist, and I can see from her torn expression that she's reluctant to let him go.

Within minutes, Nicola has returned, worry lines etched on her face. She tells me about her fruitless search of Dorothy's room, and I lay a hand on her shoulder as I explain the situation and reassure her that everything will be OK.

'Are you alright, hun?' she asks Steph, who is tearful but trying to hold it together as she rests one hand on her modest bump. The young woman nods and I feel a rush of sympathy for her. The sound of rusty bolts screeching across the door is enough to bring Dorothy to our side.

'Where do you think you're going?' Dorothy's face is pinched as she rushes into the hall, her underskirts rustling as she moves. Her voice fills the space as she calls for her husband. 'Henry? Henry! They're making a break for it!' It would be comical if the situation wasn't so dire.

Henry takes long strides from the living room, and soon we're facing him. 'Either let me make a phone call or I'm leaving,' Joey says, with a firmness I've not seen before. I've definitely underestimated him. When we first met, I thought he was a bit soft.

Henry glares down at him and presses his fingers to his throat. 'The phone lines are . . . down. No leaving.'

But Joey is resolute as he pulls another bolt across. 'I'm going. Either give me my phone back with the SIM card inside it or I'm out of here.' He tries to open the door, but it's locked.

'We don't have . . . the SIM cards,' Henry's words grate as he struggles to speak. 'You must . . . obey . . . the rules.' This whole situation is making me increasingly uncomfortable as Joey squares up to him again.

'Haven't you heard? This isn't a communist country. You've no right to keep us here.' I step between them as Joey's agitation grows. All I've done tonight is referee arguments between the hosts and guests.

'I'll smash a window if I have to, just let me the hell out of here!' Joey rattles the thick wooden door. I'm surprised at how worked up he is. Does he know something we don't?

'Hey, buddy, there's no need for that.' I turn from Joey to Henry. 'Just open the door and let him go.'

Steph stares, wordlessly, at us both.

Henry silently turns on his heel and I'm hoping he's gone to get the key. 'There's no helping some people,' Dorothy shakes her head. 'All we've done is take you in, feed you and try to keep you all safe.' We stand, transfixed, as we wait for Henry to return. I hear a key turn and what sounds like a cabinet door creaking open in one of the rooms off the hall. *What is he doing?*

I grab Nicola as she steps away. 'Where are you off to now?'

She blinks, her eyes bloodshot from tiredness. 'To look for George, of course.' But things are getting heated, and I don't want to leave Joey and Steph in case there's another showdown.

'Hang on a minute.' I tighten my grip on her arm, but she snatches it away. I'm about to tell her off when there's a collective gasp from the other guests. I've been focusing solely on Nicola and as we both turn around, we're met with the barrel of a gun.

23

Elita

Oh golly. I can't believe what's happening. One minute I'm sitting in my chair watching all the action on screen, then out of nowhere, this little guy pops up. It's George – the curious six-year-old who has managed to stumble upon my hidden spot. There's dust on the shoulders of his pyjamas, and his big clunky headphones hang loosely around his neck. He looks like a cute chubby teddy bear, now he's with me in the flesh. I'm totally caught off guard, but there is something nice about his presence that makes me relax in my seat. After a moment of awkward silence, George speaks.

'Hi. I saw you at the window before. Who are you?' His face is a mix of curiosity and fascination as he looks me up and down.

Standing at the guest room window was one of the most daring things I've done. I was so excited to see a young guest that I couldn't help but wave. 'I'm Elita,' I reply softly, trying to act cool. 'I'm impressed that you found me. What are you doing here?'

He starts shuffling his feet, a mischievous expression on his face. 'I got bored. I hid and played my game for a while, then I followed the tunnel around. I didn't want to listen to the grown-ups anymore.'

I can't help but smile. The hidden places in this house have never been described as tunnels before. I suppose if you don't know where you're going then they can seem that way. What I don't understand is why he'd want to leave his mum when she's looked after him so well. Our lives are so different. Here I am, dying for some human company while all he wants is to get away. He is staring at me, mouth open, but I feel this connection, so I don't mind. I'm happy he's here, even if everything feels a bit uncertain right now.

Then George asks the big question. 'Are you . . . are you OK?' His stockinged feet pad against the floor as he cautiously approaches me for a better look.

His reaction could have been worse, and I like his honesty. I'd rather he ask me about my looks outright than be too scared to speak.

'I don't exactly fit the model, George,' I reply, letting my swivel chair down before shuffling off the edge. 'But don't worry, I'm good. I've been hidden away here for so long, having a visitor is pretty cool.'

George glances at the shelf which is full of the lotions and eye drops that Granny makes me use. Then there's the collection of wigs and the special cushioned shoes that stop my feet hurting on the hard floor. It's not easy when you're a teenager trapped in a little girl's body, especially one like mine. I can see through George's frown that he's trying to understand. 'Does it hurt?' His words are tender, and I melt a little inside. Even though we barely know each other, he already gives a damn about me.

'I first came here when I was around your age, like, ten years ago.' I watch his face as he tries to wrap his head around the maths.

'But that means you're . . .'

'I know,' I stop him mid-sentence. 'I don't look like a teenager. I've been stuck in time.' I'm kinda relieved just to let it out. I don't want to be like this anymore.

'And you're sure it doesn't hurt?' He takes another step, inspecting me more closely beneath the light of my desk lamp. He's clutching his iPad like his life depends on it, but his big dark eyes are filled with compassion. I try hard to act normal because I don't want to frighten him off.

'Nah, it doesn't hurt,' I assure him, grateful for his kindness. 'Granny Dorothy looks after me. She's super nice.'

He nods like he understands. 'You're still you, and that's what matters.'

It sounds like something he picked up from his mum or teacher or something. But you know what? His kindness boosts my spirits. I feel like he gets me.

'Check this out.' I point at the screens and cameras, inviting him into my world. 'Wanna see?'

His eyes light up as he takes everything in. As George steps closer, he seems totally hooked on the screens. I make sure to show him some pre-recorded videos, because it would spoil things if he saw that his mum is going crazy searching for him.

As I explain all the surveillance stuff, George's fascination grows. He listens to every detail, soaking it all in. It's like this little adventure becomes an escape for him, a break from everything else going on. I sense that this isn't the first time he's run away to be on his own. 'I've been watching you, see?' I point out. 'There are little cameras everywhere. Grandad did a great job of installing them for me.' Time melts away and before we know it, we're sitting side by side before my computer screen. I'm glad that he can't hear the others calling for him. I've always felt like I'm living under the skin of the house, where nobody can find me, not even the bad people who took my mother away. But George did, and that makes me a bit nervous.

'How did you find me?' I can ask, because we're like friends now, casually chatting away.

'I saw you. First upstairs, when I got here, then a little while ago, when I was coming out of the toilet. You disappeared behind a wall. So I followed, but it took me a while to catch up with you because I got a bit lost and stopped for a rest.'

'Toilet adventures, huh?' I can't help but laugh. 'You're very brave.' He's talking about one of the wall panels which is one of many secret doors. I should have locked it behind me, but I forgot, with everything going on.

George shrugs, but these cute little dimples press into his fleshy cheeks as he smiles. 'I like exploring.'

'Well, you're a very lucky boy. I don't get to explore much, at least not while guests are here. I get to come out when the front doors are locked, and everyone goes home.' I talk about my life, and how it's not so bad. Time slips by unnoticed, now the barriers that kept us apart have faded away. George doesn't seem to want to leave, and honestly, I'm not ready to let him go. The thought of our new-found friendship ending sucks. And what if the monsters come back? I can't bear the idea of anything happening to my new friend. I'd be stuck here, unable to stop them, just like it was with my mum.

How I wish she had hidden here with me when the bad stuff began. It's something I asked Granny a hundred times over. Why didn't she just lock herself away, here with me? But Granny always gives me the same reply – she never thought that things would go as far as they did. She was tired of hiding away. She thought that if she faced them, they'd finally leave her alone. But monsters don't listen to reason. That's why George isn't safe out there. At least here, nothing bad will happen to him.

I muster the courage to ask him the question on my mind.

'Hey, George, wanna stay here a little longer? I've got a bunch of games we can play, and chocolate too. What do you say?'

He looks at me and I'm praying he says what I want to hear. I can't bear to go back to being alone again. 'It's OK, Granny will tell your mum that you're safe.'

Then, after a pause, he nods, his grin spreading wide across his face. He's so cute, I want a photo of him to hide with my other keepsakes.

'OK,' he says at last. 'I'll stay.'

This massive feeling of relief washes over me. Finally, I've found a friend. He may be ten years younger, but he's actually taller than me. Maybe that's why he seems so relaxed in my company. He knows that I'm no threat. My heart gives a little flutter in my chest as I realise, I can't let him go. Not yet, anyway. In the hidden layers of the guest house, our friendship will grow. Even if the bad people come, they can't touch us now. I've got enough supplies to last us until long after they're gone.

Mystery on the Mic Podcast

The Watts Case Series: Episode 6

Alex: Hey there, mystery enthusiasts! Welcome back to 'Mystery on the Mic'. I'm Alex, your host, and joining me is the ever-curious true crime historian, Sarah. How's it going, Sarah?

Sarah: Hey, Alex, great to be back, and boy, do we have a peculiar tale to unravel today.

Alex: You're absolutely right, Sarah. So, picture this, listeners: Caleb Watts, son of the late music mogul Ronnie Watts, has got himself caught up in a bit of a legal jam. He pleaded guilty to drug possession, and in true Watts family style, the circumstances are nothing short of bizarre.

Sarah: Bizarre is an understatement, Alex. So, Caleb returns home one day to find his mansion swarmed by sniffer dogs and cops. And instead of losing it, he just calmly offers them a tour. I mean, talk about staying composed under pressure. I'm not sure that's how I'd react if I came home to that.

Alex: Totally! And to make things even weirder, he grabs his guitar and starts serenading the officers while they search his place. He's singing about Jesus, forgiveness and love!

Can you imagine turning the place over with that going on in the background?

Sarah: I can't even ... (laughs). But we're not done yet. All the while, there's this group of people in his house, chanting that they're the 'Fellowship of Jesus Christ'. Some even claim Caleb is the 'second coming'. You couldn't make this stuff up.

Alex: Right? And during this investigation, the police find a bunch of cannabis on the premises. Plus, two young women who were reported missing by their families. These women don't want to go home though. They're quite happy where they are.

Sarah: It's a whirlwind of strange events, Alex. And what makes it even more intriguing is that Caleb's brother Ronan is away in New York when this all goes down. So, it's Caleb who takes the heat for the drugs.

Alex: Speaking of heat, when he shows up in court, Caleb's rocking this bohemian outfit, beard, sandals, the whole shebang. He's all about the spiritual vibes, blesses the courtroom and everything. This guy is on another level.

Sarah: And get this, listeners, he openly admits to the drug possession but claims it's for medicinal use. The court buys it and slaps him with a £500 fine. Case closed!

Alex: Talk about a peculiar turn of events. From a music mogul's extravagant mansion to this spiritual journey where he claims to be the second coming. It's giving off strong cult vibes.

Sarah: I agree. The Watts family's tale just keeps getting more fascinating. Caleb's got this mystique about him now, he's capable of anything as far as I'm concerned. I can't wait to see where this case goes next.

Alex: Well, mystery fans, we'll be keeping an eye on this one for sure. Thanks for tuning in to another intriguing episode of 'Mystery on the Mic'. We'll be discussing our next case right after this sponsored ad break.

Sarah: Thanks for joining us, folks. Stay curious and keep those mysteries coming!

24

Nicola

I stare at Henry's gun in disbelief. None of us know what he's capable of. As I mentally plan an escape route, the sense of our isolation expands ten-fold. The Loch House is miles from help, and we're hemmed in by the storm. But it appears a bigger danger lies inside, casting shadows upon the faces of my fellow guests.

Henry is rigid in his stance, his face stony as he stares us down. Was it *him* who murdered the hotel guests all those years ago? Am I looking at the murder weapon? I think of the religious artefacts and books I saw in his room. Could the murders have been some kind of religious offering? What about George? Are we next?

Adrenaline floods my body as I comprehend the danger we're in and my heart flutters like a small bird caught in my chest. I barely remember my firearm training, because police detectives aren't armed. We were told if such an incident occurred, to wait for armed backup and be a good witness, reporting everything to Control. But my colleagues feel a million miles away right now. What I'd give to be back in the station, with George safely at home. I thought that he was hiding, but now I'm consumed with worry for my missing son.

Henry jerks a head towards the living room. All the colour has drained from Dorothy's face, but she ushers us forward, along with the other guests. 'It's for your own good,' she witters, taking quick, dainty steps after us. 'You know the rules, nobody in or out!' But Dorothy looks scared. This wasn't part of her plans.

We follow the other guests inside, everyone except Sunita, who our hosts seem to have forgotten about. I need to do something. We're standing in a circle before the fireplace, in our usual gathering place. I ignore Matt's warning look as I take a breath to speak.

'Calm down.' I gesture with my hands as I speak to Henry in an authoritative voice. 'Put. The gun. Down.' But Henry's jaw is set firm as he trains his weapon on me. Dorothy stands behind him, her bright pink lips forming a small 'o'. She is in way over her head.

'You're only making things worse,' Matt whispers gruffly next to me. 'Just do as he says for now.'

I watch the other guests, their eyes darting nervously between one another. I'm keenly aware that this situation has the potential to go very wrong very quickly. Matt's hands are trembling, his knuckles white as he clenches them into fists. He's standing so close to me that I can smell his sweat. Bea scowls as she sits next to the fireplace, subdued for once. Earlier I would have pegged her as the first person to break down. But after what she told me in her room I see her in a different light, and much of her behaviour has been explained. I was shocked by her confession and haven't had a chance to tell anyone what I know . . . At least now I know what she's doing here.

Steph stands nearby, having sought solace in the embrace of her husband, Joey. His eyes are burning with determination. He's undone his coat, the chance of him leaving The Loch House growing smaller by the minute. The tension in the room is palpable as Dorothy and Henry stand before us, instructing us to stay put. Dorothy fidgets as she watches us closely. Henry's expression grows harder, his gaze cold and unwavering, his grip on the shotgun tight. I don't know much about guns, but it looks old. I watch Bruce as he narrows his eyes, trying to make it out. I wonder if he's worked with firearms during his time in the police. Our conversations have been brief and to the point so far.

I just hope Henry doesn't do anything stupid. Are they that desperate to keep us in here, or does he have something far darker in mind?

'We're sorry for the inconvenience, but it's for your own safety,' Dorothy's voice trembles, the strain evident as she slowly comes to terms with the situation we're in. 'You know the rules. Until the storm passes, we can't let anyone leave.'

Joey's voice cuts through the uneasy silence. 'That's not your decision to make. A child is missing and you threaten us with a gun? Can't you see how crazy this looks?' But Henry just glares, his dark eyes cold.

Steph whimpers, clutching Joey tightly. He whispers that it's OK as he tries again with Henry. 'Just . . . just let me go, mate. There's no comeback on you if something happens to me.'

His plea hangs in the air, the weight of his desperation clinging to each word. Dorothy looks to Henry as she awaits his answer. All this time, I thought that she was the one in charge, but it seems that I was wrong. He's holding the shotgun with both hands which means he can't speak. His face is stern and unwavering, and she seems to take her cue from that.

'No one is leaving!' she screeches, her voice high. Henry's shotgun glints ominously, its cold steel a stark reminder of the danger that we're in. He holds it up and trains the gun on each of us, finally resting on Joey.

There is a collective gasp, a mixture of fear and disbelief. The room seems to shrink as the walls close in. Joey takes a step back, his hands raised in surrender. 'For God's sake, man, this is crazy! You can't shoot us all!' A bitter laugh leaves his lips. 'I thought you wanted to keep us safe?'

Henry's grip on the trigger tightens. 'You don't understand,' Dorothy points to the window. 'There are things out there, bad things you couldn't possibly comprehend. They're blood thirsty. They're . . .' Dorothy covers her mouth with her hands. 'I can't. I . . . I can't even think about it.'

'Please. Lower the gun. We're listening.' Bea's voice trembles as she speaks, her eyes darting from Henry to Dorothy and back again. 'What things? Tell us. Make us understand.'

Dorothy's gaze flickers with a mix of fear and regret. 'We never intended for it to come to this,' she whispers, her voice barely audible as she rests a hand on her wrinkled chest. 'The storm has brought them, and now they're coming to finish what they started. They won't leave without her, not this time.'

I jump as Henry stamps his foot. He's trying to get Dorothy's attention but can't speak unless he takes one hand off the gun. He scowls at her with a ferocity that makes her wilt. 'Sorry, dear.' She seems to disappear into herself. 'I've said too much.'

'Wait, what do you mean?' I demand. 'Who's coming, Dorothy? Who?'

Henry stamps his foot for a second time before training his gun on me. I don't trust him not to pull the trigger, and I swallow through the tightness in my throat.

A dreadful silence settles over the room. I won't sit idly by while George is on his own somewhere in this awful place. Dorothy and Henry clearly have some serious mental health issues. If it were anyone else holding the gun, I might just call their bluff and leave, but Henry is unpredictable – and whatever is spooking Dorothy, it's real to her.

The fire crackles and spits as a whoosh of air is driven down the chimney. Now Henry's gaze is trained on Joey, but Bruce is edging closer, and he shoots Matt a conspiratorial look. My throat clicks as I try to swallow. My limbs are trembling with adrenaline, the shock of having a gun pointed in my face . . . But all I can think of is my little boy. I have to tell Henry to put down his weapon. This isn't going to end well.

I jump, as a sudden, thunderous crack of splintering wood erupts outside. A tree must have come down in the storm. It's enough to distract Henry for the briefest of moments, and there is a flurry of activity as Bruce, Matt and Joey struggle to loosen the shotgun from his grip.

'Henry!' Dorothy squeals. Head down, I launch myself towards her as she rushes to her husband's side. The woman feels stick thin, the rough material of her clothes scratchy against my face as I bring her to the floor. Bea stands, rooted to the spot as her screams fill the room. It's too late to stop Steph as she rushes towards Joey and the others. I try to shout a warning, but the words don't come. Dorothy fights against me, and she's so small and slippery that it's like wrestling with an eel and she scrambles out of my grip. I'm just trying to get to my feet when the deafening blast of a gunshot fills the air.

25

Matt

My ears are ringing from the blast of the shotgun, and I shake my head, clambering on to my knees as I try to regain control. We've all ended up on the floor, with Henry on his back at the bottom. Everything felt like it was moving in slow motion as we grappled the cold steel of the shotgun. But Hill's finger was on the trigger, and it shot out a blast which left me reeling. Bea's mouth is open, the whites of her eyes exposed. All I can hear are muffled screams. I cry out as I pull back my clothes to check my chest, legs and arms. There's blood . . . but it's not mine.

The air crackles with tension. It takes me a couple of seconds to orientate myself before I realise what's going on. I exhale in relief as I realise that Joey has control of the shotgun. He's on his feet, and now Nicola is beside me asking me for my belt. I can barely hear what she's saying through the humming in my ears. Frustrated, she takes it anyway, quickly unbuckling it and pulling it through the loops. I'm about to ask what she's playing at, but I see her pressing a knee in the small of Hill's back and securing each of his wrists. Bruce is sitting on the ground, cradling his arm. Blood seeps through his shirt onto the carpeted floor. I push the butt of my palms against my ears, but it makes no difference. I must have been close to the blast.

Nicola is in full police mode as she assesses the aftermath of the shot. She helps me up off the floor and guides me to a chair. 'My ears . . . I can't hear,' I say, but my voice sounds weird in my head. She signals at me to stay put, and I watch as she turns to Bruce.

Joey is with Steph. Mascara-stained tears are rolling down her face. I can't hear what he's saying as he removes the bullets from the gun to make it safe. Bea is standing nearby. She's stopped screaming but her face is like chalk as she watches on. Dorothy lunges towards her husband, and I can barely make out her protests as she tries to undo the belt that Nicola has secured around his wrists. He could have shot any one of us.

I'm not having this. I wobble to my feet, pulling her off him, shouting that he could have killed any one of us tonight. But I sound like I'm underwater and the ringing in my ears isn't going away. Now Joey is at my side, and I help him get Bruce to his feet. I didn't realise that Nicola had gone until she returns with a dining room chair. Her face is flushed with determination. Steph approaches her with what looks like a curtain tie, and they get to work. Knots are tied with trembling hands. It seems Dorothy flounced off before anyone could get to her, and I pray to God that she doesn't return with another gun.

Bruce winces as he shifts onto the sofa, and I notice that someone has crudely bandaged his arm. 'We need a doctor,' I manage to say, but Nicola points to the ceiling coving and I notice a chunk missing from the corner, which tells me that he'll be OK. Bruce has been grazed by the gunfire, but he was lucky – this time. He nods to Nicola, clutching his wound, the arm of his shirt ragged, his expression one of relief.

Hill, dishevelled and disoriented, glares back at all of us as he sits, knees parted wide on the chair. His eyes are filled with a mix of defiance and regret. I can't make sense of what's going on . . . What are they frightened of? Everything they've told us has been cryptic. Do the problems with this guest house lie within? I'm glad he's tied up, and I'll feel better when Dorothy is under control. I just wish that the police were involved. Now we have no choice. Someone needs to get help.

Joey wastes no time in setting his plan into motion. Supplies are gathered and Hill offers little resistance as he sits quietly, unable to speak. Nicola tells me she's found the empty gun cabinet and that, according to paperwork kept in a nearby drawer, Hill had a licence for one gun. It's not uncommon out in the highlands, but it doesn't make me feel any better about things. My head is swimming, and I take a breath as a wave of nausea overcomes me. The back of my head is throbbing from when I hit the deck.

By the time Joey is ready I'm feeling steadier and, despite the ringing, my hearing has improved. Soon it will be midnight. I wish it was morning and this awful night was behind us. At least Joey is trying to sort out some help.

'Sorry,' I say, as I face him at the front door. He found the key to the door catch in Hill's pocket, and now he's ready to face the storm.

'For what?' He seems more like himself, despite the situation we've found ourselves in.

'I wasn't much use when the gun went off, it deafened me . . .' I'm about to say more but he raises his hand.

'You're kidding me, right? The way you jumped on him . . . it was crazy. I was only able to grab the gun because you tackled him to the floor. Jeez . . .' He shakes his arms and legs. 'I'm still buzzing. It was a hell of a rush.'

I'm grateful that he's helped me save face. I don't want Nicola to think any less of me. Dorothy still hasn't returned, and I'm wondering if she's with George somewhere. I've seen how she's been with him. As crazy as her husband is, I don't think she'd cause George harm. This house is a labyrinth of dark corridors. It wouldn't surprise me if she's disappeared into a basement room. Joey opens the heavy door, pushing against the howling wind. A sudden icy gust steals my breath away. It will be a long time before dawn greets us, and the landscape is a chilling blanket of snow.

'Are you sure about this?' I ask, as Nicola and Steph join us.

'I'm sure,' he replies, hugging his wife one last time. He steps out into the storm, casting one final glance back at us all, his resolve unyielding. 'I'll be back, as Arnie would say.' A blast of icy wind gusts through the open doorway as Joey disappears into the snowy abyss. We close the doors, but the air is fraught with uncertainty.

'Right.' Nicola holds up the bunch of Henry's keys. 'Time for a proper search for George.'

26

Elita

I can't believe this is happening. George is sobbing like a baby and I'm freaking out. A massive bang shook the walls, and it felt like our place had been hit by lightning. But when I checked the outside camera I could see one of the big pine trees had fallen down outside. It's not the first time it's happened. The place is surrounded by them and Grandad has explained that the storms we get up here sometimes loosen their roots. At least it didn't come crashing into the house.

But when I checked the living room camera screen I nearly fell off my chair with fright. A fight had broken out and Grandad had his gun! Some of the guests were grabbing for it, with poor Grandad underneath them on the floor. My first thought was that the monsters were back. I forgot all about George being next to me and I couldn't help but scream. That set *him* off, and then he saw his mum holding onto Granny, which made him even worse.

Now I take a deep breath, feeling helpless as we watch. Thank goodness Grandad hasn't been seriously hurt. He never takes out his gun. Granny hates having it in the house. But now Bruce is holding his bleeding arm and Bea is screaming like a crazy woman. I click my mouse as I search each room on the cameras but there are no outsiders to be seen. Sunita's room cameras have been blacked out. Has she covered it up? Nobody's ever noticed them before, hidden deep in the dark coving of the ceiling, but I guess that when you notice one, you see them all. The living room camera is bigger than the others – it has to be, to fit everything in. And sometimes the glass reflects the flames of the fire which kinda makes it stand out.

Now I stare at the flickering screen as Nicola secures my grandad to the chair with a belt. Joey is holding a shotgun. The bang that shook the walls of the house must have been Grandad's gun going off. But what the heck is going on? I've watched these cameras day and night for years. Today I turned my back for minutes and all this happens.

I blink and see a flash of Granny running down the hall. It's too dark to make out her face, but at least she seems OK. I turn back to George. His shoulders jerk as he cries.

'I . . . want . . . my . . . mummy,' he says between sobs. I feel like crying now too, because these are the words I said after I lost my mum. He clambers off the chair to leave. I can't let him go, which is why I've already pressed the door firmly shut. All the panels look the same. He won't find his way back without me.

'George, you have to stay here.' I'm trying to sound all grown up and brave, but my voice is shaking because I'm scared to let him go. 'It's not safe out there. The bad people, they're coming. I can feel it. It won't be long.' It's true. The house feels different. Just like it did when Mum hid me, all those years ago.

George looks up at me, his big brown eyes wet with tears, and my heart breaks. I never wanted to make the little guy cry. He points to the screen. 'Mu . . . mummy's lo . . . looking for me. I have to go back.'

I grab his arm to hold onto him, but all I get is the sleeve of his pyjamas as he pulls away. 'George, please, don't go yet. We have to hide, just for a little while, until the bad people go away.' I feel like the worst person in the world.

'I want my mum . . . mummy,' he sobs, wiping away his tears with his chubby hand. 'I miss her.'

I don't want to hear this. He can't leave me alone. Not now. I grab him for a second time, and dig my fingers into his arm. 'I get it. I miss my family too. But they can't protect you out there. We *have* to stay hidden. The bad people, they're dangerous. They want to hurt us. I won't let that happen to you.'

'Mummy's a police officer,' he says, as if she has superpowers.

I feel sick to my stomach. How can I make him understand how dangerous these people are without frightening him even more? I set my jaw firm because I'm angry that my new-found friend wants to abandon me so soon. 'Yeah, well, my mum was pretty tough, and they killed her in minutes. Not just her, but everyone who stayed here that night.' I stare into his eyes. 'Everyone except me.'

I hate that I'm scaring him, but I'm scared too. I know I'm asking too much, but I can't bear the thought of being alone again. George wriggles free from my grip. Despite our age difference, he's much stronger than me.

'Come with me,' he says, taking a few steps back. 'Mummy will look after us both.'

A bitter laugh leaves my lips. He's so innocent, is George. I'll never get out of this place. The world isn't ready to meet me yet. I watch as he walks away and my heart sinks like a stone in my chest.

'How . . . how do I get back?' He turns back to me as he presses each panel on the wall. Because he didn't come in through a clearly defined door. There's no handle and you need to know exactly where and how to press. The little guy may have been lucky getting in, but he'll never make it out, not by himself. I watch in silence as he presses each panel in the wrong place. George isn't going home. Not tonight.

27

Matt

The living room feels cloaked in a haze, the fire casting shadows on the worn wallpaper. Steph's restless energy fills the air as she paces the floor. Everybody's unsettled, half worrying that Dorothy and Henry are insane, half wondering if they are being truthful about the killers' return. But wouldn't that mean they know more about the murders than they're letting on? Killers don't suddenly appear out of nowhere. Not unless they've been right under your nose all along.

I can't help but wonder if the answer to the mystery of The Loch House is staring us in the face. Henry can handle a gun and isn't afraid to use it, when the situation escalates. I can't believe he loaded it with bullets – all because Joey asked to leave. Why allow us in here in the first place if they were so scared? None of it makes any sense. But then they're living in a museum of memories – and they are far from good.

Bea's voice rises over my thoughts, her words laden with dire predictions. 'This isn't right. I can feel it in my bones. Joey's going to get lost in the belly of that snowstorm. His aura was all wrong when he left.'

Steph whimpers, her eyes swimming with guilt. Her hands have disappeared up the sleeves of her jumper. Her voice trembles as she says, 'Maybe . . . maybe this is my fault. I shouldn't have let him go. What if something awful happens to him?'

'Don't listen to her.' Bruce exhales a thin sigh. 'Bea, for God's sake, calm down. You're only making things worse.'

Bea regards Bruce coolly as she reaches into her sparkly bag and retrieves a cigarette. Bruce grumbles in protest, but Bea pays him no mind. With defiance, she lights it and takes a long drag, the smoke mingling with the smell of burning logs. This is unacceptable. I reach out, gently prying the cigarette from Bea's grip. In one fluid movement, I throw it into the nearby fireplace.

'Steph's pregnant, she shouldn't have to breathe in your second-hand smoke.'

'I really don't mind.' Steph delivers a watery smile. She looks longingly at the cigarette as it evaporates in the fire and I'm guessing that she's recently given up herself.

I clear my throat as Bea gives me a dirty look. 'Well, enough health and safety rules have been broken here tonight,' I say. 'We can't afford to start a fire. Things are bad enough as it is.'

'Oh, I don't know…' Undeterred, Bea fishes out a pink vape from her bag. 'The smoke might attract some attention.' She gives me a sly smile as she inhales its artificial vapor, locking it in her lungs. The glowing dot illuminates as she stands by the window, out of my reach. She exhales the vapour from the corner of her mouth and the smell of mangos fills the air. My patience wavers, concern for our well-being mingling with growing annoyance. I remind myself that this isn't easy on any of us, Bea included. I should be helping Nicola with her search, but I want to monitor the situation, because everything feels on a knife edge.

The storm is slowly abating, but giant snow drifts line the front of the guest house where our cars are parked. I can't see the winding road beyond it, or the loch on the other side. The world is dead outside. I find it odd that Sunita hasn't joined us, if only to see what all the noise was about. I imagine her alone in her room. She's probably just as scared as the rest of us, locking herself in to feel a little more secure. I rub my temple as the beginnings of a headache bloom. My hearing may have cleared, but I still feel the aftershock of the gunshot. I can't believe how close I came to death.

28

Nicola

Steph is mournful as she stares out of the living room window. Joey has long since disappeared into the snow-covered landscape. She looks lost, on her own as her husband leaves The Loch House behind.

'He'll be back before you know it,' I say, trying to offer comfort. Matt didn't let me search for long. He insisted that it wasn't safe for me to be roaming the corridors alone. He's gone to look for George on the condition that I stay with Steph. I agreed, to get him off my back, but I've every intention of asking her to search with me. Two sets of eyes are better than one and I need to find my son.

'And then there were five.' Bruce's morbid voice sends a chill to my bones.

I blink as my eyelids grow heavy. A wave of tiredness has overcome me, but there's no way I'm sleeping now.

Steph turns to face me, her eyes moist. 'He's right.' She is holding onto the thick velvet drape as if it's a cloak which offers protection. 'There's just five of us left. You, me, Matt, Bea and Bruce.'

I shake my head at Bruce before returning my attention to Steph, who is growing more panicked by the second. 'Oh, c'mon now. Joey will be back soon. Sunita's asleep in her room. George is probably exploring, and Dorothy hasn't got far.'

But Bruce seems intent on stirring things up. 'Really? Like Sunita wouldn't come running after hearing that shot? Something's going on here, Nicola. You're a police officer. You've thought it too. You don't need to sugar-coat things.'

'Bruce,' I say, 'we don't know anything at this point. And I don't think you should have any more to drink.'

He responds with a snort as he sips the whisky he has poured for himself. I thought that I knew what he was about, but now I'm not so sure. There's something off about him. A real police officer wouldn't try to frighten the other guests.

Steph releases the curtain and cradles her bump. Like me, she is consumed with worry for her child. Each passing second feels like an eternity, my worry mounting with every creak of the floorboards, or rattle of the pipes in the walls. This building has swallowed my son. He's in here, somewhere, but I'm running out of places to search. I cast an anxious glance towards the door, longing for Matt to return, hopefully holding George's hand.

'Will you help me look for George? Matt's got keys. He might find something.'

Steph comes to my side and delivers a smile. 'I thought you'd never ask. Sometimes our men treat us like we're invalids, don't they? I know they care but . . .' She sighs.

'I hear you,' I agree. 'If Matt had his way I'd be giving in my notice to the police.' The mention of my job reminds me that I've lost my way. This isn't me, standing here, waiting for someone else to save the day. What would my colleagues say if they could see me now? What I'd give to be able to speak to them. Liam would know exactly what to do. I've never felt safer than when I'm in his company. I push back all of my doubt, fear and concern and turn to Bea. She's sitting on the sofa, staring into the fire. 'Will you be OK, staying with Bruce and Henry while we have a look around?'

Bea appears to be in a dream world, which is hardly surprising, given why she's here. She snaps out of her thoughts and looks at us both. 'Sure. It's not as if I'm going anywhere. But get back soon. I don't want to be left on my own for long.' I could point out that she's not exactly on her own, but I know what she means. It's unsettling, how our numbers are going down. There's no love lost between her and Bruce and it seems she has her reservations about him too.

'We'll be back in a minute,' I reassure her. 'We're not going far.'

'Are you OK?' I look to Bruce, whose complexion is grey.

'Just light-headed,' he says. He's lost quite a bit of blood, but thanks to a well-stocked first-aid kit, I've managed to stem his wound for now. Henry is staring at the floor, his hands tied behind the dining room chair. His eyelids are half-closed and he's so still that I wonder if he's fallen asleep. His eye sockets are deep and shadowed, and his skin has taken on a grey hue. It makes me uncomfortable, keeping him here like this, but we haven't got much choice. I didn't sign up for this when I came for my break-up holiday with Matt. Because that's what it would have been had things not taken such a crazy turn. If Matt hadn't insisted on dragging me here . . . I hate the train of thought. The first step in self-improvement is being responsible for my own actions. Blaming the world for your problems gets you nowhere.

'C'mon,' I say to Steph. But we've only taken two steps before Matt calls my name. His voice is urgent, and my heart jolts in my chest as I pick up pace. He's found something.

29

Nicola

We follow the sound of Matt's voice, his words cutting through the stillness of the hallway. A desperate hope rises within me as I make my way down the hall for the hundredth time. I yearn for a glimpse of my missing boy, but instead I'm faced with Matt standing in the doorway of a room at the end of the corridor. 'George?' I call out, unable to see my son. I swallow down the lump in my throat as I see that he's not there. Instead, I'm met with a pungent smell of something herby hanging heavy in the air. The place is filled with religious artefacts, pictures and crosses of every kind. The skin on my arms prickles as a layer of goosebumps break free. This was locked the last time I tried it, and now I can see why.

'Stinks in here,' Matt remarks, his voice laced with unease. It's clear that he's out of his comfort zone too. I follow his gaze to the peculiar objects filling the dank space. There must be dozens of reed crosses hanging from the cobwebbed ceiling. Each one twists slowly in the draught as I breathe in the overpowering scent of herbs lingering in the air. I peer closer, taking in the sight of dozens of small stick figures eerily suspended from the ceiling.

'It's just incense,' Steph says softly as she remarks on the smell. Her hand gently touches the crosses with a reverence that hints at a deeper meaning. It is as if they have special importance to her. 'They're St Brigid's crosses. They keep out evil.' She smiles as she catches my expression of curiosity. 'They're bringing back memories . . . I went to an all-girls Catholic school.'

I've heard of St Brigid's crosses. I think they're Irish, as the name suggests. I wonder if Henry originates from there. Even if he did have an accent, it wouldn't be evident now.

'What about the stick figures?' I ask, at a loss as I try to make sense of this strange room.

Steph simply shrugs. 'You've lost me there.'

'Well, I think they're creepy,' Matt looks apprehensive, his hands on his hips as his gaze sweeps the room. He's dishevelled since the incident, his hair messy, the tail of his shirt rumpled and hanging out.

This room feels and smells like a funeral home. The worn brown carpet has seen better days, and . . . are there nails driven into the shuttered windows keeping them tightly closed? Is that to keep people from getting in or getting out? I don't know which prospect frightens me more. Some windows in the guest house have curtains, others have blinds and some, shutters. Everything is mismatched. But they're all similar in one way – the windows are all nailed tightly shut. As far as décor goes, no two rooms in this place are alike. There's a continuing theme of royal portraits and hand carved mahogany ceiling coving, but that's as far as it goes. The carpets are mismatched, and in some rooms the floors have creaky and scratched floorboards. The walls are damp and dirty, and I doubt the place has had a lick of paint in decades.

As for this room . . . Matt is right. It *does* stink. This is more than incense. I cast an eye over a wood wormed dresser to see a smudging stick in a bowl. I only know what it is from watching too many episodes of *Most Haunted* back in the day. Yet another tool to keep out evil spirits. My steps falter as I navigate the religious imagery adorning the walls, the weight of Christian history bearing down on me. My pulse speeds up as I'm overcome with a sudden need to escape this claustrophobic space. I stumble over a hefty velvet cushion on the floor. My gaze is drawn upwards to a haunting depiction of a bloodied Jesus on a cross. This is a place of prayer, a sanctuary steeped in secrets, and I can't shake the feeling that it is Henry who kneels upon this cushion, his bony hands clutched in prayer, his soundless whispers lost in desperate pleas.

'Are you alright?' Matt asks, for the hundredth time tonight. I nod, too tired to speak.

As we venture deeper into the room, my sense of unease grows. Dusty mahogany shelves line one wall, heavily burdened by books. I see hardbacks on Christianity, with tomes about the occult, magic and demonology jostling for space alongside the sacred texts. I scan the spines of the books as I try to make out the titles, but many are written in languages I don't recognise.

A thin wind sweeps through the room, causing the reed crosses to sway and bump against the stick figures. What do they represent? I recall the tatty bogle on the outskirts of the guest house. The hairs stiffen on my arms as a hollow rattling fills the space. I can't help but feel that we're not alone.

'George?' I call, checking each corner of the oppressive room. I press my ear against the wall, looking for any hint of his presence. Silence. I kneel, placing my ear against the dusty carpeted floor, wrinkling my nose at the smell.

He's here, somewhere in this house. I can feel his presence.

I continue to explore, my footsteps cautious. Steph is leafing through the books while Matt roots in the drawers of a small mahogany cupboard.

'Have you found anything?' I ask. The furniture could hold a clue, a tiny breadcrumb that will lead us closer to my missing child. The shake of Matt's head quells my hope.

'No, nothing here,' he replies sombrely, pressing the heel of his palm to his back as he straightens. 'We can try the loft next.' This scares me, not because we can't reach such a high ceiling, but because it's the last place that we haven't searched. What if he's not there? What if George and Dorothy have done something terrible to him and my baby boy is buried in the snow? He'll always be my baby. And life isn't worth living without my son.

My stomach rolls over as nausea takes hold. I follow Matt out, throwing one last glance into the room before the door creaks shut.

Mystery on the Mic Podcast

The Watts Case Series: Episode 7

Alex: Welcome back to 'Mystery on the Mic', everyone. I'm your host, Alex. Today, we're diving headfirst into a chilling, and quite baffling case. It took place on the picturesque Isle of Skye, in an old, lonely establishment known as The Loch House guest house. Ten years have passed since the owner and all the guests of this house were discovered dead under murky circumstances. And while the case itself is frightening, the real intrigue lies in the man who supposedly led the investigation. Joining me today to shed light on this complex tale is our true crime historian, Sarah. Hello, Sarah.

Sarah: Hi, Alex. It's great to be back, even if the story we're exploring today is anything but cheery.

Alex: Absolutely, Sarah. So, we promised our listeners something juicy this week and there's been lots of talk on social media about a little publicised incident involving a man who became obsessed with the case. Now we know what it means to be obsessed by true crime (chuckles) but while we enjoy going down the old rabbit hole, none of us have gone as far as impersonating a police officer to find out more.

Sarah: Let's hope not, although I did dress up as a WPC on a hen night one weekend.

Alex: What you do in your spare time is your business, Sarah. That sounds like a story for another day!

Sarah: Hmm, I'm not sure it's for public consumption. Let's talk about what we've found instead.

Alex: Ha! Good swerve. Let's begin with this unusual character, Bruce Hawthorn. Could you tell our listeners a bit about him?

Sarah: Happy to. Bruce was . . . well, eccentric, to put it mildly. He was a loner, residing on the Isle of Skye. His interest in police work and solving crimes was something that I found fascinating. He became known for his intricate knowledge of policing methods and procedures, as well as an uncanny ability to play the part of a police officer convincingly.

Alex: But he was not a law enforcement official himself, correct?

Sarah: That's correct, Alex. Bruce was an imposter. He went to great lengths to make a fake warrant card then impersonated an officer, going from house to house, interviewing locals about The Loch House case. His obsession was . . . unsettling, to say the least.

Alex: And this wasn't just some harmless hobby. Impersonating an officer is a criminal offence. But Bruce's obsession went beyond role play. His in-depth involvement in The Loch House case seems downright suspicious.

Sarah: You've hit the nail on the head, Alex. Bruce's actions were undeniably strange. When the deaths at The Loch House occurred, he seemed to latch onto the case with a disturbing enthusiasm, even camping out in a tent in freezing temperatures nearby when he couldn't gain access to the property. He took it upon himself to lead his own investigation, conducting detailed interviews and gathering evidence. He even recreated a miniature model of The Loch House, pinning photos, maps and notes to a giant corkboard in his living room.

Alex: It's strange to think about, isn't it? You have this guy, with no official authority, going around, questioning people, gathering evidence. And doing it so well, that he fooled the locals into thinking he was the real deal. But he lived on the Isle of Skye? Didn't they know who he was?

Sarah: That's a good point, it's a small island, but no, they didn't. He was a total loner, lived with his mum who apparently did everything for him. Then she died and he focused all his attention on the case. Maybe it was a coping mechanism. He'd tried to join the police when he was young, but rumour has it that he didn't get past the initial stages due to issues with his mental health. But locals said he was very convincing, saying that they believed him when he said he was a police officer who happened to live on the island when the murders occurred.

Alex: And who could blame them? I mean, why would he lie?

Sarah: That's the big question. It was his attention to detail that was perhaps the most frightening aspect of his charade. He knew police protocol intimately, he had a solid grasp of the terminology, and he even carried a warrant card and shoulder harness with various other police paraphernalia he had somehow sourced. Bruce Hawthorn was a convincing actor and he prepared well for the part.

Alex: It's uncanny. Chilling, even. But eventually, the truth about Bruce was discovered, correct?

Sarah: Yes, it was. It took some time, but in the end the actual police realised what was going on. They checked with outside forces to confirm that there was no Bruce Hawthorn working the case. The man who had been investigating The Loch House case, who had been speaking with locals and collecting evidence, was an imposter.

Alex: What an unbelievable revelation! So, what happened to Bruce?

Sarah: It was all very low key, hence why it wasn't reported to the media. I imagine it was embarrassing to the police force involved. Naturally, Bruce was arrested. As we said, impersonating an officer is a serious crime, and he was tried and sentenced. He received an eighteen month suspended sentence due to his remorse and impeccable record. Apparently, he came across as quite convincing in court, but from what I've heard about Bruce, this is where he excels – being able to convincingly role play.

Alex: They say that murderers often return to the scene of the crime. It's not unusual for them to want to relive it repeatedly. Did police think this was the case with Bruce?

Sarah: It seems so. He was interviewed at length and police even extended his time in custody beyond the normal twenty-four hours, so they must have had justification to get the necessary permissions. But from what I've found out, the CPS didn't believe the case was strong enough to go to trial. A fascination with murder is not against the law – thankfully! So, despite his conviction, there was no concrete evidence linking him to the deaths at The Loch House. His obsession, as alarming as it was, seemed just that – an obsession – to replace the hole in his life after his mother died. Some people in the community still believed he was using the investigation as a cover, and that he may have been involved in the murders, but without solid proof, the truth remains elusive.

Alex: And what's your opinion about his obsession with the case? Was it just the thrill of playing cop, or was there something more?

Sarah: It's hard to say. There's no denying Bruce's fixation was excessive. He was a bit of a strange one too. Before his mother died, he spent his spare time making tatty bogles, those weird Scottish scarecrows, which he'd put up in various parts of the island. Again, it's not against the law but I've seen pictures of these things and they're disconcerting to say the least. Makes you wonder what went on in his head.

Alex: But he seemed normal enough when dealing with locals? I guess he'd have had to, to pass himself off as police.

Sarah: Oh yeah, he was very convincing, authoritative, well spoken and well dressed. Even charismatic. It's surprising, given how much of a recluse he was, although some say he took his cues from the countless hours of police dramas that he watched on TV. He also spent hours poring over the home-made case files he'd created and going over witness statements he'd recorded from locals, although they hadn't actually seen anything of value as The Loch House was so remote. He also took hundreds of photographs and pinned them to a board in his living room. It was as though he was living and breathing The Loch House case. Even after his arrest, Bruce seemed unable to let the case go. He continued to declare that he was on the brink of a breakthrough, and that he was close to solving the mystery.

Alex: Sounds like he was protesting a little too much. It's equal parts fascinating and disturbing if you ask me. A mystery that remains unresolved, shrouded in questions and haunted by an obsession. And at the centre of it all, a man whose dedication to a case crossed the line into the realm of the bizarre.

Sarah: That's right. The story of The Loch House remains one of the most intriguing cases in the annals of Scottish true crime. But it's also one of the least publicised cases I've come across. It's like the police want to bury it because it's such an embarrassment to them. It's certainly a stark reminder that sometimes the pursuit of truth can lead to a darker path than one might anticipate.

Alex: Absolutely, Sarah. A truly bizarre tale. Makes you wonder where Bruce is now.

Sarah: It's said he left the island after he was arrested and rented a flat on the mainland. But surely someone that obsessed would have a hard time letting it go.

Alex: Indeed. And if our listeners know anything more about Bruce Hawthorn, or if he's listening to this podcast, we'd love to hear his side of the story.

   Thank you for sharing this chilling case with us. And to our listeners, stay tuned for more unsolved mysteries and true crime history here on 'Mystery on the Mic'. Remember: the strangest stories are often true.

30

Elita

It took me some time to calm George down, but honestly, he's become a lifeline in the little time that he's been here. But now the little guy is staring at me with his big, curious eyes.

'When can I go home?'

'In the morning,' I tell him, making room next to me on my bed. 'Get some shut-eye.' I pull the quilt over his shoulders, savouring the moment of having my first friend over. I'm not a great liar but I've never had a sleepover before, and this might be my one shot. Tomorrow I'll have to decide. Do I hang onto him and keep him safe here with me, or let him go and risk his life? These decisions feel too grown-up for me. I know, right, I'm a teenager now. But aren't life experiences meant to shape you as a person and teach you how to grow? I haven't had many of them so I can't always figure things out. I muster my best smile and tell George everything's going to be OK.

Doubt crosses his face, and his breath smells chocolate sweet as he speaks.

'But I want to go back now.'

His words hit me hard, but I keep my best smile fixed on my face.

'In the morning. Don't worry, George. Granny has told your mum that you're having a sleepover. It's after midnight. Everyone's asleep. Now get some z's. You can go home tomorrow, back to your regular life.' Granny once said that I speak with too many Americanisms, but what does she expect when all I have to watch are old reruns of *The Simpsons* on TV.

I feel a mixture of relief and guilt as George accepts my lie. He nestles into the pillow beside me, all warm and cosy. I get why he wants to leave, and no number of treats can make up for it. There is no night or day in this room. No sun, no rain. Just stale air. It sucks big time, and it hits me just how much I want to leave too.

George yawns and soon he's softly snoring next to me. I know he needs to be back with his mum but I can't bear the thought of losing my only friend. Tears threaten to spill over because I'm doing to George what was done to me – keeping him a prisoner here and away from his normal life. This isn't some soap opera on TV. The outside world is scary and messy but I'm still jealous of his life. He has a mum, for a start.

As I put my hands to my eyes to stop the tears, the panel swings open and Granny quietly creeps in. I'm used to her coming and going whenever she wants. She looks tired, her clothes are dusty, her hair all tangled. I don't know why she wears wigs when her own hair isn't all that bad. Not like me. I don't like the sight of my scalp without my blonde wig. The first time Granny bought it for me, I was so happy, I cried. Mum always taught me to accept who I was, but with her thick wavy hair and pretty face, that was easy for her to say. Granny sweeps a hand over her head to tidy herself up. The corridors which lead to this room are basically like spider central, covered with webs and dust. Grandad's too big to fit through easily, which is why his suits are always covered in dirt. As she comes close, Granny puts a finger to her lips, telling me to stay quiet because we need to chat first. I have broken a big rule by having a friend in my room. Her face shows her disappointment, which makes me feel ashamed. Quietly, I scoot off the end of the bed without waking George and follow her to the chair where I sit, hardly able to look at her. She shakes her head as she whispers. 'Honestly, Elita, what were you thinking, bringing him here?'

I'm trembling, not because I know I'm in trouble, but because I can't bear to let George go. 'I didn't. He found me. One of the panels must have come loose.' I let out a sigh because lying isn't my thing. 'OK, he followed me. But I didn't know about it until he got here.'

Granny quietly tuts. 'What have I told you about being out of your room when there are guests in the house? You know it's against the rules.'

'But, Granny, I just wanted to . . .'

'To what? Sneak into their rooms? Touch their things? I'm not stupid, Elita. I know what you've been up to when they're in the dining room.' She opens the drawers of my desk, revealing a treasure trove of things – snatched magazines, receipts, soaps, nail polish, whatever catches my eye. A discarded bus ticket is a gateway to another world. Food receipts can be stories in themselves. I imagine what the food tasted like, daydream about trying it myself one day. When you live in a black and white world, your imagination is like a getaway. But now I have the best prize of all, a real-life person – and Granny wants to take him away.

'Please,' I say in a quiet voice, so quiet that she has to lean in. 'Please don't take him.' My voice wavers with desperation as I grab her hand. Her skin is cold and her hand feels bony, which reminds me that my time with her won't last forever. 'George gets me. He's all I've got.'

Granny squeezes my hand back, her touch grounding me. 'I know, Elita. But we can't keep him here forever, now, can we? He's not like you. He'll grow up. One day, he'll be a big hairy man! Can you imagine that?' She chuckles, but her face falls when she sees that I'm not joining in. 'When the guests have gone, we'll find a way of getting you out of here. We'll travel. I'll bring you to London. You'll love it there. Trust me.'

'But how?' I say, because I'm different. 'People will stare. And what about the bad people? What if they come back?'

'Don't you see?' Granny whispers. 'If we don't get George back to his mummy, the bad people will kill us all. It's bad enough that they've taken Grandad's gun. How can he defend us if he's tied up in a chair?'

'Dorothy?' George murmurs, sitting up. He sounds so relieved to see her that it tugs at my heart. I want to ask her about the bad people, because I don't understand. Why would they come back here after all these years? What would they want with me?

'Hello, George.' She greets him with a smile but I know that she's still not thrilled about me keeping him here. 'How did you get here?'

He swings his legs off the bed, yawning. 'I snuck in. Can I see Mummy now?'

'In a bit,' she replies.

I struggle to hold back my tears. My heart is heavy, knowing I'm losing the only friend I've ever had. He looks so cute as he rubs his eyes, his dimples on show.

'Are you good at keeping secrets?' Granny asks, and I bite my bottom lip as everything hinges on his answer. But he nods, and I exhale in relief. There's nothing Grandad wouldn't do to keep me safe. I hate to say it but it's a part of him that frightens me sometimes. I know my grandparents aren't what you'd call normal. I've learned this from memories of my mum and watching programmes about families on TV. But Granny and Grandad are the only family that I have. I'm also not what you'd call conventional. I've never seen anyone like me. Kids grow up, change physically. I still fit in the same clothes that I did when I was six. Even then, I was tiny for my age. I'm not stunted. I'm special. But I wish that I was like everybody else.

I don't understand why I have to hide away. Grandad prays a lot. He says that God speaks to him, but I think it's just voices in his head. I've seen the crosses that he hangs in his prayer room, and the special stick dolls he's made which represent each of us. There's another stick doll in a box wrapped in muslin cloth. It's named after my mother. He says she's in a special place. It hurts my heart to think about her, and the other stick figures which represent the guests that died in this house. He's making more, one for everyone here tonight. There's a small one for George. I hope that my new buddy will be OK.

Granny has finished her lecture on secrets, and the importance of keeping our 'special hiding place' safe. George is ready to leave now. He knows what he has to do. Everything hinges on how he'll act when he leaves this place. I can't bring myself to say goodbye. I'm going to go to bed where I can pull my blanket over my head and block out the rest of the world. Sometimes I feel like a mole, living in the dark, only coming out when it's safe. I have my monitors but I don't want to see what happens tonight, not to him . . . He rushes forward to hug me one last time.

'Bye bye, Elita,' he mutters into my wispy blonde hair.

Reluctantly, I let him go. It feels like part of me is being torn away, leaving just emptiness inside.

Granny wraps her arms around me in a gentle hug. 'It's late. Get some sleep,' she whispers. 'Soon, it will all be over, and we'll get you out of here. We'll move away. Maybe we could go abroad – somewhere sunny, where you can be yourself.' I cling on to her promise before the inevitable warning comes. 'Just don't leave now, whatever happens. Not until I say it's OK.' I nod as she breaks away. George gives me a little wave before they disappear into the panel from which he came.

The room falls into a heavy silence, shadows dancing upon the walls. George's footsteps fade away. Solitary confinement looms ahead of me, and I hang on to the hope that someday, I won't have to be alone anymore.

Mystery on the Mic Podcast

The Watts Case Series: Episode 8

Alex: Hey, mystery enthusiasts! Welcome back to another intriguing episode of 'Mystery on the Mic'. I'm Alex, your host, and joining me today is the indomitable true crime historian, Sarah. How's it going, Sarah?

Sarah: Hey, Alex! Ready to dive deep into the enigma of the Watts family and their eerie mansion?

Alex: Absolutely, Sarah. Today's story is like something out of a psychological thriller. So, picture this, folks: Ronnie Watts' magnificent fourteen-bedroom mansion is up for sale for a jaw-dropping £9.5 million. This Grade II listed beauty is sitting pretty in the serene Surrey countryside, surrounded by three lush acres.

Sarah: But here's the twist, listeners. Ever since Ronnie and his new wife Heather passed away under very mysterious circumstances, there's been this eerie vibe around the place. And it's not just the high price tag that has potential buyers thinking twice.

Alex: You've got that right, Sarah. The house itself is like a millionaire's dream. We're talking open-plan lounges, a fancy glass dining room, Italian designer kitchens, eight swanky bathrooms and even an indoor pool, complete with a sauna and state of the art gym!

Sarah: It's got all the bells and whistles, but there's history here too, Alex, and that's where things start to get . . . strange.

Alex: Yeah, apparently the neighbours are spooked. They say Caleb, Ronnie's son, has these constant visitors, all dressed like they stepped out of the same weird fashion catalogue. They roam around in groups, trying to recruit people, and some folks are downright scared to leave their homes!

Sarah: One neighbour even mentioned they knocked on their door, demanding that they repent! It seems to be some kind of cult.

Alex: And here's the real head-scratcher: there are lots of reported missing people showing up at the mansion. Concerned parents are frantically searching for their sons and daughters who've fallen into this 'fellowship' thing.

Sarah: One parent told reporters that their daughter dropped out of university because of these 'spiritual warriors' and cut off all contact with her family on their advice. It's heart-wrenching, really. It was only down to the sheer doggedness of her mother that she managed to get her back.

Alex: Yes, and now the mansion's up for sale, and the estate agent says it's because Caleb and Ronan want a fresh start. But let's be real, Caleb's been spotted in white robes, and his 'fellowship' has raised more than a few eyebrows. They're probably moving because too many angry parents are turning up at their door.

Sarah: The sale isn't just about bricks and mortar. It's a big deal, and demonstrates how much the Watts family legacy has changed. This mansion, once a symbol of wealth and success, now carries the weight of a troubled family's history.

Alex: And the big question is, who'll buy it? Will it get a fresh start, or will it forever echo with the tragedy of Ronnie and Heather Watts?

Sarah: That's the question, Alex. And speaking of money, let's not forget the Watts family fortune. Ronnie Watts left quite the legacy, and his sons, Caleb and Ronan, are set to inherit a considerable sum. It's known that Heather, Ronnie's young wife, was giving some hefty donations to charity before she mysteriously died. Makes you wonder, doesn't it?

Alex: Indeed. It's a classic case of wealth and privilege, but it's also a story of a family torn apart by tragedy and, dare I say, madness.

Sarah: It's fascinating, isn't it? The psychology behind families like the Watts is like peeling back the layers of an onion. There's always more to uncover.

Alex: Absolutely. You know, in the world of true crime, we often find these elements of wealth and privilege intertwined with darkness. The Watts mansion is a physical representation of that paradox.

Sarah: It's not uncommon. Many wealthy families have skeletons in their closets, secrets they try to bury beneath their opulent lifestyles. But these secrets have a way of resurfacing, as we've seen with the Watts family.

Alex: And speaking of secrets, let's dive a bit deeper into the psychology of the Watts family. Ronnie Watts' career was the stuff of legend in the music industry, but it came at a price. He immersed himself in his work, neglecting his sons, Caleb and Ronan.

Sarah: That's right. Loss, neglect and the relentless pursuit of fame all played a role in shaping the lives of these two young men. Caleb himself shared that there were endless parties and a lack of love in his early years.

Alex: And when his mother died, he wasn't even allowed to grieve. Instead, he buried his emotions. But as we know, emotions have a way of resurfacing, often in destructive ways.

Sarah: Absolutely. And that's when we see the rebellious phase, the alcohol, the drugs. Caleb said he managed to straighten himself out for a while, but those demons were always lurking.

Alex: It's a pattern we've seen in many true crime stories, isn't it? The struggle to cope with pain and trauma often leads to substance abuse and self-destructive behaviour.

Sarah: Yes, it's a coping mechanism, albeit a destructive one. But now Caleb's found his personal path to redemption through religion, an extreme one at that.

Alex: That's right, and if I'm honest, the wider implications concern me. He's immersed himself in spirituality, describing his deep connection to Christ. Music has now become a means of self-reflection and healing. It wouldn't be too bad if it only involved him. But his devotees grow daily, and they're . . . how do you say . . . forceful in their opinions. Makes you wonder how far they'd go to get their own way.

Sarah: Good or bad, it's been a powerful transformation. He's transitioned from what he calls a 'sinner' to a 'saint'. And he's found a community of like-minded individuals who provide him with unwavering support and love.

Alex: But, of course, there are sceptics. Some wonder about the influence of this new-found fellowship on Caleb's already complex psyche. I don't mean to sound morose, but I have a bad feeling about this.

Sarah: You have every right to. Let's face it, some of these cults don't end well. And that's the thing about true crime. It's not just about the crime itself; it's about the people, the psychology, the human element. It's about understanding what drives individuals to make the choices they do.

Alex: Absolutely, Sarah. The mansion's sale signifies the end of an era, but what lies ahead for Caleb and Ronan? The legacy of Ronnie and Heather Watts' unsolved deaths still remains.

Sarah: Only time will reveal the fate that awaits this iconic estate, as it seeks a buyer who will surely have to embrace both its grandeur and its haunting history.

Alex: Poetically said, Sarah. And as always, folks, stay curious, we'll be back after this sponsored break for more mysteries on the mic!

Sarah: Stay curious, indeed!

31

Nicola

It's 1 a.m. and I'm beyond the point of tiredness. I'm running on adrenaline since finding that creepy prayer room. What was the idea of all those crosses and stick figures hanging from the ceiling? No wonder he keeps the room locked.

There's no sign of Dorothy and if I'm honest, I don't really care. I don't have the energy for her right now. Being apart from my son is tearing me up. I've searched every inch of this house. I've even been up in the loft. So why do I feel like I've left something out? I need to keep busy. Matt mentions making some rounds of toast when I hear noises coming from the hall. My heart skips a beat in my chest. Is that . . . I'm not imagining the sound of George's low chatter, am I? Matt is standing by the window next to Steph, and immediately our eyes lock.

'Mummy!' George calls, as Dorothy escorts him into the living room. She looks directly at me, her blue eyes sparking with what appears to be defiance as she tilts her chin upwards. 'I found him in the linen basket,' she says. 'In the laundry room.'

My knees weaken with relief. I vaguely hear Matt muttering that he already checked there, but I'm so happy to see George that I don't care. He looks tired but no worse for wear as he runs towards me. 'George!' I call, wrapping my arms around him and lifting him up off the floor. 'Oh my word, where have you been? Are you alright?' My chest burns with love for my child as I squeeze him tight. He's still clutching his iPad, his headphones around his neck.

'I'm OK, Mummy,' he says, squirming beneath my grip. I set George back on his feet. I'm babbling now, smoothing over his hair. I tell him how scared I was as I check him up and down. Matt is by my side.

'Glad you're back, kiddo. You gave us quite the fright.'

George looks up at us both, his dimples pressed into his cheeks as he gives us a hesitant smile. 'I was hiding, but then I fell asleep. Sorry, Mummy.' I catch sight of what looks like the remnants of chocolate on his face.

'You frightened the life out of me,' I sniffle once more, wiping away a tear. 'I'm never letting you out of my sight again.'

Matt glares at Dorothy. 'What's really going on here? I rummaged through all of those baskets, calling George's name.'

Dorothy remains silent. Now isn't the time for questions. I'm overwhelmed by a mix of emotions as Matt turns to my son. 'Don't you go missing again, George, you hear?'

Bea has gone to bed. Bruce is somewhat subdued since his brush with death. His bandaged arm has stopped bleeding at last. Dried blood is caked on his trousers, and although he's washed his face, there are still specks in his grey hair. Weary, he gets up from the sofa, limping slightly as Henry watches on.

'Didn't you hear us calling, young man?' Bruce reaches out his hand, gently resting it on George's shoulder as I stand. 'George, where were you really? Did you see or talk to anyone while you were gone?'

I don't like his tone, but these questions do need to be asked and perhaps it's better not coming from me. George clings to my waist, his eyes shifting nervously. He shakes his head slowly, his voice barely audible. 'N-no, I didn't see anyone. Dorothy found me. She woke me up.' He looks at the woman, as if seeking her approval, and I see an almost imperceptible nod of the head.

Steph is smiling, no doubt because George's presence has given her hope. Nothing bad has happened to him while he was away. If only Joey had waited a bit longer before disappearing off into the snow. Matt is convinced Joey is a young man trying to prove his masculinity, and I've seen the way he acts around Steph. I just hope that he's OK.

I sense George's discomfort and pick him up for the second time. He's getting a bit old for such mollycoddling but I have good reason tonight. It's way past his bedtime, and he looks utterly exhausted. 'Alright, little man,' I murmur gently, flooded with relief as I hold him tight. 'Let's get you to bed.'

Matt seems like he's about to join us when Dorothy grabs his arm. 'I want a word with you,' she says to him. 'I've brought your son back, so now you can let Henry go. You know he's not a well man. It's inhumane, that's what it is.'

She has a point. I look at Matt. 'You stay,' I say, knowing he can deal with this. 'I'll put George to bed.' I start moving towards the stairs with George, heavy and tired, on my hip.

'Wait . . .' Matt calls after me, but Steph interrupts, offering to go with me instead. Matt looks mildly aggrieved but she means well, and we did promise Joey that we'd keep an eye on her.

'Alright.' He turns back to Dorothy. 'This wasn't a quid pro quo situation, you know. We tied up Henry because he pulled a gun on us.'

'Oh please,' Dorothy snaps. 'Must we keep going around in circles? He was trying to protect you. You've got what you wanted and invaded our privacy in the process. Henry's a cancer survivor. He should be resting. He's already skipped his medication because of you lot.'

'Well, I suppose,' Matt begins, but as I glance over my shoulder I see Bruce standing in his way. I wait. I don't want any more trouble. I just want to take my son to bed. George's head is on my shoulder as he grows drowsy in my embrace.

'Are you sure this is wise?' I hear Bruce say. 'The man's off his head.'

'I know.' Matt lowers his voice, as Dorothy goes to her husband. 'But look at him. What if he dies on our watch? We could be done for manslaughter.'

'As long as he doesn't produce any more guns,' Bruce warns.

Dorothy has already untied him. She mumbles words that only he can hear. I watch as he delivers a slow nod and I hope we're all doing the right thing. Henry may appear frail but after what I saw in his prayer room, I'm not sure that I trust him. Perhaps he's devoted to his faith, but he's also unpredictable and that makes him dangerous. He's on his feet again now, rubbing his wrists as he delivers an angry sideways glance. Matt sighs as he sits on the sofa. It's safer if he keeps an eye on things here.

'C'mon, sweetie.' I smooth my son's hair. 'Let's get you to bed.' Steph follows me out into the hall and I glance over at the front door as we head up. I'll be counting down the minutes until we leave this godforsaken place.

32

Nicola

I'm still riding the high of having my son back in my arms. My emotions are all over the place, and I never want to let him go. The tightness in my chest is finally easing. As parents, we take our children for granted. We imagine their futures and map everything out. Losing George felt like being on the edge of a high cliff – one I would have stepped off, had I not found him again. The love I feel for my child is all encompassing. I could never survive his loss.

I appreciate Steph's offer to keep me company because despite George being safely returned, I still feel uneasy in this place. Together, we enter my bedroom, the air heavy with the weight of the night's events. As Steph scopes the rooms, I gently tuck George into our double bed. He squirms as I fuss over him, giggling as I kiss his pink cheeks. He's not sleeping on his own tonight. I'm satisfied that he's unharmed. We can talk about what happened tomorrow after he's got some sleep.

'Nothing in the wardrobes, no bogey man under the beds.' Steph is only half joking as she settles on one side of the mattress. Our eyes meet, conveying a silent understanding. Together we'll watch over George until her husband Joey returns. Matt stresses me out with his constant fussing, and I prefer some female company tonight.

I glance around the room that was meant to be a sanctuary. The bedside lamp offers weak light. Outside, the storm is relentless as it seems to find a second breath. The wind is battering the windows so hard that it feels like the glass is going to break. I can't shake the nagging feeling that our troubles are far from over. At least here, in the bedroom, we're able to lock the door. Every creak and groan of this old building amplifies my unease, magnifying the weight of my worries.

'Can't forget Ted,' I say, getting off the bed to get George his teddy from his adjoining room. I'm searching under his pillow when I hear Steph's voice.

'George,' she whispers. 'Where were you tonight?'

Why is she asking him that?

George sleepily mumbles something about hiding in the laundry basket. I'm not sure if what he's saying is true, but he's had a hell of a long day and I can ask him about it tomorrow after he's had a chance to rest. Perhaps Steph is just nervous because Joey hasn't returned, but to be fair, he's not been gone that long.

I linger at the door, listening in to Steph's voice. 'Sometimes, we tell fibs to protect people,' she says, the hint of a challenge in her voice. 'Dorothy told you to lie, didn't she? It's OK. Joey has gone to get the police because Dorothy and Henry are bad people. They might act like they're good, but they're not. They shouldn't make you tell fibs.'

There is no answer from my son as she presses on. 'George? Do you hear me? Don't fall asleep just yet. The police will want to know where you were, so no other little boy or girl has to be scared again.'

I've had enough of this, and I walk in just as she is giving his shoulder a little shake.

'What do you think you're doing?'

She looks up at me, her face flushed with guilt. I slide George's teddy under his arm. 'There you go, sweetheart.' I cover him up with the duvet and kiss his forehead. 'Go back to sleep, everything is fine. The door is locked and you're safe. We can talk about it tomorrow.'

He presses his face into the teddy and keeps his eyes shut.

I signal at Steph, and she follows me to his bedroom where we won't be heard.

'Sorry,' she whispers, before I say another word. 'I was just trying to find out what was going on.'

'That's *my* job, not yours.' My jaw is set firm. 'You were frightening him.'

Steph looks like she's about to cry as she becomes overwhelmed with emotion. 'That's the last thing I want. He's such a sweet little boy. But, Nicola, why aren't you thinking like a police officer? Surely you can see something's not right. Don't you think it's strange how Dorothy knew exactly where George was? As for Henry . . .' Steph shakes her head. 'Have you forgotten that he pulled a gun? And what were those stick people all about? They're clearly not right in the head. What else have they got up their sleeves? And why are they so scared about what's outside? What if there are evil people coming here to hurt us?' She's speaking faster now, each question tripping over the one before.

'Steph, it's OK. Take a breath. Everything's going to be alright. We're in Scotland, in the middle of nowhere. Nobody's going to hurt us here.' But thoughts race around my head because I know she's more worried about the danger beneath this roof. I can still feel the presence of violence as it lingers in the air. Steph has a point. I've been so consumed with worry for George that I'm not thinking like a police officer – I'm thinking like a mum.

She whispers conspiratorially. 'There are secret rooms in this place, and God knows what else. What if there are other kids hidden away, like George was? Or worse, dead bodies under the floorboards?'

'Steph, you need to calm down,' I advise, as she stares at me, wide-eyed. 'Things always seem worse in the dead of night. We're free to go as soon as the snow clears. Dorothy and Henry may have some mental health issues, or maybe they're just scared, like us. Yes, the gun was dangerous, but I've seen his licence and he wouldn't have been given it if the police had any concerns.'

I watch her face closely to see if she's paying attention. 'He'll lose it now, mind,' I continue. 'Now he's been waving it about. The police will take it and he'll be charged with God knows how many offences for what they've done tonight. But their daughter was murdered under this roof. The anniversary of her death probably triggered something in them both.'

Steph appears unconvinced. Her breathing is shallow and rapid as she drives her point home. 'The night her daughter died was just like this one. Bruce said they were all snowed in. Can't you see? What if *they* were responsible for her death?'

I don't want to comprehend that thought. 'I'm no psychologist, but I've dealt with mental health issues plenty of times in the police. Dorothy and Henry . . . They're clearly not well. But I don't think either of them are capable of that. I won't let you frighten George. He's just a little boy with a vivid imagination who likes to explore.'

Steph blinks twice as she takes a breath. 'He didn't seem scared to you?'

'No, not at all.' I recall how he looked tired but happy holding Dorothy's hand. I rely on my instinct a lot when it comes to George. After his dad was sent to prison, it was just the two of us. And when he got out . . . I lived on my wits for months. I give Steph a reassuring smile. 'Everything will seem better in the morning.' My gaze falls on her bump. 'Your bump is so cute, any kicks today?' I reach out my hand to touch her belly, but she covers it with her hands and turns away. Silly me. I loved every minute of my pregnancy, but not everyone wants a stranger touching their skin.

'Sorry,' I give an awkward smile. 'I didn't mean to make you uncomfortable. I forget what it's like sometimes.'

Steph waves my apology away. 'That's OK. I get the ick when other people touch my belly, I don't know why.'

It explains why I've never seen Joey rest a hand on her bump. I swiftly change the subject. 'Why don't you get your head down for an hour? All this stress . . . it's not good for you or the baby. Matt will wake you when Joey comes.'

But Steph shakes her head. 'I couldn't sleep now, not while Joey is gone.' She wanders to the doorway and watches George, who is fast asleep in the other room. 'And I'm sorry about earlier with George. I didn't mean to interrogate him. My hormones have been all over the place this week.'

'Don't be so hard on yourself. I know what it's like.'

Steph settles herself back next to George on the bed and fixes a pillow as she makes herself comfortable. 'I can watch him, if you'd like to grab a cuppa with Matt?'

But the thought of George being locked into a room with anyone but me fills me with unease. 'That's OK,' I shift my weight, grateful for the generous sized bed. We settle into a steady silence, listening to the wind outside. Steph closes her eyes as she lies back on the pillow, but I don't want to fall asleep – not yet. I drag myself up and wander to the window.

And that's when I see two figures approaching the front door.

Mystery on the Mic Podcast

The Watts Case Series: Episode 9

Alex: Welcome, mystery lovers, to another thrilling episode of 'Mystery on the Mic'. I'm your host, Alex, and joining me is the amazing true crime historian, Sarah. How's it going, Sarah?

Sarah: Hey, Alex! It's always a wild ride exploring these mysteries, and today's story is no exception.

Alex: Absolutely, Sarah. So, let's dive right in, folks. We're talking about cults today, but not the kind you might be picturing. We're not in the jungles of South America or some remote compound in Texas. Nope, we're right in the heart of Surrey, in an opulent mansion owned by millionaire Ronnie Watts.

Sarah: That's right, Alex. It just goes to show that cults can emerge from the most unexpected places. Ronnie Watts' mansion, while picturesque, hides a dark secret – The Fellowship of Jesus Christ, or TFJC as it's commonly known.

Alex: So, my curious listeners, you might have heard us mention the Watts family in several of our previous podcasts, and we've had a whole host of new subscribers join us since the Netflix documentary which shed light on the Watts family's strange dynamics and the unsolved deaths of Ronnie and Heather Watts. But what's even more unsettling is the dark underbelly of The Fellowship of Jesus Christ, which seems to have sprouted from this twisted family tree.

Sarah: It's like a classic horror movie setup, isn't it? Fear of the Watts family's influential legal team has kept many people silent, but as the family wealth dwindles, so does the number of individuals willing to protect them from scrutiny.

Alex: And that's where Dina Harris comes in, folks. She's a talented singer-songwriter, and her story is a jaw-dropper. She went from awestruck fan to being trapped in this bizarre cult.

Sarah: Dina shared that it all started when a friend introduced her to Caleb Watts. Picture this, listeners: the mansion, the celebrity pictures on the walls, and Caleb, bathed in sunlight, serenading her about love. It must have felt like a dream come true.

Alex: And that's how these cults often work, Sarah. They lure you in with charisma and charm before things take a dark turn.

Sarah: Exactly, Alex. Dina thought she'd found her true home, but little did she know what lay ahead. Apparently Caleb had an eerie way of creating staged introductions, manipulating the person into thinking he was picking his 'chosen ones.'

Alex: But it wasn't just about religion. Dina said they bonded over their love of music, and Caleb seemed like a troubled soul searching for purpose, just like her.

Sarah: That's how it often starts. But then the atmosphere in that mansion turned sour when Ronan, Caleb's brother, entered the scene. Apparently Dina said Ronan gave her the creeps. She mentioned that he was strangely protective of his brother, too.

Alex: And then came Dina's invitation to move into the mansion. It must have felt like an adventure at first. But, of course, there were rules. Behaviour and clothes were regulated, and they had these bizarre group sessions where someone would be singled out for 'spiritual cleansing'.

Sarah: It's manipulation, pure and simple. Dina fell under Caleb's spell, and LSD was a constant presence during their night time chanting sessions. And then there were the so-called 'blessed rituals' for female members that Dina wouldn't go into detail about. Things were spiralling out of control, and Caleb was becoming more erratic. He believed he was the second coming, and Dina even saw him lead a chant with a halo of thorns on his head!

Alex: It sounds so unbelievable, but we've no reason to doubt her account. She went on to describe the doomsday talk. It's a classic cult move, creating a sense of impending disaster to keep members loyal and afraid to leave. Dina knew she had to escape. She pretended to be sick, and was brought to the hospital, and from there, she contacted her mum.

Sarah: It's amazing how she managed to build enough trust to escape. She's incredibly brave. Since then, more members have come forward with allegations of abuse. But Caleb still has followers, and they believe in retribution.

Alex: And it's chilling that Dina had to go into hiding. She went on to describe how she was worried about a baby girl that was born within the cult. She said she feared for its safety, as the brothers had a strange fascination with her, and believed that she had some kind of superpowers.

Sarah: Cults like these can be so destructive, and it's a testament to Dina's strength that she got out. I just hope the baby she spoke about is OK. Police haven't been able to find a trace, although it's possible that its birth wasn't registered to begin with. Another classic cult move. It's a reminder to stay vigilant, stay curious, and be aware of the people and groups we get involved with.

Alex: Well said. And to our listeners, stay tuned for more true crime after this short break!

Sarah: Enjoy your time on the mystery train!

33

Matt

I've been trying to stay awake in the living room, but time is crawling at a snail's pace. Bruce and Dorothy are keeping me company. I don't particularly like them, but I'd rather have them where I can see them. Their faces are filled with trepidation. Dorothy is convinced that any minute now, there will be a booming knock on the door. I don't understand that woman. If something terrible is due to happen tonight, then why doesn't she just hide? There are clearly spaces in this crumbling old house that we don't know about.

I put the question to her. She said that they can't hide forever, and some things have to be faced head on. She muttered something about the most 'important thing' being safe from the outside world. As usual, when asked about it, she closed down, switching the subject to something I have little interest in. She blabbered on about the royal family and security at the palace for ten whole minutes before I sighed and told her I had a headache. I'm not lying. I hit the back of my head against the hearth of the fireplace in the tussle. Then the gun went off near my ear and I've been feeling disorientated ever since.

Normally I'd politely listen to such boring conversations, with the occasional smile and throw in a 'really?' and a 'how interesting' every now and again for good measure. Nicola thinks she has the monopoly on dealing with strange people, but I deal with parents all the time in my job. Every now and again you come across folk who aren't quite right. Dorothy and her husband are clearly unhinged. I press my fingers to my temples as my headache closes in.

The evening has taken its toll on everyone. I'm glad that Henry has gone to bed. I still feel bad about tying up a cancer survivor, but we had no choice at the time. I only hope the authorities understand when the time comes to explain. George is back and that's all that matters.

Dorothy and I have come to a temporary truce while some of the others sleep. The experience with the gun has taken the wind out of Bruce's sails and he's said very little since his graze with death. I don't want to be here, and the tug to be by Nicola's side is strong, but I promised Joey that we'd look after Steph. I can't leave her on her own and equally, I'd feel awkward, lying in our bedroom with her there too. I sensed that Nicola was in need of some female company, so I thought it best that I keep watch. Joey's not the only man capable of taking control.

I jump as a heavy set of fists bang on the door. Someone's outside. I'm on my feet, grasping the side of the couch as dizziness leaves me reeling and starbursts float in my vision.

'Are you alright?' Bruce groans, slowly getting to his feet. I nod, guessing it's my blood pressure.

'I'm OK. I got up too quick.' I take a breath, ready to let our visitors in. But Dorothy is quicker, and she blocks my path as I try to leave the room.

'They're here!' She stares at me with a glint of madness in her eyes. 'They've come to finish what they started! Don't let them in!' There's no point in asking her what she's on about, because I've questioned her before. There's no clarification about who these 'bad people' are, no explanation, which suggests it's all in her head. There are footsteps on the landing and Steph is sprinting down the stairs at a speed faster than I imagined her pregnant body capable of.

Dorothy emits a cry as I push past her and head for the door. It's almost 2 a.m. My nerves are frayed, my head is thumping and exhaustion has crept into my bones. I don't have time for theatrics tonight.

'Who is it?' I hold my breath as I await a response from the other side of the door.

'Mate, it's me, Joey. Open the door. I'm freezing my nuts off out here.'

'Joey!' Steph calls, impatient as I pull across each bolt. Bedroom doors open and close and I wonder who else is going to join us for his welcome home party. Has Joey brought the police? Bruce stands ominously behind me, and we all hold a collective breath. Truth be told, other than Nicola, Joey and Steph are the only people I trust among the hosts and guests.

I swing the heavy door open and a burst of outside air chills my skin. Joey is not alone. A figure lingers at the edge of the porch, in the dim light cast from the hall. The stranger's features are obscured by shadows, leaving only a glimpse of their face.

Joey steps aside, his voice tinged with weariness as he shakes the snow from his clothes. 'I walked for miles, but the roads are completely blocked. There's no sign of anyone about. No snow ploughs, nothing.' He pats the snow off his knees and pulls off his beanie hat. 'I was about to turn back when I met Larry.' He jabs a thumb behind him. 'His car skidded off the road. I couldn't leave him out there in this storm.'

Dorothy's eyes narrow with suspicion as she glances from the stranger to Joey, her voice firm and resolute. 'No! He can't come in. It's not safe.'

Larry steps forward and pushes his hood from his face. 'I was on my way home from visiting my mum when my car got stuck in the snow. Please. I mean you no harm.' He shakes his hands which are red from the cold. 'I can't feel my fingers or toes.' He is softly spoken and keeps his gaze downwards.

'Come in,' I say, and as Dorothy pinches my arm with her impossibly pointy fingers, I swivel and whisper in her ear. 'Get off me, will you? You lost all right to tell us what to do when your husband pulled a gun on us.' She visibly wilts before me, and I feel another stab of guilt. We're all stuck in this crazy situation and need to look after each other.

Dorothy's voice is filled with caution, and she speaks with a stern yet compassionate tone. 'Come inside if you must, but we'll be watching you. Any sign of trouble, and you'll be out the door before you can blink.' She glances up at me with an 'are you satisfied now?' expression on her face. I try to smile but it feels like there's a little man with a jackhammer drilling inside my brain.

'Come in. We'll heat up some soup for you.' I push through the pain as I usher the stranger inside. Joey pulls the locks and bolts across the door and a tiny bit of me feels a sliver of unease. We don't know this man. Why would anyone venture out on a night like tonight? What if Dorothy's telling the truth? But then I look at Joey, who seems relaxed in his company. It's not as if we could turn the guy away.

I turn to Steph as she follows Joey down the hallway. 'Is Nicola OK?'

'Fast asleep, they both are.' There is literally a bounce in her step as she flashes me a smile. I glance up at the stairwell before following Joey and the others. The last thing I want is to wake Nicola or George up. Besides, sleep would evade me now that there's a stranger under our roof.

As we step into the warmth of the living room, a palpable tension settles in the air. I watch from a distance as, weary yet grateful, Larry takes a seat by the crackling fire. The warmth casts a soft glow upon his features. He's tall and broad-shouldered, with a light brown beard. I'm guessing he's in his forties. I notice his expensive watch and look away as he catches me staring. Bea is standing in the doorway, watching us. She enters cautiously and takes my side as we observe the others. 'I thought nobody was allowed in or out.' She speaks low enough that Larry can't hear. She's changed into a loose fitting tracksuit and the skin around her eyes is smudged with mascara.

'His car broke down,' I explain, crossing my arms over my chest. 'It's Baltic out there.'

Bea's face shifts subtly, her brow creasing in displeasure.

'Have you seen any of the others?' I ask, wondering how Sunita can sleep through everything that's going on.

Bea shakes her head. 'They're probably asleep. I wish I was. I just lay there, wondering what was going on downstairs. Then I heard the door, and I thought maybe Joey was back.' She throws a displeased glance at Larry, who sits quietly as Joey tells Dorothy about his short-lived expedition in the snow.

Bea exhales a long sigh. 'I had hoped Joey would come back with the police. We've got enough to worry about without throwing a stranger into the mix.'

'I'm keeping an eye on things, you can go back to bed if you like.'

'No offence, hun, but I don't know you from Adam.' She listens in as Joey talks about the ferocious weather and how isolated the island appears to be.

'I kept hoping I'd see some sign of civilisation . . .' He rubs his hands together as he warms them before the fire. 'But there was nothing. No houses, no traffic measures, nothing. It was disorientating, I was worried that I'd get lost. I was about to turn back when I saw the outline of Larry's car in the ditch. The snow was up to the windows. I nearly walked right past.'

'Do you have a phone?' Bea asks Larry, not bothering to introduce herself. 'We could do with one right now.'

'Battery's dead,' Joey answers on his behalf. 'Happens in low temperatures with iPhones. Completely zapped.'

'I doubt the cops would reach us even if it *was* working.' Steph cosies up next to Joey, her smile permanently fixed on her face. 'All we can do is sit it out.' Her attitude has completely changed, which makes no sense. She was distraught before, which is why Joey left. Now he's back with a stranger in tow and she's suddenly relaxed. Perhaps it's because we've found George and she's feeling happier under this roof. Or maybe the time she spent with Nicola did her good. The urge to check up on her is strong, but I need to suss out our new guest first. I wince as another thunderbolt of pain hits the back of my skull.

'Are you OK?' Bea asks as she picks up on my discomfort. 'You're looking a little peaky.'

'I've got a migraine coming on. I've not felt right since the gun went off.' Larry doesn't say a word, or even look in the slightest bit worried by the mention of a gun. I'm guessing Joey told him all about it before they got here. His expression of steady acceptance is disconcerting. It's not how I would act.

In the moments that follow, Bea finds some codeine in her bag, and I gratefully take them with a glass of water. Bruce finally finds his voice and interrogates Larry as Bea busies herself, serving us bowls of hot soup. Conversations about the weather follow, and Larry answers Bruce's questions about his broken-down Mercedes. He paints a picture of misfortune as he explains how he tried to make it home before the storm. As the words flow, Dorothy's scepticism seems to remain steadfast, her gaze never straying far from the newcomer. To be honest, I don't blame her. Larry speaks like his words are carefully orchestrated and it doesn't escape me that he never meets her eyes. Joey, on the other hand, watches Larry like a parent watching their child recite their lines during the school play. Perhaps I'm being paranoid. What harm is Larry actually doing, other than taking shelter from the storm?

We settle into the worn furniture. 'I'm a spiritual healer and psychic,' Bea shares after Larry finishes answering Bruce's many questions. 'I've travelled the world working with light and dark energies. The moment I stepped foot in this guest house, I sensed the vibration of violence in its walls.' Her words hang in the air, and a new-found interest stirs within me. Here is a self-proclaimed loner, devoid of the familial ties and the comforts of home. What drew her to travel to such places? I can't imagine never wanting to settle down. I should be joining Nicola, but I can't help but wonder about Bea's history and what caused her to come here tonight.

Steph quickly changes the subject, her voice filled with a mix of resignation and dreams. 'I'm a beautician. Been working long hours to save up for a deposit on a house. But the housing market is brutal. Sometimes it feels like we're chasing a dream.'

My gaze wanders to Joey, another member of this ragtag group. A musician, striving to make his mark on the world, earning meagre wages as a barman. Steph's unwavering support echoes the idealism of youth.

'We all have our struggles,' I interject. 'I'm a headmaster, and all I want is to settle down. But Nicola . . . she lives for her job in the police. It consumes her, defines her. Sometimes, it feels like we're drifting apart.' I blink. I can't believe I've voiced my thoughts aloud.

Bea offers up seconds, and everyone finishes their soup. The room falls into a contemplative silence, the hiss and spit of the fire the only companion to our thoughts. Tonight has been a journey in more ways than one. Deep down, I know that Nicola doesn't want to marry me yet, but one day she'll think differently. In the meantime, I'll do whatever it takes to keep us together. Nicola and George are my life. I'm nothing without them. I'm never letting them go.

34

Elita

A bitter feeling creeps over me as I sit at my desk watching the guests chit-chat. I burn with jealousy as I watch them share stories. What would I say if I found myself in their inner circle? 'Hi, I'm Elita. My mum was murdered, and I've been hiding in these walls ever since.' Yeah, right. They wouldn't hear any of that cos they'd be too busy gawking. I doubt they've ever met anyone like me.

From what I've learned, children who never grow up are in short supply in the real world. But then I think of how quickly George accepted me – a teenager with great big blue eyes wrapped in the body of a wrinkled little child. Would they accept me or freak out? Grandad said that I'm a miracle. He treats me like I'm different and doesn't know how to talk to me.

I miss George so much that it hurts. I know it sounds stupid, because he was only here for a little while, but I'm so mad with Granny for taking him away. Besides, that's not how grandmothers act, at least not from the books I've read or stuff that I've watched on TV. They're meant to look after you, not hide you away like you're something to be ashamed of. Mum never would have wanted this for me. But what can I do? I thought about following George, I even made it as far as the panel in the hall. But then our front door opened as somebody turned up and I ran back to my computer to see what was going on.

Now there's a stranger in the mix and I'm so torn, I don't know who or what to believe. I've heard how guests talk about Granny and Grandad. They say that they're crazy – both of them. Does that mean that everything they told me was a lie? Have I been stuck in The Loch House all these years for nothing?

I try to pick through what I know to be true. According to Mum's journals, I was an angry baby who kept her awake at night. I wasn't like other children, but she loved me just the same. She came with my dad to The Loch House and started a life here. They were running away from something. It turned out that my father wasn't my biological dad. Granny had to spill that secret before I read it in her diary. I wasn't too upset because we weren't what you'd call close. I guess that's why he left. Maybe he couldn't stand to look at me. Mum stayed to raise me on my own.

I tried to find out more, but Granny doesn't like talking about it because it hurts her too much. But she told me that the people Mum ran away from caught up with her, and that's why she died. They didn't want to let me go. She said Mum always knew that this could happen, but she didn't think that they would go that far. All of this stuff is true, I've no reason to doubt it. These people are dangerous. They murdered everyone in this guest house to get to me. But what about now? Ten years have passed. Are the same people still hunting me down? And what makes me so special, apart from my appearance? Grandad said that my name Elita means 'chosen one' and that I'm too good for this wicked world. But if I'm that special, then it comes back to the same question – why am I hidden away?

I look at the stranger huddled by the fire. He says his name is Larry. Does he mean to do me harm? Did his car really break down? What's in that leather bag that he's carrying around? Everything feels like it's been building to this night. I don't know what it is about this guy, but I feel like I've seen him before.

Then it hits me like a comet as he speaks again. Oh my golly God. It can't be. I can't blink. I can't breathe. I am paralysed by fear as the memory returns in terrifying clarity. *This* is the man who killed my mother. None of these people are getting out of here alive.

35

Nicola

I stand at the bedroom door straining to hear voices downstairs. Why hasn't Matt come to check up on us both? It's unlike him to leave me alone for this long. The second Steph heard the front door open, she leapt off the bed without a word and ran out of the room so fast that I was afraid she'd hurt herself. I remember what it was like, being pregnant with George, when my balance was all over the place, but she was out of the door like a gazelle. Something about her feels off. I listen through the door. I've only opened it a crack in case I need to lock it in a hurry. I can't believe that Dorothy let the stranger in.

The group have left the hall, and they're in the living room now. From what I've gathered, Joey has returned – and he's not alone. But it's not the police in his company – it's a stranger whose car left the road. Dorothy's words play a warning in my mind. I return to George, waiting for Matt to pop in with an update. But he seems to have forgotten about me, and I'm half tempted to go downstairs. Bloody keyless rooms. What is the point of that? I'd never leave George alone, not after what happened tonight.

I watch him sleep peacefully, totally out for the count. He's always been a heavy sleeper. There could be a screaming match going on downstairs and it wouldn't wake him – I should know. Although most of the arguments I had with his dad were one-sided. After the first time he hit me, I knew better than to answer back. I should have left him then. But he was so damned sorry, blaming his awful

183

upbringing and swearing that he'd get help. He even promised to go for therapy – anything for me to take him back. I should have seen the warning signs, but I was stuck in my own childhood rut.

I think, deep down, I took a leaf out of my mother's book, believing that jealousy to the point of violence was a sign that someone cared. And after all, it *was* my fault for upsetting him in the first place – wasn't it? I sigh, knowing there's no excuse for my inability to see the truth. I used to safeguard victims of domestic abuse, for God's sake.

The only thing that made that relationship worthwhile was George. But what mental scars has the past left? I stand over him, my chest tight. He's six years old but still sucks his thumb when he sleeps. Trauma brings coping mechanisms. Hiding and sucking his thumb are just two. There are others. Things I don't wish to think about now. Guilt closes in on many levels. I need to put him first. I think about Matt and his need to settle down . . . If Mum was here, she'd tell me that I should put George first and marry him.

With a sinking feeling in my chest, I imagine my future. Matt wants children of his own, but the minute I fell pregnant he'd insist that I gave up my job. What other stipulations would he have? I already keep my hair long for him, even though I wanted to cut it months ago. He likes me to dress conservatively when his colleagues come around, and talking about some of the racier police jobs I've been to is frowned upon. The truth is, I stopped loving Matt a long time ago. But then I think about it and wonder, did I ever love him at all?

Thoughts of my shift colleague come to mind and immediately, I smile. I've been working with Liam for years now. Matt disapproves of our friendship and asks why I can't be partnered with a woman, but then he relaxes when I tell him that I'm physically safer with my male partner, who is a lot stronger than me. The truth is, spending time in Liam's company brightens my working day. I think of his thoughtful gestures and the times he's brought me a cup of coffee, or one of my favourite macadamia cookies from Subway. Then there's other times, when he's been a shoulder to cry on after a tough job. Liam understands me in a way that Matt never could . . .

I inhale a soft breath as I suddenly realise what's been happening.

How could I have been this blind for so long? I care about Liam far more than I should, but Matt has always stood in my way. Liam has often joked about me being his 'work wife' and how we may as well date and be done with it. I remember when I told him that I was moving in with Matt and he was quiet for the rest of the day. I shift on the bed beside George as I'm hit with a clarity that I should have had months ago. *I can't commit to Matt because I'm in love with someone else.* My hand touches my mouth as I think of all Liam's kind gestures, and the many times he's offered to take me out for a meal. There's more than friendship between us. I can see that now.

The bedroom door opens. Finally. It's Matt. Heat rises to my cheeks as if I've been caught out.

'Hey,' he says softly. 'Steph said that you were going to sleep.'

'In this place?' I whisper as he sits on the edge of the mattress. 'No chance. I don't know why she thought I'd sleep now. What's happening downstairs?'

He rubs the side of his temple. There are dark circles beneath his eyes and from under the dim light his skin has taken on a grey hue. He looks beat. 'Joey didn't get far because the roads were too bad. He was about to head back when he came across a car in the ditch. The guy was half frozen, so he brought him back here to thaw out.'

'Was he hurt?' Matt looks at me in confusion and I clarify. 'From the car coming off the road. Was he injured? The ditches look pretty deep around here.'

Matt rubs his chin. 'I don't know. I didn't ask. He seemed OK, just cold.'

'I'm surprised Dorothy let him in.' After everything she put us through when we got here, it seems like a strange about-turn. The wind whistles through our windowpanes as George snores peacefully on the bed.

'We didn't give her a lot of choice.' Matt sighs, hunched on the bed. 'But I dunno . . . he's very quiet. A bit too quiet.' He glances at George and smiles. 'Manage to get anything out of him?'

I shake my head. 'Steph annoyed me a bit. She tried waking him up when I went into his room to get his teddy.'

Matt's face darkens. 'For what?'

'To ask him where he had been. I told her off. It wasn't her place.'

'Well, she seems quite happy now, snuggled up next to Joey on the sofa.' He reaches out to touch my leg and before I realise it, I've pulled away.

'Sorry,' I quickly say. 'It's been a long night.' The truth is, we will never be Steph and Joey, and we both deserve more. I'm about to broach the subject when he speaks first.

'Why don't you go downstairs? Take a break. I'll keep an eye on George.'

'Are you sure?' I say. I do need to move around a bit to keep myself awake, so I swing my legs off the bed and stand. I can't deny that I want to know what's going on down there either . . . My police instinct tells me something is not right. 'Just as long as you don't fall asleep and lock me out.'

'I'll leave the door off the latch.' He kicks off his shoes and takes my place on the bed.

'Are you OK?' I say, catching him wince as he lies down.

'Headache. Well, more of a migraine really. Bea gave me some codeine, but it's barely touched the sides.'

'Oh, you poor thing. Need anything?'

He closes his eyes, exhaling a tired breath. 'Just a lie down. There's soup in the kitchen if you're hungry. We've all had some.'

But food is the last thing I want. My stomach still feels tied up in knots. I quietly close the door, leaving George in Matt's capable hands. Despite my tiredness, I press on, fuelled by curiosity as I head for the stairs.

I take quiet, cautious steps upon the aged floorboards. Night shadows dance and sway, taunting my frayed nerves. It's gone 2 a.m., still a few hours until dawn. I am met with a heavy silence in the living room. Steph is whispering something to Joey, and it looks like Dorothy has fallen asleep on a wide armchair. Bea is watching the stranger intensely. If he feels her gaze, he doesn't acknowledge it. He stares into the fire. He hasn't noticed me yet.

He's not a bad looking man, with his neatly trimmed beard and shoulder-length brown hair streaked with slivers of grey at the temples. As he looks up from the fire and meets my eyes with his gaze, I immediately sense that something is off. I can't quite pinpoint it, but I am cautious as I take a seat across from him. Maybe it's this place, or Dorothy and Matt's misgivings, but I don't feel safe in the presence of this man. It feels strange for another person to enter our orbit out of nowhere like this.

'Hey, Nicola, how's George?' Steph is happier now, brighter in Joey's presence, and I return her smile.

'Out like a light. Are you OK, Joey? Matt filled me in.'

'Yeah,' Joey gestures at the stranger. 'This is Larry. He's hanging out with us until the storm passes.' He talks about the weather as he pokes at the fire. Larry doesn't speak, but my gut twists with suspicion as I catch him looking me up and down. I take an instant dislike to the man and rise from my seat. 'Anyone want anything from the kitchen? I'm going to put on the kettle.' They respond with a shake of the head.

I amble down the hall, lost in thought. As a police officer, I'm normally on the ball. But George's sudden disappearance and reappearance has left me out of sync. As I reach the kitchen, I realised that Bea has followed me in. 'I don't like that guy,' she whispers. 'Can you stick around a little longer, sound him out? His aura is all wrong.'

I turn the kettle on to boil and look for teabags. For once, I agree with her. 'It's weird, I've not even heard him speak, but he gives me the creeps too. Maybe it's just tiredness. Things will look brighter in the morning when the storm has passed.' I spoon some sugar into my cup and take the milk from the fridge.

Bea doesn't look reassured. 'I've tried sleeping, but I keep turning things over in my mind. Someone almost got shot tonight. Henry's trying to hide a secret that's worth going to prison for. Even with my bedroom door locked, I don't feel safe in this place. I like everyone to be where I can keep an eye on them. Answers. That's what I want.'

'I know. Me too. I'll be glad when we leave here. In the meantime, I won't leave George on his own.' I imagine Matt beside him, he's probably asleep by now. He's a very light sleeper so if anyone so much as tries to open our creaky bedroom door he'll be wide awake. I yawn and stir my tea. I can't wait for morning to come. Maybe I'll feel better if I talk to Larry and sound him out. I carry my cup into the living room, orchestrating the questions in my mind. But he's gone.

Mystery on the Mic Podcast

The Watts Case Series: Episode 10

Alex: Hey, mystery enthusiasts! Welcome back to another intriguing episode of 'Mystery on the Mic'. I'm your host, Alex, and joining me is the ever-astute true crime historian, Sarah. How's it going, Sarah?

Sarah: Hey, Alex! I'm thrilled to be diving into this mind-boggling case with you today.

Alex: Absolutely, Sarah. Today, we're back unearthing the eerie and perplexing tale of Caleb Watts, the enigmatic leader of The Fellowship of Jesus Christ. We've shared the links to previous podcast episodes on this family, but the story never seems to end. Now, it takes us on a rollercoaster through secrecy, delusions, and the unsettling world of cults.

Sarah: That's right, Alex. Who knew when we first reported on this case how it would unfold? It's a tale that reminds us that even the most outlandish and sinister cults can emerge from the most unexpected places. Caleb Watts first formed his church after inheriting his Surrey family estate with his brother.

Alex: I can't wait for the day when this case reaches its full conclusion. Let's hope it happens while we're still on air!

But back to the story. In true cult style, the Watts brothers used their wealth to entice young musicians with promises of fame and fortune.

Sarah: Yes, and as we've said before, the cult members were predominantly female, with a sprinkle of selected couples. But it all went underground after a police drug raid in 2008 forced them out of their lavish Surrey mansion.

Alex: And then, they lived this nomadic, secretive existence. By 2010, their 'family' had grown, with over a dozen children, many fathered by Watts himself.

Sarah: Watts was a truly deluded individual, Alex. He believed he possessed supernatural powers and commanded his followers to engage in sexual activity with him. It's horrifying how these charismatic leaders manipulate their followers.

Alex: Indeed, Sarah. Couples in the group were promised special spiritual favours if the female was 'chosen' by Watts for procreation. This went on until 2010, when Watts started preaching about a doomsday event.

Sarah: And his delusions got even darker, Alex. Apparently his brother would torture anyone trying to escape, leaving distraught parents unable to rescue their children from the clutches of this cult.

Alex: But there had been a glimmer of hope in 2003 when a brave couple, Amelia and John Evans, managed to escape. John reportedly smuggled out his wife and her daughter, fathered by Watts, while taking another cult member to the hospital.

Sarah: Watts believed that this specific child was the 'chosen one' who would lead them to salvation when they'd 'follow him into the light'. It's chilling to think about.

Alex: And let's not forget the stockpiled poison, Sarah. Watts was preparing for a mass murder-suicide.

Sarah: Thankfully, the plan never came to fruition. After a police raid, social services uncovered several unregistered children at the farmhouse, leading to the disbandment of The Fellowship.

Alex: Caleb Watts received a life sentence for a litany of heinous crimes, including sexual assault, rape, cruelty, false imprisonment, and murder.

Sarah: His brother Ronan, on the other hand, served less time in prison in exchange for testifying against Watts and other cult members.

Alex: But here's the twist, folks. Some former cult members described Ronan as even more dangerous than Caleb, calling him 'manipulative', 'dangerous', 'violent' and 'unhinged'. They claim his remorse in court was all an act.

Sarah: Rumours abound that the cult might still exist. But with Caleb on life support after being beaten up in prison, what's left of this enigmatic group? And what happened to Watts' 'chosen one', the child who would be sixteen years old now?

Alex: Those are some mind-boggling questions, Sarah. And regardless of what remains of the cult, there's no denying the trail of devastation they've left behind.

Sarah: Indeed, Alex. This case serves as a stark reminder of the power charismatic leaders can wield and the profound impact they can have on their followers.

Alex: You know, Sarah, cults have always fascinated me in a rather morbid way. How do individuals, often seemingly normal people, get ensnared in these web-like organisations?

Sarah: That's a great point, Alex. Cults are often shrouded in mystery, and understanding the psychology behind them is important.

Alex: Absolutely. I mean, here's Caleb Watts, a seemingly charismatic figure, convincing people to follow him, to the point where they'd willingly partake in rituals that, in any other context, would be unthinkable.

Sarah: As we've mentioned before, cult leaders like Watts often employ manipulation tactics that prey on the vulnerabilities of their followers. They offer a sense of belonging, purpose and identity, which can be incredibly enticing, especially to those who feel lost or adrift in their lives.

Alex: Right, it's like they create this alternate reality where they're the saviour, and everyone else is lost without them.

Sarah: Exactly, Alex. They often use isolation from friends and family to strengthen the group identity. In a way, it's like a psychological trap where the leader controls every aspect of their followers' lives.

Alex: And that's what makes escape so difficult. We heard from Dina earlier, who faked an illness just to get out. It's terrifying to think about the lengths these cult leaders go to to maintain their control. I've heard of a technique called 'shunning' that's used on anyone who leaves but then tries to return. They're outcasts for life.

Sarah: And what's even scarier is that, for many, the escape is just the beginning of a long and painful journey towards recovery. The psychological scars can linger for a lifetime.

Alex: Absolutely. But it's also incredibly courageous of those who do manage to escape and then share their stories, shedding light on these dark corners of society.

Sarah: You're right. It's through their courage that we can learn more about the inner workings of cults and hopefully prevent others from falling into the same traps.

Alex: And that's why we do what we do here on 'Mystery on the Mic'. To shed light on these mysteries, learn from them, and, in some small way, make the world a safer place.

Sarah: That's the goal, Alex. So, to all our listeners out there, stay curious, stay vigilant and keep unravelling those mysteries.

Alex: Stay tuned, dear listeners! We'll be back with a new case after this sponsored break.

36

Matt

It's the smell that makes me realise I'm no longer at home. In the brief second before I open my eyes, I inhale a stale, earthy stench from the pillow I've been drooling into. My pillows at home smell of lavender. Nicola uses the fabric conditioner because she swears that it helps her drift off to sleep. But not here, in this alien environment with its rattling pipes and shuddering windowpanes.

I wake, wiping my mouth. My head is thick with brain fog. How long have I been asleep? I blink as I look at my watch and I realise that only twenty minutes have passed. It's nearly half two. George is still deep in slumber, so I slide off the bed and pad into our en suite. It's a relief that the codeine has finally kicked in, my migraine now reduced to a dull throb at the back of my head. I taste sourness on my tongue – a by-product of not brushing my teeth. I make it quick, as my head feels sensitive, and I can't bear the vibration of the electric toothbrush rattling against my molars. I've just finished when I hear a voice in my bedroom. My senses heightened, I push open the door of my en suite to see Joey and Larry standing over George.

Confusion washes over me as I take in the scene. 'What the hell are you doing?'

Joey jumps at the sound of my voice. He looks as if he's been caught in the act. 'Shit, sorry man. I thought you were asleep in the other room.' He exhales a strange, forced laugh and looks from Larry to George.

I recall George's bed and the toys he always insists on bringing, which are bundled beneath the blankets on his bed. They must have thought that I was in there, asleep. They've been checking, seeing if the coast was clear. I'm about to repeat my question when Larry turns, his face a mask of false innocence. 'Oh, hey, Matt, don't sweat it. Just checking up on the kid, you know? Making sure he's alright. Nicola said he went AWOL earlier on.'

My jaw tightens as anger simmers beneath the surface. 'You're checking up on him? Why? What gives you the right to come in here and invade our space?' I launch myself towards him, but a wave of dizziness makes me stumble and Joey stands in my way. I steady myself. Didn't Nicola say that Steph tried to wake George earlier? What do they want from him?

George stirs, his long lashes fluttering as he unplugs his thumb from his mouth. He is unaware of the tension in the air.

Larry's gaze shifts, his voice taking on an unsettling tone. 'George, hey kid, wake up.'

The sight of him shaking his shoulder leaves me furious as George wakes. 'Hey there, champ,' Larry continues. 'I'm looking for a special little girl. Can you tell me where she is?'

'Hey! Leave him alone!' I shout, outraged. But as I approach Larry for the second time, Joey holds me back. He's clearly stronger than me, and his tight grip on my forearm takes me by surprise. I don't want to frighten George, so I keep my voice low. 'Get out, do you hear me? Leave. Now.' I growl at Joey, as Larry leans over George. But his grip on me is strong.

'Mummy?' George says, looking beyond the three of us at Nicola, who has just come in. She is white with worry, her eyes wide as she watches us all.

'Shit.' Larry glares at Joey, his tone carrying an edge. 'I thought I told you to lock the door.'

'What's going on?' Nicola demands, dodging us as she approaches George. She takes him in her arms and looks to me for answers. 'Matt? What are they doing?'

'I was in the bathroom,' I say, shaking my head. 'And when I came out, they were standing over George asking him about some girl.'

This isn't good. I think of Dorothy's warnings and feel physically sick. Who have we allowed inside? Whatever they're after, Joey, Steph and this Larry are in it together because Steph woke up George to ask him a similar thing. Now Steph has followed Nicola in, and as she speaks in a high-pitched screech, George hangs on tight to Nicola.

'Everything alright? Joey? What's going on?' Her hand rests on her bump as she approaches her husband, who finally lets go of my arm.

Nicola's gaze darts between Steph and Joey, her eyes burning with suspicion. 'You two . . . you're in on this, aren't you? With Larry? If that's his real name.'

I've no doubt that Nicola's right. Joey was playing me all this time, acting all innocent as he asked for my advice. No wonder he was desperate to leave. The whole thing was a ploy to get Larry inside.

Steph turns her doe eyes towards Nicola, her voice filled with feigned innocence. 'What are you on about? Sorry, I'm not with you, hun.'

Hun? My disbelief quickly turns to outrage. 'Don't play *dumb*, Steph. It doesn't suit you. Nicola's right, I know you've been playing us both.'

It's frightening, how her face changes as her mask finally drops.

'At least I won't need this anymore.' She whips off her top, shaking her hair after she's pulled it over her head. A strange giggle leaves her lips. 'I've been sweating like a pig all evening in this get-up.' She's not in the slightest bit self-conscious as she stands there in her pink satin bra. I can't believe my eyes as I take in the sight of the round cushioned padding strapped around her thin frame. With a click, she undoes the padding straps, allowing the cushion to fall with a small thud to the floor. 'That's a relief.'

She gives me a cheeky smile as she catches me staring at her, standing there in her leggings and bra. Joey thrusts her top into her hand and tells her to put it back on. Things have immediately cooled between them. Are they even a couple?

'It's OK,' she says, shoving her arms through her top, which is now baggy for her slight frame. 'There's nothing to worry about. We're here for the girl, that's all. Nobody needs to get hurt.'

'Then what do you want with my son?' Nicola stares at Larry. 'This has nothing to do with him.'

'It has everything to do with him!' Larry roars. 'When he knows exactly where she is. Oh, we know old Dorothy and Henry won't speak, but he will.' He turns back to face Joey. 'Bring him downstairs.'

'Over my dead body!' Nicola stares at them both.

'Mummy?' George whimpers as Joey approaches him on the bed.

'It's OK,' Nicola smooths over his hair as she holds onto him tightly. 'Nobody's going to hurt you.'

I lunge towards George and Nicola, desperate to keep them safe. But Larry is quicker as he turns and punches me square in the stomach. The blow feels like the force of a steam train, and I gasp as I fall to my knees, unable to breathe. Nicola's screams fill the air.

I've never been hit so hard. I'm dizzy and feel like I'm going to throw up as I'm left winded on the floor. Then Steph leaves, only to return with Henry's shotgun. My heart pumps an extra beat as she thrusts the weapon into Joey's hand. He's waving it at Nicola and George. 'Downstairs, both of you.'

Nicola is silent as she gathers up George and does as she's told. He clings to her like a spider monkey, his head buried in her chest. There's no arguing with a gun, and I finally manage to inhale some air into my lungs as Larry drags me to my feet. He picks me up like I'm made of paper and pushes me ahead. I don't know what they're planning, or who they're looking for. I only hope that we come out of this alive.

37

Nicola

I feel sick to my stomach as George trembles in my arms. Why the hell did I let Joey take Henry's gun? I'm meant to be a cop for God's sake, I should have confiscated it after the incident. Why haven't I protected my son? Slowly, we descend the stairs. We were too vulnerable in the bedroom, but I'm keenly aware of the victims who died in the very living room we're heading to years before. I feel for Matt, who has already taken a punch to the gut. To think that hours before, Joey was hanging on his every word. Lies, all of it. I'm furious that I was taken in. It seems obvious now that they were planted in the guest house, scouting the location before bringing the stranger in.

As we enter the living room Matt glances at me, his expression pained. He may be broad-shouldered, but he's not cut out for conflict of this nature. Bea is next to the window, her face flushed with anxiety. Bruce holds his arm as he watches Larry with mistrust, while Henry and Dorothy look fit to kill. The threat of a gun does not silence Dorothy as she throws herself at the man that we allowed into her home.

'Killer!' she screams, launching herself at him. Bruce lunges forward, trying to hold onto her, but as he winces in pain, she makes her escape. 'Bastard!' 'Murderer!' Each word is followed by a string of expletives as she accuses the stranger of murdering her daughter ten years ago. Larry pushes her away and she staggers backwards for a few steps, barely managing to keep her balance on her spindly legs. Her eyes bulge as she rounds on us.

'I told you he'd come back. But would you listen?' She jabs a bony finger in the air. 'Whatever happens now . . . it's all *your* fault.'

Larry delivers a nod of the head and within seconds, a remorseless Steph has grappled Dorothy's arms behind her back. 'Bitch! Traitor!' Dorothy spits the words, until Steph shoves a cloth into her mouth. She is pushed onto a chair, and further restrained as she screams into her gag.

'Stop!' Henry approaches, one hand pressed against his throat. 'Please!' He begs Steph not to hurt her, but she screams at him to get back.

'This is so undignified,' the stranger finally says as he stands with the confidence of a man who has done this before. 'There really is no need for it.' He casts his eyes over us as he takes a pistol from his backpack. 'Now. Are you going to sit in silence, or do I have to use this?' The firearm is sleek, black, and appears modern. I've no way of knowing if it's real, but I've seen similar guns seized in drug raids. How many guns do they have, and what is so important that they felt the need to hold us all hostage using firearms?

I finally manage to calm George's crying, and he hiccups in my arms. I scout the room. Everyone except Sunita is here. Joey has gone to get her, while Steph trains Henry's shotgun on us. Firearms are the only thing capable of keeping us compliant, without it I'd be tearing her hair out by now. She looks ill at ease with the weapon as she grapples to get the proper grip. I'm guessing she's never held one before, but one squeeze of the trigger is all it takes.

As I keep my eye on the shotgun, I'm more furious than scared. To think that I swallowed her act whole. Passing herself off as pregnant, then pretending she was scared and vulnerable – I am incensed by her betrayal. How could a woman do this to a mother? George hasn't harmed anyone. What do these people want?

Larry settles into a worn armchair by the fire as he watches us with a new-found confidence in his eyes. He's not a stranger whose car came off the side of the road. He's come here with a purpose. Steph and Joey had to come first to scope out the place before he arrived. Were they the ones who were snooping in our rooms?

I exchange a glance with Matt. His muscles are tensed, and I deliver a warning shake of the head. I don't want him doing anything stupid. Everything feels on a knife edge. We don't understand these people, or what they're capable of. All I know is that it centres around a little girl that they're looking for, and the murders that took place here before. But how can that be?

They're convinced that George has spent time with the child in question. Judging by the warning looks that Dorothy's shooting in his direction I'm guessing that he has. That story about him being in the laundry basket obviously wasn't his lie – it was hers. I remember the child George mentioned, a blonde girl waving in the window . . . Who or what are Dorothy and Henry covering up?

For now, the stranger has gained our compliance as he holds us hostage. But this must end soon. I take a seat on the sofa across from Larry, with George on my lap, as he gestures at me to sit down. It feels like we're in a pressure cabin and the air is running out. I try to steady my breath as every instinct screams at me to take George and run. I'm jumpy from the sudden onset of adrenaline and my mouth is arid. I tap the heel of my foot against the floor as I struggle to keep still. Larry's presence looms large as he sits, watching us all.

'What do you want?' Matt sits next to George and me on the sofa, a protective arm around us both as he directs his question at Larry. My little boy is sucking his thumb now, his head buried in my chest.

But Larry ignores the question as Joey makes an entrance, with Sunita by his side. But this isn't meek and mild Sunita, who barely speaks a word. This is a woman who strides in with confidence as she takes in the scene. Joey seems wary around her. He's watching her every movement, and Steph takes a couple of steps back as she approaches us all. She's dressed now, having discarded her earlier nightwear for jeans and a thick sweatshirt. They are travelling clothes, suited to the cold weather, and I have a feeling she doesn't plan on staying here for long. She joins Larry's side, looking at him with a mixture of admiration and trepidation.

'What kept you?' she says, examining his face. He mumbles something about the weather, and I'm floored by yet another betrayal. To think that not long before, she sat me on the bed and calmed me down when I was upset. He leans down and mumbles a response that only she can hear.

'Really? Sunita? You too?' I say in disbelief. Matt squeezes my arm, the way he always does when he believes that I've spoken out of turn.

Sunita smiles but her eyes are dark with warning. 'There's no need for anyone to get hurt. We just want what we've come for and then we'll be on our way.'

'And what *have* you come for?' Bea speaks from where she's standing next to the window.

'What's rightfully ours.' Sunita approaches Steph, who visibly withers beneath her gaze. 'I heard you put on quite the show.' Steph lowers her head as she continues. 'Just remember why you're here.'

'Yes . . . I . . .' Steph stutters. 'Sorry.'

'And if you're going to hold a gun at least do it properly.' She yanks the firearm upwards, making Bea gasp as it is temporarily trained on her. '*This* is how you hold a gun.' She fixes Steph's position, pushing her shoulders back.

'Don't make me regret bringing you here.' Sunita's words are low as she utters a warning. I can't hear Steph's response but it's obvious the woman has a hold over her. Sunita wastes no time in approaching Dorothy, and looks down at her with disdain. It seems Sunita is the matriarch of this dark band of travellers, and will stop at nothing to get what she wants. Dorothy flinches as she roughly pulls down her gag. 'Where is she?'

'Go to hell!' Dorothy screams, before taking a breath and spitting on her captor. Sunita responds with an open hand and slaps her hard on the face. I'm shocked at this sudden act of violence against someone of Dorothy's age, and a gasp escapes my lips. Henry groans, unable to voice his upset. What have we brought upon those people by allowing Larry inside? I feel terrible for my earlier assessment of them. I judged them both from the beginning, when with their own wonky thinking, they were trying to keep us safe. But then Steph, Sunita and Joey were already guests by then. I exchange a glance with Bruce. He warned me from the beginning that things weren't right. Could I have done things any differently? I wish we'd taken our chances with the storm and just gone home.

'Fine,' Sunita's annoyance is evident, her face pinched. 'If you won't tell us where she is, then we have no choice but to start with the child.' Her expression is fierce as she turns to me. The determination in her eyes terrifies me. I'll fight her if I have to. But then Steph steps forward, and this time her stance is firm as she trains Henry's shotgun on my head.

38

Matt

'Hang on a minute!' I bellow, as the strangers approach George. I don't know what the hell they are doing here, or where in God's name they came from, but they're not having my son.

When Larry touches Sunita's arm to still her movements, she delivers a small bow of the head in reverence and backs away. There's something odd about the way she looks at him, as if he's some sort of God. She may command the others, but she is second in line to him. Steph and Joey seem uneasy around them both. It's not that they're scared of them as such, although I see that too. It's that they have an unusual level of respect. As if they would do anything they asked them to. Perhaps they already have. What did Sunita mean when she told Steph to remember why they were here? Just how far will they go?

Larry steps forward as Sunita retreats. 'As I said . . . there's no need for any of this. We don't mean you harm.' He is well spoken, but an undercurrent of darkness robs any confidence I might have in his words.

'You don't mean us harm?' I say. 'Tell that to the person aiming the guns.'

Larry nods and Steph lowers the shotgun. Larry holsters his pistol in the back pocket of his jeans. I can't believe that there are firearms involved. We're in Scotland, for God's sake.

Larry turns to face Nicola, his gaze softening. 'I need to tell you something. By the time you've finished listening, you'll understand why I've had to go to such desperate measures to find my little girl.'

'Your little girl?' I interrupt. Everything has been cloak and dagger so far.

The man ignores my question, his gaze focused on Nicola, as if she is the most important person in the world. For a fleeting second, I feel like I've seen him somewhere before.

'My real name is Ronan,' he continues. 'I met Dorothy's daughter, Amelia, over twenty years ago. She was friends with my brother, Caleb. She was a musician, like many of the people he encountered back then.' A small smile creeps onto his lips. 'They were starstruck by my brother. He was a good soul who just wanted to help. He didn't turn anyone away. Have you heard of Ronnie Watts?' He watches as Nicola frowns. 'You're probably too young . . .'

'No,' she corrects him. 'Wasn't he the music producer who was found dead with his wife?'

Ronan emits a soft chuckle. 'Yes, I should have known you'd remember that, being a police officer. I'm Ronnie's son, Caleb is my younger brother.'

I vaguely recall the family because they were always in the news. Filthy rich, but always the victim of one tragedy or another. I remember my father remarking upon it when Ronnie's first wife died, saying money couldn't buy you happiness and that the family were cursed. Nicola seems more relaxed now and soothes George in her arms, softly rubbing his back. At least we're getting answers. I listen as Ronan continues.

'I formed a relationship with Dorothy's daughter. She got pregnant shortly afterwards, but Caleb thought the baby was his. I loved my brother, so I let it lie. Then Amelia had Elita.' He pauses, his gaze distant. 'Caleb wouldn't allow anyone to come near her. He said she was the chosen one.'

'Chosen for what?' I ask, because my head is bursting at the seams with questions. 'And why couldn't you have come here like normal people and asked to see her?'

But Ronan continues to act as if I'm not even here. As he smooth talks Nicola, it feels like he's getting under her skin.

'What happened?' she asks, when Ronan fails to answer.

His smile is almost hypnotic, and the room falls quiet as he continues with his story. 'It all got too much for Amelia. She was in a relationship with this other guy and, well . . . the pair of them took off. Elita was four years old. It was the last straw for Caleb, who had been suffering with mental health issues. He went on the hunt for Elita, but it took years for him to track Amelia down. Just over two, in fact.' Ronan's voice is steady as he recounts events of the past. He speaks of a family torn apart by darkness, of the delusions that had ensnared his brother and the tragic outcome when Caleb finally caught up with Amelia and she failed to give him their child.

My headache has returned with a vengeance, and I struggle to process his words. Ronan's face is etched with sorrow and determination. But something tells me that the foundation of this story is built on lies.

'Then all those people died.' He punctuates his words with a sigh. 'Caleb swore they were still alive when he left . . . a part of me wonders if he was responsible for it. Even then, he didn't find Elita, my lost little girl.' He finally breaks his contact with Nicola and looks up at Dorothy. 'All this time, they've kept us apart. It's cruel, that's what it is. Child cruelty in its worse form. She's here. I know it. But this house is a maze. We don't know where to start. All I want is to take my daughter home.'

His face is twisted with emotion as he glares at Dorothy and Henry. 'You. You imprisoned my little girl.' His gaze focused on Henry. 'And you're meant to be a man of God! You, more than anyone, should understand how important this is. Don't act like you don't know how special she is!' They utter no response.

He stops to take a breath and composes himself before returning his attention to Nicola. 'They took your son, too. So you know what I'm going through.' A beat falls between them. All that can be heard is the low hiss of burning timber and the whistle of wind through the windowpanes.

'You expect us to trust you?' Nicola's voice carries a mixture of fear and anger. 'After everything that has happened here, can we really believe what you say?'

'I understand your doubts,' Ronan says. 'But Elita's being kept prisoner somewhere in this awful place. She's not in the system so nobody's looking for her. She doesn't deserve to be hidden away.' His gaze travels over the walls of the house. 'She's here, and thanks to Steph and Joey, I know it for sure. I've been searching for her all these years, and now I need your son's help.' He emits a playful gasp and runs a hand through his hair. 'I know I've gone about this all wrong. I get . . .' he pauses to find the words, '. . . over emotional when it comes to family. Elita's my only child, and I can't stand to think of her locked away.'

I glance at Nicola, and our eyes lock in a shared understanding of the gravity of the situation. Even if there was a sliver of truth in Ronan's words, we have to keep George safe.

The pieces of the puzzle are slowly coming together, revealing a disturbing truth. I've been watching George's face. Mention of Elita has got his attention. He wasn't hiding in the laundry basket. He's been with her. Should we keep quiet and help him deny the truth, or it is safer for George to give them what they want? But what happens to Elita then?

39

Nicola

As Ronan's story unfolds, I find myself caught between my instinct to protect my son and the possibility of helping a young girl trapped in a nightmarish existence. I've sacrificed a lot of things to protect George over the years, and I won't let anything stand in my way. Ronan's story might be entirely reasonable, if he and his cohorts weren't holding guns . . . Ronan's eyes are the deepest brown I've ever seen. His gaze is hypnotic. I hadn't noticed it until he started talking. He has a way of holding my attention that I've never experienced before. I'm aware that I've relaxed, despite the threat. Perhaps a part of me *wants* to believe him. I listen as he speaks, my mind painting a story – but how much of it is true? I can't help but sit and listen as he tries to win me round. Because he's right. He didn't take George. I'm pretty sure that Dorothy and Henry did.

'I know it's hard to believe, but my brother was lost in his own delusions. I've been searching for Elita ever since, hoping to bring her home.'

I have to challenge his account. 'What about the murders? Are you really telling me that Amelia's death wasn't your doing? And what about the rest of the people who died under this roof?'

'I don't blame you for being dubious.' Ronan's gaze drops, his voice filled with remorse. 'But Caleb is a good man. He might have sedated those people, but he'd no intention of murdering them. If you're looking for the killers, then look closer to home.'

'Lies!' Henry manages to shout, his voice making me jump.

'I've read the reports,' Ronan counters. 'You were there, you called the police! Amelia always said that you were a control freak. What happened, Henry? Did you have an argument? Did you want to keep Elita for yourself?'

I can't believe what I'm hearing. Is it possible that Dorothy and Henry were the killers all along? I know that they're unbalanced, but would they really go that far? But now my mind paints a picture of them turning up after Caleb left. What if Ronan's telling the truth? What if Henry lost his mind and finished everyone off?

My mind reels as Caleb continues.

'I couldn't save Amelia, but Elita deserves a life. We're not the monsters here . . .' His gaze narrows as he stares at Dorothy and Henry. 'All these years, they've kept her hidden away, imprisoned. What kind of life is that for a child? I've tried going through official channels, but her birth was never registered. They wouldn't listen to a word I said.'

'And you think this will help you? Orchestrating all this?' I shake my head in disbelief. 'Using a section five firearm is a serious offence. Then you're looking at kidnapping . . .' I begin, but Matt gives me a sharp dig in the ribs. He's right. I'm in no position to be making things harder for him. We've seen his face. We know who he is.

The room falls into a heavy silence, the weight of our doubts hanging like a dark cloud. 'What happens if you find her? What next?'

Ronan is smiling now, his eyes glinting with amusement, as if I've asked him something cheeky.

'I'm hardly likely to tell you where I'm going now, am I, Nicola? But I will say that Elita will be well cared for. She needs rehabilitation.'

'But how is that any better for her? Surely taking her away for rehabilitation means hiding her away again . . .' I ignore Matt as he sighs beside me. 'And if George does tell you where Elita is, how can I be sure that he won't be harmed?'

Ronan just shakes his head. 'Now why would I harm your child when I'm here trying to find my own?'

My gaze shifts down to George, and I'm torn between the need to protect my son and the possibility of uncovering the truth. 'George, sweetheart, do you know anything about Elita? Have you seen her?' But before he can reply, Dorothy begins another tirade. She's managed to loosen her gag and is vocal about her opinion.

'Don't listen to him, he's a liar! He wants to kill Elita too. Don't tell him, George, whatever you do!' She gulps back a breath as Sunita advances upon her. 'That family ran a cult. My daughter came here to escape them. But they hunted her down and *killed* her because she wouldn't let them sacrifice her child. Why do you think they're all here? They're part of The Fellowship of Jesus Christ! Fanatics and killers, the lot of them!'

And suddenly everything clicks into place. That's why there are so many people involved. Why they behave so strangely. They're all still following Caleb. They'd follow him to the ends of the earth.

Steph's face contorts, a mask of fury replacing the once-charming facade she had worn. 'Shut up, you old hag! You've no idea what The Fellowship is about.' She stuffs the rag back into Dorothy's mouth.

George whimpers, his eyes glistening with fear as he watches the grown-ups in front of him arguing and hurting each other. He is far too young to be part of something like this, and something breaks inside me as I think about what this is doing to him. I wrap my arms around him like a protective shield. I'm under no illusion as to the danger we're in here. Henry and Dorothy may be odd, but I can't see any motive for them killing their flesh and blood . . . It doesn't make sense.

'We've wasted enough time,' Ronan says, his niceties dismissed. 'Tell us where Elita is, or somebody gets hurt.'

'No!' Matt shouts, gesticulating with his hands, but the movement means Steph's gun is now trained on him.

'You think you can defy me?' Ronan's veneer of patience is cracking. 'You think I won't do whatever it takes to find Elita? Caleb is dying in hospital. She's the key to my brother's salvation.'

'George,' I whisper to my child. 'Just tell him. Tell him where she is.' I'm scared, because I know where this has the potential to end.

Dorothy's eyes meet mine. They're bright with desperation. 'I'm sorry,' I say quietly. 'I have to protect my son.'

But George isn't speaking, and he gives a tight shake of the head. I release a guttural scream as he is forcefully wrenched from my arms.

40

Elita

I'm totally frozen in front of my computer screen, my mouth hanging open because I can't make sense of it. What is even going on? This guy is supposed to be my dad? But he . . . he's a killer, isn't he? So why is he saying that Granny and Grandad did those things? Now I'm wondering if I can trust my memory at all. Mum's journals were always super honest about how I didn't belong to her husband back then. I kinda always thought *he* was my dad – until Granny showed me her diaries and then BOOM, everything changed. Now I know why he barely looked at me – they even split up because of me. And it's not like I had room for anyone else other than Mum in my life. My grandparents have always felt more like babysitters over the years. Now this guy has stepped up to say that he's been looking for me all along. He's saying he'll do anything to set me free. But what about the awful things that Granny's just blurted out? Did I come from a cult? Did Caleb really want to sacrifice me? There were pages of the diary that were torn out. Was Granny trying to protect me? Can I trust what she said at all?

I try to remember that awful day when my mother died. I strained to see through the air vent in the wall, but I remember the guy's voice. It was smooth, even when he was angry. He was demanding to see me. Then I blacked out. When I woke up, Granny and Grandad were in the house. I went to them. She told me my mother was dead. All these years . . . I made up a story in my head. The story that this man had finished her off. But now I'm wondering if it *was* him.

My heart's going totally crazy, and I'm freaked out, seriously. I don't know who the real monsters are anymore. Granny said that she and Grandad stashed me here to protect me. But what if *they're* the ones I need protecting from? All the times I begged them to let me live out in the open, and they said no. It's all so confusing, and I don't know what to do.

My emotions are all over the place as I think about going to him. Confusion is eating me up, and Granny's warnings play on a loop in my head. She always said that I was special, that there would be people who'd want to exploit me for their own gain. But seriously, what's so special about me? And now, the idea of meeting the man who claims to be my dad, who shares my blood, is weirdly pulling me in, even though I've got major doubts.

I sneak a look at the image of my grandparents, tied up and helpless in the living room. It feels like history is repeating itself and I don't know who to trust. Ronan is carrying a gun. I may not be super savvy socially, but it's clear that this guy isn't good. At first, I thought I recognised him, but I get what he's saying now. That when his brother left, everyone was still alive. But that would mean that Granny and Grandad were the last ones to see Mum alive. The thought makes my stomach churn. Grandad wouldn't have hurt her . . . would he? I shake my head, because I can't make sense of this. No. They'd never do that. But then how many times has he said he would do anything to protect me?

I stare at the image of Ronan. How can I trust someone who threatens to hurt a little boy? All my instincts scream at me to stay away, to protect myself and those I care about. That's what my mother died for . . .

I'm drowning in doubts as I listen to him speak. Part of me wants to believe him, as he swears he's spent years searching for me, even reporting me missing to the police. Memories of them showing up at The Loch House searching for me come flooding back. It's all because of him. And why did my grandparents never register my birth? Why keep me hidden from the cops? Was it really to protect me – or to stop me from being taken away? I know that Mum was religious once, and Grandad is a bible basher too. It's probably where she got it from. She ran away from home to get away from his lectures but ended up joining a cult. What if Grandad made me hide so I wouldn't run away like her? He keeps yapping on about me being special, yet he's never even given me a hug!

I'm on such shaky ground. Part of me craves the sense of belonging, being part of a family. Yet another part screams at me to be careful, that there are big-time dangers behind Ronan's story.

My buddy George, is in danger too. I can't just watch him get hurt. Granny should have left him here, safe with me. I cover my mouth as I watch Ronan drag George over, making all these demands for my whereabouts. He says he doesn't want to harm George, but there's nothing he won't do to get me back. I guess he's ready to save me, but at what cost?

Nicola is shouting at him to leave George alone, but he's talking about starting fresh, a life away from this madness. It's super tempting, but when I see George crying I can't watch. It's just too much. What am I supposed to do? I feel like I'm suffocating in this room, all alone.

I climb down from my chair. It's after three in the morning. In a few hours it will be dawn. The chance of a new life dangles in front of me. Should I trust Ronan, or play it safe and stay put? What if I stay and they murder everyone? This time, there will be nobody to save me because my grandparents will be dead. I walk to the exit panel on shaky legs. Should I go through?

41

Matt

I had to pull Nicola back as Ronan grabbed George from her arms. One wrong move and George could be seriously hurt. These people don't care about us. All they want is this kid that Dorothy and Henry would give up their lives to hide. What makes this girl so special that everyone wants her so badly? I feel useless as another wave of nausea washes over me. My headache has returned as a full blown migraine, and it couldn't have happened at a worse time. It's chaos as Steph and Joey shout at everyone not to move. I try to lunge forward to take George from Ronan's grip, but the icy touch of the muzzle of Henry's shotgun against my temple is a reminder of the danger we're in.

'Tell us where she is!' Steph's voice trembles with desperation and anger. She's getting increasingly agitated as George refuses to speak. 'Don't make us hurt the boy!' she warns, pointing her gun at anyone who dares to move.

'I don't know who you're talking about,' Nicola cries. 'I was out of my mind when George went missing. You were there! I didn't know where he went.'

'For fuck's sake,' I shout at Joey. 'You're frightening him half to death.'

'George,' Steph continues, a tremble in her voice. 'Just tell us where the little girl is. Then you can be with your mummy and soon you can all go home.' But George doesn't respond. His face is wet with tears, and his eyes are filled with a blankness that I've seen before. In the face of trauma, George has two reactions – he either runs away, or withdraws into himself. He's not taking anything in now. Life with an abusive father has made him this way. Nicola and I have worked hard to make him feel safe and loved, but now he's back to that time in his life when he was so scared he had to disappear deep inside himself. I want to make Ronan understand, but my head feels like it's trapped in a vice.

'Listen to me, kid. If you don't tell me where Elita is, we'll shoot.' Joey roars the spittle-laden threat to George, who has gone limp in Ronan's grip.

'Let him go.'

The voice comes from behind us. It sounds incredibly young, somewhat fractured, yet female and determined.

'Elita!' Ronan says, joyful as he loosens his grip. George runs into Nicola's arms and, through my pain, I heave a sigh of relief. I return my attention to the reunion taking place in front of me. He came here looking for his daughter, but the person standing in the doorway isn't a sixteen-year-old girl.

42

Nicola

In the middle of all the chaos, a female voice rings clear.

'I'm Elita,' she says quietly. She looks like a doll. She walks with a wobbly gait on matchstick legs, her frilly blue dress a miniature version of the clothes Dorothy wears, and a similar blonde wig is perched oddly on her head. Dorothy is sobbing now, choking on her tears. The room feels like a pressure cooker as Elita, a frail yet defiant figure, emerges from the shadows, her eyes burning with a wisdom far beyond her years.

Sunita's voice conveys awe and uncertainty.

'Elita . . . You're here. After all this time . . .'

'Is it true?' Elita takes a hesitant step towards Ronan. 'You're my father?'

Her voice, delicate yet filled with a quiet strength, pierces the newly formed silence.

'You can't hurt Granny and Grandad. Or these other people. Or George. I mean it. Let them go.'

'We won't hurt them,' Ronan says, his eyes moist. The colour has left his face. Seeing his daughter appears to have taken its toll. 'Joey, take off their gags.' I notice that he doesn't mention the bindings. He returns his attention to Elita. 'Oh my God, I can't believe that it's true. It's all true. You never grew up.'

Steph is crying as she chants the low hum of a mantra, while Joey keeps a watchful eye on the rest of us. I find it hard to believe that the child standing before us is sixteen years old. She clearly has a medical condition, yet this band of people are treating her as if she's some kind of ageless messiah.

I glance around the room. Bea is standing with her fists clenched, her face tense. Steph has lowered the shotgun and Joey's resolve seems to have weakened as they exchange bewildered glances. The revelation of Elita's presence has unsettled them, their confidence wavering in the face of an enigmatic force. Perhaps they were just going along with Ronan and Sunita's instructions and never truly believed that she was here.

Bea's eyes are locked on Elita, her voice laced with a mix of sorrow and anger. 'You . . . You're the reason my sister is gone.'

I've been expecting this. Bea confided in me when she brought me up to her room.

She throws a glance over the rest of us as we wait for her to explain. 'My sister was an artist. She came to The Loch House to paint. She stayed here ten years ago when she was murdered by these animals. I told her on the day of her funeral that I'd get to the root of it. I heard the rumours about a secret child. All these years, and I was right.' She stares at Ronan. 'You. You killed my sister.'

'It was his brother, Caleb,' Elita says, a little shyly as she clutches her thin hands together. 'They look alike, but now I'm here I can see the difference.'

But Bea doesn't look so sure. 'People change, honey,' she says in a sarcastic tone. 'It's been ten years. Not everybody's like you. We don't all stay the same.'

Her words are bitter, and I watch as Elita's expression changes. There is doubt there, as she surveys Ronan's face. 'No . . .' But she speaks with less resolve. 'You're wrong.'

'Then where is this brother? Tell me. I deserve to know,' Bea insists.

I should be asking the questions, but George is back in my arms and that's all I need for now.

'Caleb's dying,' Ronan bends down to give Elita his full attention. Sweat has broken out on his brow. 'We need to bring you to him. He can't make the journey on his own.' I've noticed Ronan's habit of ignoring the people he doesn't want to talk to while immersing others in a conversation that's hard to find a way out of. There's something otherworldly about him. When he looks at you, his gaze is hard to break.

'What journey?' Bea's words are stringent. 'What are you talking about?'

'Get her ready to go,' Ronan instructs Sunita as he slowly gets to his feet. 'It'll be dawn soon. We don't have much time.'

'Wait!' Elita cries as she is swept off the ground with ease. 'Where are you taking me?'

Sunita gives Elita a gracious smile. 'On your journey to eternity. You are the chosen one. We can't do it without you.'

I don't like the sound of this.

'Mummy,' George whispers. 'Don't let them take her.'

My son's words pull at my heart, but I'm helpless against three people. What can I do? I've taken in every aspect of their physical appearance. I've memorised every aspect in case I'm needed to give a witness statement later on. It doesn't look like they're going to hurt us. I'm hoping that they'll just take Elita and go. I look at Bruce for guidance, but his expression is one of resignation. He wants them to leave too. I know this makes me a bad person, but we stand a better chance this way . . . The police will track them down.

They gather up their things, but minutes later, Ronan staggers, then shakes his head.

'Are you alright?' Joey takes his arm to steady him.

'Oh, Ronan,' Bea's voice is cold. 'Did you really think I'd let you go?'

'What . . . what have you done?' Steph says, as Ronan staggers forward. He only makes two steps before he collapses onto his knees.

Bea exhales a bitter laugh. 'I knew who he was the second you let him in here. Do you think I'd let you get away with murdering my sister? You came here for Elita because you think that she will save you, but all you want is a bloodbath.' I watch, open mouthed, as she turns to Steph. 'I'm glad you're not pregnant. Makes me feel better about poisoning you.'

'What the fuck!' Steph screams, grappling with her shotgun.

'Enjoy your soup, did you? It was taking too long to work, so I put some in your tea for good measure too.'

'You fucking bitch, I'll kill you!' Steph screams.

'Shoot me and you won't get the antidote.' Bea speaks in a tone that isn't to be messed with.

There's so much going on here, I need to get George away, and I wonder if he can show me his hiding place. I bend down to my son's level and whisper in his ear. 'Can you show me where you were hiding?' He nods, his gaze on the others. Sunita is busy holding Elita, who is struggling in her arms for escape. Ronan is retching, trying to make himself sick. Steph and Joey have turned on Bea, who seems to have a death wish. Dorothy is screaming for Elita, and as Bruce edges towards me, nobody can hear us speak. 'Ronan's pistol,' he says. 'I'm pretty sure it's fake.'

But the shotgun isn't, and Steph is holding on to it tight. I nod at Bruce, ready to make a run for it. I'm trying to get Matt's attention, but he's sitting on the sofa, holding his head. I only hope he hasn't drunk whatever Bea has laced the tea with. I've got no choice but to leave. I only hope that he follows me out.

'C'mon,' Bruce whispers. 'If we stay here, they'll kill us all.' I don't want to leave the others, but soon it will be dawn and there's a chance that we can go for help. I don't want to hide in this house anymore, I want to go outside. Even if I run with George in my arms, we might be able to flag someone down.

'The front door is bolted,' I whisper. 'It'll take us too long to open it. George knows where we can hide.'

But Bruce shakes his head. 'They'll chase us, we won't have time. Go to the kitchen. Shove something up against the door once we get through. I've got the key to the back door.'

My throat clicks as I try to swallow. I noticed Bruce hanging around Henry earlier on. He must have taken the keys from him. A flare of hope lights in my chest. If we can make it to the kitchen . . . the dining room door is heavy. If we can get it closed in time, they won't be able to get through. I deliver a stiff nod of the head. Steph is swearing at Bea, who is laughing at Ronan as he stumbles groggily, trying to get to his feet. Joey is screaming for an antidote and I'm desperately trying to signal to Matt who doesn't appear to see me. This isn't like him at all, but there is no time to wait.

I whisper my plan to George. 'If anything happens to me,' I say with a tremble on my breath. 'Just run. Go to your hiding space and don't come out until the police get here.' He clings tightly to me as I slowly follow Bruce out. I catch Dorothy's eye and she screams to distract them as she calls Elita's name. We're almost at the door, but Steph has seen us leave. 'No!' I gasp, as she takes aim. *No, please God no*, I silently pray as we run for cover. But it's too late for prayers as the boom of the shotgun delivers a final shot.

43

Nicola

The snow-laden landscape glistens under the pale morning light. The storm that held us captive for so long has finally subsided. I'm outside The Loch House clutching my son, my breath forming delicate puffs in the frigid air. There aren't enough police officers to deal with us all, and backup is on the way. I wait with the rest of the group. They huddle together, their faces etched with a mixture of weariness and relief.

I can't believe that Matt's dead, his lifeless body lying on the living room floor. I don't understand how it happened. He saved our lives as he grabbed the rifle from Steph's hands. But as the shot went off, he was showered with plaster dust from the ceiling. Matt wasn't wounded, but neither was he breathing after he crumpled to the floor. The only sign that something was wrong was the blood trickling from his ears and nose.

Bruce had been right about Caleb's pistol – it was fake. In the moments that followed the gunshot, Bruce took control of the shotgun while Joey and Steph grew sluggish from the drugs that had laced their soup. I'd barely made it to the hall with George when Sunita tried to make a run for it, with poor little Elita in her arms. At last, I was free to do something as Bea followed her out, screaming bloody murder not to let Sunita get away. After leaving George in Bea's care, I took after that awful woman, all my pent-up frustration fuelling me as I grabbed a handful of her hair and yanked hard. It was enough to send her reeling. As

Sunita stumbled, I managed to snatch the little girl from her arms. I placed Elita on the floor. Within seconds, she was by George's side and it melted my heart to see him place a protective arm around her.

'You don't understand!' Sunita had screamed. 'She's our saviour!'

I wasn't in the mood for madness as I paid her no notice and ushered the children into the living room. With George safely on the sofa, Elita and I undid Dorothy and Henry's bindings. Only then could I return to Matt. His skin was still warm as I touched his face, but his lifeless eyes stared at the ceiling as I checked for a pulse. Nothing. 'I don't understand,' I cried to Bea, as she joined me by his side. 'Did you . . . did you poison him?'

'Of course not!' She looked at me, horrified. 'They're just sleeping tablets. But I made sure that Matt didn't get any. I'm sorry, sweetheart . . .' she sniffed, as her eyes filled with tears. 'But this isn't down to me.'

With trembling fingers, Bea dialled the emergency number on Ronan's phone, which had been working perfectly all along. Ronan was lying on the floor by then, his movements sluggish as he reached for Elita. But he got little mercy from Bea, who kicked him in the stomach for what he and his kind had done. With a shaky voice she spoke to the police and recounted the harrowing events that had unfolded within the walls of The Loch House. The words spilled out in a rush, her desperate pleas for help mingling with her sobs. She'd come across so hard when she fought with the others, but it turned out that it was all a front. I'm grateful that she had only crushed sedatives into their drinks. In one last ditch attempt, I pumped Matt's chest as I delivered CPR. But two rounds in, I knew it was in vain. He was gone.

Now I'm being bundled into a car, and a blanket is being wrapped around my son. The police officer is Scottish, and she tells me her name is Mel. She knows that I'm a police constable and she speaks to me like a friend.

'I'm sorry for your loss,' she says, glancing in the rear-view mirror to speak to me.

I know that this is terrible . . . utterly unforgiveable . . . but a big part of me is grateful to finally be free. 'Thank you,' I say, cradling George in my arms. I've told him to go to sleep, and he's resting his head on my lap. He's just happy that Elita is safe. It's all he wanted, in the end. Perhaps he could relate to her having to hide away.

'What's happening now?' I ask, as Mel negotiates the recently snow-ploughed roads with care.

'Same as you'd expect. We'll take statements from everyone, get you some food. Sort everyone out.' She throws George and me another glance. 'Sounds like all hell broke loose in there.'

I squint against the morning sun as it bounces off the snow. 'I feel numb,' I say, unable to cry. 'It's been the night from hell, I'm just thankful we're alive.'

Mel looks at me with concern. 'I could call someone when we get to the nick. Family? Friends? One of your colleagues, maybe?' Her soft Scottish accent is soothing. I think of Liam, and the urge to hear his voice is strong. But it feels like it would be a betrayal somehow. Matt died trying to protect me. I owe him my life.

'What about Matt's family . . .' I say. 'Do they know?'

'Aye,' Mel nods. 'We're arranging for someone to deliver the agony now.' I've delivered many 'agonies' during my time in the police. Each one has stayed with me. I never thought that the police would end up arranging one for Matt's mum.

Perhaps Liam already knows about the incident. I don't have my phone. He could be trying to ring me for all I know.

I just want to get the next twenty-four hours over with, so George and I can go home. I know that Matt has left a will. It was his grand declaration of commitment to us, although I'd told him there was no need at the time. It's our place now. At least my son will have some security, stability, keeping the home he loves and his room. I feel terrible for what he's been through tonight, after our history . . . I did everything in my power to protect him from my ex, but the mental scars remain. I vow to put George first from now on. The car bumps along the recently snow-ploughed road, and I kiss the top of his head. He's exhausted, we all are, but the chance of getting some sleep seems very far away.

I don't want to spend a second longer in Scotland than I have to. I never imagined that I would be going home without Matt. I still can't believe that he's gone. I can write my own account of events when we get to the station. God knows I've had enough practice with the five-part statement over the years. George will be spoken to and handled sensitively. I just want to go home.

Home. How empty our place will be without Matt. The second I found his engagement ring hidden in his pocket, I knew my future life had been all mapped out.

Like I said, mental scars run deep. I didn't realise how much until my ex, Gav, found me again. Returning to that memory causes me physical pain as a hard ball lodges in my chest. He turned up at my door one night and forced his way in. I only thank God that George was at my mum's. Gav was a mean drunk, and after taking the breadknife from the kitchen, he'd dragged me upstairs. I knew what he was planning, that he'd presumed that I would be helpless against his strength. But time had passed since he'd been to prison, and I'd grown strong. All I could think of was my son. So, when I got the opportunity to fight back, I did it for George.

Thanks to countless cans of Stella, Gav was unsteady on his feet. It took just one hefty push to send him reeling down the stairs. I remember the sounds of his snapping bones, as he hit each step, and praying that one of them would be his neck. Because I knew that if he got back up from that, he'd kill me for sure. As he lay at the bottom of the stairs, groaning, I took the knife from his hand and finished him off. I'll never forget that last look on his face as the light left his eyes.

I knew just how to position him, so it looked like he'd fallen on top. Then I made it look like he'd broken in through the back door. I lived down a secluded lane back then. Nobody saw me come or go. Mum gave me an alibi. She said I'd been with her the whole time that Gav had been 'lying in wait'. Officers said that he must have fallen down the stairs, drunk.

But what I did to Gav haunted me, and I needed to get it off my chest. I was a *killer*. Was my soul damaged forever? I was desperate to talk to someone. That's when I met Matt. The one person who could offer me redemption. Because he was a good man. Solid. Respected. Dependable. He treated me like royalty. He bought me flowers, left me little romantic notes. He wanted to know where I was every minute of the day, so he could keep me safe. Matt was a shoulder to cry on, and he knew all about Gav. I drank a lot back then. Enough to make me pour my heart out and confess what I had done. I know how stupid this sounds. I'm a police officer for God's sake. But unless you've been in this circle of control then you won't understand. I safeguard victims of abuse. I give them the talks I wish someone had given me. And like them, I understand how hard it is to break away from the repetitive cycle of being kept under control.

But somehow, even with Matt, I ended up in that spiral all over again. As we drive away from The Loch House, I catch sight of the rotting tatty bogle who we met on the way in. Someone has placed him standing upright against the tree. His features are distorted, but he carries the same lopsided grin. I inwardly shudder. I'm never travelling to Scotland again. But if there's one thing it's given me, it's freedom to carry on.

Matt was not a monster. He was a man with deep-rooted insecurities. Someone who desperately needed to be loved – whatever it took to keep that person by his side. He didn't grow up in an abusive childhood. I don't know why he clung onto me like that. But something in his psyche just wasn't right. Matt made his terms abundantly clear. If I ever tried to leave, he'd tell the world what I had done. It wasn't just his word against mine, I had given him details about Gav's death that nobody else could know. Yet I was desperate to leave, and ready to take that chance. The relief of my secret being safe is immeasurable.

I couldn't bear for my son to learn that his mother was a murderer. That would hurt me more than losing everything, or ending up in jail. It's the reason I was helpless when it came to standing up for myself. Matt's hold over me was strong. Each time

I tried to make the break, he reminded me of what I had to lose. That's not love. It's just another form of control. I smooth down my son's hair. Perhaps our trip to The Loch House wasn't such a bad thing after all.

44

Elita

I thought I'd be happy to be free, but it's sensory overload. People in the outside world look at me differently to everyone else. There are the people who blatantly stare, the ones who recoil, then the ones who can't look at me at all. I am special. I'm the little girl who never grew up. At least, I thought I was. Now, it seems that I'm not alone. There are others like me. What I have is a medical condition. I'm not so special after all. I'm certainly not a religious icon brought to the earth to bring Caleb and his kind home . . . Is Ronan even really my father? It seems that way. Is he a murderer? I don't know, I'm just glad he's not dead. Because I still need answers about what happened to my mum.

I'm finally given some alone time, but it won't be for long. The police have been kind, and my social worker is called Izzy. She's outgoing and bubbly, with bright red curly hair and she wears blue dungarees and a rainbow top. She's gone to get me some food, but what I really need is sleep. My grandparents are in the building, talking to the police. I saw so much on camera, but thanks to a glitch in the system, not all of it was recorded, which is just as well, given some of the stuff I heard. I guess Steph and Joey knew about the cameras somehow. It's why they put on such a show for me: talking about the baby and their perfect lives. Sunita knew too, which is why she apparently climbed up onto the dresser and covered hers up with a washcloth. I don't know how they knew, I guess they must have noticed them when they came in. Most people don't see them, but if you go into a room with a suspicious mind, then I guess you pick stuff up. The Loch House isn't a regular place to stay. They must have been on their guard.

As for Nicola . . . she didn't know about her bedroom camera, at least not when they first arrived. The conversation I overheard between her and Matt was a bombshell. George deserves to have his mother with him, not in a prison cell. Nicola's not a bad person, and that horrible man she killed deserved to die. But while she stands up to people in her job, she was the underdog at home.

George told me all about it, how his real daddy, Gav, used to hurt his mum. He told me that he'd died after falling down the stairs when he was in the house, all alone. He also said that he was glad that his daddy was dead. Nicola had told him a story about troubled souls getting another chance when they pass on to a better place. He seemed happy with that, and he liked his new daddy, Matt. But George didn't see what I picked up on camera when Nicola and Matt were whispering in their room. Matt had two sides, and from what I saw, he wasn't as good as George thought. It's not right to blackmail someone to stay with you. From what George told me about his daddy, I don't blame Nicola for pushing him down the stairs. At least now he won't be able to hurt her again. I don't know how Matt died, but Nicola and George will be able to start again. It's a time for new beginnings for both of us. My grandparents meant well, but living behind the walls of The Loch House was no life at all.

Mystery on the Mic Podcast

The Watts Case Series: Episode 11

Alex: Welcome back to 'Mystery on the Mic', everyone. I'm your host, Alex. And I'm joined, as always, by our true crime historian, Sarah. Today, we're revisiting the chilling case of The Loch House guest house on the Isle of Skye, and hold on tight, folks, because we've got a shocking long awaited resolution to this case – don't we, Sarah?

Sarah: We sure do, Alex. And you're not kidding about the shock factor. I was working on my laptop on the train when I discovered the news and I literally squealed out loud. I've been studying this field for years, and this case is unlike any I've seen before.

Alex: I'm with you, Sarah. This isn't just a plot twist; it's like an entire new book. Let's not keep our listeners in suspense any longer – but if you're new to the case then I recommend that you go back to episode one and work your way through the podcasts. It's *so* worth it. But if you want to keep listening, we're excited to share that the case of The Loch House guest house has finally been solved. Tell us more, Sarah.

Sarah: It all came to an explosive climax last weekend, during the tenth anniversary of the murders of The Loch House owner

Amelia Evans, and her guests. History seemed to be repeating itself as, just like before, guests and hosts were snowed in by an almighty blizzard. And just like ten years ago, the night ended in bloodshed. As well as a key revelation that I've barely been able to wrap my head around.

Alex: Let's dive in first with the people who were staying in The Loch House when it all kicked off. And I can tell you, folks, we have a mystery guest that nobody except the hosts, Dorothy and Henry Hill, were aware of. I'm barely able to catch my breath as I reveal that . . . Amelia Evans, the previous owner of The Loch House, had a secret daughter named Elita, who . . . get this, listeners . . . was living *inside* the walls of The Loch House. All. This. Time. Sarah, how do you feel about Dorothy and Henry's secret granddaughter? Because this news just blew me away.

Sarah: It was a *huge* bombshell. According to my sources, Elita's birth was never registered, so to all intents and purposes, the sixteen-year-old girl didn't exist. Amelia managed to keep her daughter Elita a secret, and when guests came to stay, she not only moved around within the walls of The Loch House, but had her own secret room. She even visited guest rooms when they sat down for dinner, and stole trinkets to keep for herself. The poor child. It's hard to believe that she was right under everyone's noses all this time.

Alex: I'm still trying to comprehend it. Is it really possible to live like that?

Sarah: Believe it or not, yes. Some of these old houses were built to protect smugglers or all manner of persecuted people. Only those with a keen eye would have noticed that the house is a bit like a reverse Tardis: smaller on the inside than out. It's astonishing that the police never picked up on this ten years ago. The crime scene would have been thoroughly searched.

Alex: It's not the first time the team investigating this case have been embarrassed by their failures. Remember Bruce Hawthorn, the man who posed as a police detective as he interviewed locals? Keep listening, folks because we've got more on *him* later on. I don't want to jump ahead though as we have so much to cover. First, we've got to discuss Amelia's desperate attempts to protect her child.

Sarah: Yes, Alex. Elita was homeschooled and never mixed with children her own age. She had books and a TV, but no Wi-Fi, so she didn't communicate with the outside world. But this case takes another strange turn as officers discovered monitors in Elita's hidden room. She kept herself occupied by spying on the guests through several covert cameras dotted around the house.

Alex: That gives me the shivers. I wonder how many people have stayed in those rooms over the years? No wonder Tripadvisor reviewers complained of feeling like they were being watched. But why was Elita kept a prisoner?

Sarah: Hmm, I'm not sure that she was. It's said that Elita could come and go through the passages as she pleased, but she lived in constant fear of the people who killed her mother and wasn't allowed contact with the guests. Not only that, but Elita is said to have a disability, which would have made it harder for her to move about. She's not really grown since the age of six, when her mother died.

Alex: Can this case get any more tragic?

Sarah: I'm afraid it can. So, in order to be able to understand this latest update, we need to go back to Amelia, and the reasons she went to The Loch House in the first place. Remember we had a theory that Amelia was hiding from someone? Turns out we were right. I knew there had to be a reason why she stayed in such an isolated place after her husband left. She was protecting her daughter from a cult – The Fellowship of Jesus Christ, to be specific. Amelia and her partner escaped the cult with Elita when she was just a baby, and it appears that one of its leaders, a man named Ronan Watts, was searching for the child, who he claims is his.

Alex: Woah. So, Ronan Watts, son of deceased music producer Ronnie Watts who we've mentioned in previous episodes, is Elita's biological father? Excuse me while I fall off my chair.

Sarah: (Chuckles) Yes, I thought I'd keep that in my back pocket for the show. I'd guessed that Amelia was running from something, but I never had her down for being in a cult. And not just any cult. We're talking about The Fellowship of Jesus Christ, run by brothers Caleb and Ronan Watts. Listeners may remember that we've discussed this pair in previous episodes, due to the suspicious deaths of their father Ronnie Watts, and his young wife Heather, who was due to inherit the Watts fortune when her husband died. Incidentally, each of the tragic pair died from a single shot to the temple – the same way that Amelia Evans was murdered. A suicide note was found at the scene. Police had their suspicions that Caleb and Ronan were involved but they lacked the evidence to make it stick.

Alex: Well, The Fellowship of Jesus Christ is a new player in this story. Just when you think this case can't get any murkier there's a real life cult thrown into the mix.

Sarah: It's hard to believe that these things go on, but they do, and The Fellowship still has a strong following in the UK. Amelia and her musician husband were former members of the cult before they escaped. We've previously covered interviews with some of the members who claimed that Caleb Watts was planning a mass suicide. It supposedly disbanded after officials got involved, but many say that it went underground. That is, until Ronan Watts and some other members of The Fellowship turned up at The Loch House Hotel last weekend.

Alex: Let's not jump ahead. I know listeners are screaming for the low-down but let's talk about the other guests who stayed in The Loch House last weekend. What do we know about them?

Sarah: Well, we have hosts Henry and Dorothy Hill and their granddaughter Elita. Then we have Nicola McKenna, an off duty police officer, her six-year-old son George, and her partner Matt Barber, who booked The Loch House at the last minute because other hotels were full. These are the only people staying there who didn't have a vested interest in the case.

Alex: Yes, it's a shame they got caught up in it all. What about the others?

Sarah: Bea Alderman was there because her sister was one of the guests who died ten years before. It's believed that she went to The Loch House looking for answers.

Alex: She certainly found them. Who else have we got?

Sarah: Surprise surprise, we have Bruce Hawthorn. We've discussed Bruce at length in the past. He's known for having an unhealthy interest in the case. Then we have Joey and Steph Coombs, cult members posing as newlyweds who were planted in The Loch House to look for Elita.

Alex: They weren't the only members of the cult to stay there that night, were they?

Sarah: No, there was a yoga instructor who booked in under a false name. I've not been able to source her real identity yet, but she called herself Sunita and she's linked to Ronan Watts. She was also planted there to assist him when he got into The Loch House.

Alex: So now we've set the scene, we can share what we know about that night.

Sarah: Some of the details are sketchy, but I'm sure everything will eventually come out. What we know is that the guests were snowed in that night, Ronan Watts gained entry thanks to his cohorts, and the other people in the guest house were threatened as they searched for Elita. History seemed about to repeat itself, until the little girl made herself known.

Alex: Ronan Watts was all ready to leave with his alleged daughter, wasn't he?

Sarah: Apparently so, but here comes the explosive part. According to a reliable source, someone let it slip that Caleb Watts was dying and that he needed to take Elita with him 'on his eternal journey'. You see, the cult had always believed that Elita was some kind of 'chosen one' due to her being different. Remember the movie, *The Curious Case of Benjamin Button*? Well, it gives us an idea of what life was like for Elita. She suffered from progeria, a rare and sadly fatal genetic condition in which the body ages prematurely, stunting growth from an early age. It also causes poor weight gain, and a characteristic appearance of a large head on a small body, with a small jaw, chin and mouth. So, while Elita was in fact ageing prematurely, she could also be seen as *unnaturally childlike*, or should we say supernaturally childlike, for those who didn't understand. According to my sources, her grandparents had no knowledge of her condition and Elita was revered by her grandad Henry, who was a very religious man.

Alex: That poor girl, to be shut away for so much of her life when she's done nothing wrong. But moving back to that night – from what we know, it seems that things really kicked off in the guest house and, as a result, Matt Barber died at the scene?

Sarah: I'm afraid so. It's a tragic end to the story of The Loch House, although we don't yet know how he died. Police arrived at around 6 a.m., but it was too late to help Matt Barber. It's certainly good news, however, that cult members Joey, Steph and Ronan were arrested.

Alex: And there's an implication here, isn't there, Sarah? That Ronan Watts and his cult could be responsible for the deaths at The Loch House ten years ago?

Sarah: We have to be careful what we say right now, Alex, but it certainly looks that way. The pieces of the puzzle are starting to fit together in a chilling picture. Ronan Watts and his cult members could well be the ones who orchestrated the horrific event at The Loch House ten years ago. It's been said that Ronan was the more violent of the two brothers, and possessive over his brother, who he revered. Perhaps they've been looking for Elita all this time, or maybe his brother Caleb was involved the first time around and Ronan came on the scene to clean up his mess.

Alex: We can only imagine. Now, Sarah, let's bring back into focus a character from our earlier episodes – Bruce Hawthorn. How does he fit into this turn of events?

Sarah: It's possible that Bruce Hawthorn had a suspicion that something was going to happen that night. It's said that he sustained a flesh wound but we've no clear details on that yet. He was more than just an eccentric bystander, that's for sure. He threw himself into the heart of the investigation that he's obsessed over for years.

Alex: And as for poor Elita . . . I'm still wrapping my head around the fact that she exists.

Sarah: Yes, it's heartbreaking to think about Elita, the young woman who grew up hidden away in the walls of The Loch House. Not just hidden in the walls, but she must have felt like a prisoner of her own body too. It's a distressing thought.

Alex: Indeed. Also, you have to think about the lengths Amelia went to in order to protect her daughter. The sacrifices she made. It adds another layer of tragedy to this already grim case. But let's shift gears a bit. The Isle of Skye is a peaceful, idyllic place known for its natural beauty. How has this case affected the community there?

Sarah: The impact has been significant. Imagine living in a small, closely-knit community where everyone knows everyone, and then such a shocking crime occurs not once, but twice. Many residents can't believe that something so heinous could happen in their backyard. Some feel guilty, knowing that little Elita has spent a great deal of her life behind walls, and nobody picked up on it. There's a certain level of anger towards Elita's grandparents, who should have done more. I hope Elita finds some semblance of peace in all this chaos.

Alex: (Sighs) It's a stark reminder of how the darkness of crime can touch anyone, anywhere.

Sarah: Absolutely. It's been a harrowing journey, but hopefully, it's nearing its conclusion. I'm sure we'll cover more in another episode when everything comes out. It's amazing how long we've been investigating this case.

Alex: You can say that again. This case feels such a huge part of our podcast over the years. Little did we know when we started off how much it would grow!

Sarah: To think we used to record at that tiny little kitchen table, with the sound of traffic outside. Looking around our studio now, I'm amazed at how far we've come.

Alex: Our love of true crime knows no bounds (chuckles) and with almost a million listeners, it seems we're not alone.

Sarah: This case has been enough to reel anyone in. I'm just glad we've found some closure at last.

Alex: I'm sure I speak on behalf of our listeners when I say thank you for helping us dissect these latest developments. It's been enlightening, albeit chilling. And to our listeners, thank you for being part of this journey as we unravel the truth behind the mysteries that surround us. It seems there's always more to the story than meets the eye.

45

Nicola

Six months later

I said I'd never return to Scotland, but here I am, back at The Loch House where it all began. Call it closure, I suppose.

Liam is waiting in the car. We're not dating, not yet, but we have grown closer and it's obvious that he'd like more. But this time it's my choice. He's been patient and supportive. I've come to know a whole new side of him. He wants me to take my time and do what's right for me and George. So much of my life has been stumbling from one disaster to another. Having George, and joining the police, are the only things I've got right so far. He's even introduced me to a therapist – who knew that Liam went to therapy! He made me swear to keep it to myself. But you can't be in the police as long as he has and not experience a trauma of some kind.

George isn't here this time, he's in school. He's having therapy too. I'm learning to cope with the shame I feel for not parenting him properly so far. We're moving forward. We're healing. We're learning to use our experiences to grow. I sold Matt's place in the end, and split the profits with his mother. It felt like the right thing to do. It felt too strange, living there after what happened. It's odd how you can simultaneously miss and not miss someone, but at least Matt has taken my secret to the grave. There are some things I can't talk about in my therapy sessions, but I did say that he'd been emotionally manipulating me to stay with him. Had he not died of a brain aneurysm, I'd either be married to him or in prison by now.

The doctors said that there was nothing anyone could have done, and that he'd most likely suffered from a bleed on the brain after his initial tussle when he fell. I remember him complaining about a migraine, and by then the damage was done. He died a hero in the end, saving us from Steph's gun. I owe him my thanks, which is why I'm here, standing outside The Loch House with a bunch of white lilies in my arms. I stare up at the shuttered windows and a cold feeling snakes down my spine. The 'For Sale' sign is chipped and battered as it flaps in the wind. I can't see anyone taking over this place . . . Locals have started up a petition to have it razed to the ground.

George, my sensitive soul of a son, visited Elita regularly until she was fostered. She's part of a big family now and moving on with her life. I think it's best for both of them if they focus on the future. Elita's genetic condition means that her life won't be long, but thanks to Jane and Laurie, her new foster parents, she's packing the most into every day. They're saints, the pair of them, dedicating their lives to help kids like Elita, and giving them the best of care. Elita still gets to see Dorothy, who has moved back to London with her husband. I think it all got too much for her in the end. It's said that Henry will receive a suspended sentence for the part he had to play that day. Given his frail condition, I think that it's best. One thing's for sure, they won't be taking in any more guests.

I lay the flowers on the doorstep of The Loch House. There are other bouquets here, some withered and some recent, alongside the tealight candles which have now gone out. It's why I waited until evening to come. I read Bea's card, which is a tribute to her sister. I'm half expecting to bump into Bruce, which is why Liam volunteered to come along. Bruce lied about his past. He was never in the police, but he *was* touched by the darkness of The Loch House. Apparently, he had a bit of a thing for Amelia when they both lived on the island and admired her from afar. But this isn't a place for romance. It's a house where darkness blooms. I think about the tatty bogle, and the windows which were nailed shut. There's something unsettling about this place, and the land that it's built on. I hope they do knock it to the ground.

A sharp wind starts to whip around me when my attention is drawn to another bunch of flowers, their petals curling at the edges. Rain has smeared the writing on the card, but the words cut through me, bringing back the old feelings of dread.

To Elita, from Ronan. May we meet again.

Ronan's in prison, which means one of his followers has left it here . . . Caleb is dead. Much was made about The Fellowship on the news when this all came to light. I was right in my estimation of Ronan, it was widely reported that he was the more violent of the two. They'd been planning a mass suicide when Amelia fled the cult with her daughter. Plans and stocks of poisons were found after police raids. No wonder she came to the ends of the earth to escape them. If only they hadn't caught up with her.

At least now we know what happened, and Bea has been given closure. Caleb gave an account on his deathbed. Perhaps he was hoping for redemption, or maybe he finally saw sense, but he confessed that the deaths were down to him and his brother after all. He hadn't wanted to kill Amelia and the guests on that awful night, but Ronan persuaded him it was the only way to save their souls. It was Ronan who pulled the trigger, and Caleb who administered the poison. What a waste of life. And it wasn't their first kill. According to Caleb, they were responsible for the deaths of their father and his young bride, too. It was all down to money, and the fear of losing their inheritance. Again Caleb administered the drug, while Ronan pulled the trigger – and they got away with it, for all these years.

Ronan didn't find Elita because he wanted to be a father. He said he'd been searching for her for years, but in reality, he wanted to take her to his brother to fulfil his dying wish. But he wouldn't have stopped there. The thought of so many people being under their spell is frightening. My gaze flickers over the other cards which are left on the expansive doorstep. Some are held down with stones, a few are standing in the wind. But they're all signed *with love, The Fellowship of Jesus Christ*. My shoulders rise an inch at the thought of all these people standing where I am now.

I startle as I hear movement from inside the building. It could be a wild animal, or squatters perhaps, but I'm not hanging around to find out. I pivot on my heel and fight the urge to run back to the car.

'You alright?' Liam says, turning over the engine.

'Fine.' I offer a tight smile, and slowly exhale. 'Let's go, eh?'

This time, I'm keeping my promise. I'm never coming back here again.

Acknowledgements

No author works alone, and I'm truly grateful to the team of people who have brought my latest book to fruition. Thanks to my hugely talented editors Jane Snelgrove, Cara Chimirri, and the wonderful team at Embla books for doing such an amazing job. I'm thankful to the brilliant copy editors, proof-readers, cover designer, audio book producers and narrators as well as all the people behind the scenes who have helped to bring this book to you today.

Thanks as always to my passionate and hard working agent and her team at the Madeleine Milburn Literary, TV and Film Agency. I pinch myself that I get to work with such remarkable people. Speaking of remarkable people, a special mention goes to my author friends Mel Sherratt and Angela Marsons, as well as so many generous and supportive authors that I am fortunate enough to know.

A special shout out to the bloggers and book club members who have read, reviewed and spread the word about my books. I am hugely grateful for their support, especially the wonderful people who have championed my books from the off.

A huge thanks to my biggest supporters – my family, both in Ireland and the UK. Thanks to my husband Neil, for being my rock, and to my children, although they aren't children anymore. It warms my heart that they're still proud of their old mum.

Thanks also to my readers, who are always in the forefront of my mind when I write my books.

I do hope you enjoyed your stay at The Guest House.

I love hearing from my readers and you can find me on social media at
    Facebook: @CMitchellauthor
    X: @Caroline_writes
    Instagram: @Caroline_writes

You can sign up to my free VIP reader's club here:
    www.caroline-writes.com

A Note from the Author

Thank you for reading *The Last Guest House*. It feels different from my other books, and I hope you enjoyed trying to solve the mystery along the way. The podcast sections were inspired by my YouTube channel, True Crime Detective. I ran the channel for a while as I reported on various true crimes. When an update came in on a famous case, I'd report on that too.

I wrote 'Mystery on the Mic' in the same fashion, with the episodes stretching out over years, from early on when the crimes occurred, right up to when they were resolved. The hosts report on many true crime cases, but each time an update on the Watts family came in, they added it to the Watts family playlist. I preferred not to date the podcast episodes, so I hope this was clear. I enjoyed writing the fictional podcast episodes as it added a fresh perspective to the story.

Until next time, my dear reader,
   Caroline

About the Author

Caroline is a *New York Times*, *USA Today*, *Washington Post* and international number one bestselling author, with over 1.5 million books sold. To date her books have been shortlisted for the International Thriller Awards, the Killer Nashville Silver Falchion Awards and the Audie Awards, and her 2018 thriller *Silent Victim* won the US Readers' Favorite Award in the 'Psychological Thriller' category.

Caroline originates from Ireland and now lives with her family in a village just outside Lincoln. A former police detective, she specialised in roles dealing with vulnerable victims, victims of domestic abuse, and serious sexual offences. The people she dealt with are a huge source of inspiration for her writing today. Caroline writes full time.

About Embla Books

Embla Books is a digital-first publisher of standout commercial adult fiction. Passionate about storytelling, the team at Embla publish books that will make you 'laugh, love, look over your shoulder and lose sleep'. Launched by Bonnier Books UK in 2021, the imprint is named after the first woman from the creation myth in Norse mythology, who was carved by the gods from a tree trunk found on the seashore – an image of the kind of creative work and crafting that writers do, and a symbol of how stories shape our lives.

Find out about some of our other books and stay in touch:

X, Facebook, Instagram: @emblabooks
Newsletter: https://bit.ly/emblanewsletter